THE LOST AND THE CHOSEN

THE LOST SENTINEL BOOK ONE

IVY ASHER

COPYRIGHT

Copyright © 2018 Ivy Asher
All rights reserved. This book or parts thereof may not be reproduced in any form, stored in any retrieval system, or transmitted in any form by any means—electronic, mechanical, photocopy, recording, or otherwise—without prior written permission of the author, except in cases of a reviewer quoting brief passages in a review.

This is a work of fiction. Names, characters, places, and incidents either are the products of the author's imagination or are used fictitiously. Any resemblance to actual persons, living or dead, businesses, companies, events, or locales is entirely coincidental.

Edited by Polished Perfection
Cover Design by Story Wrappers

DEDICATION

For the ones who believed I could,
so I did.

1

I shut the locker door, the sound echoing off the concrete walls of the empty room. I tuck earbuds into my ears, press play on my phone, and my playlist picks up where it left off at the end of yesterday's workout. Flyleaf's "All Around Me" trickles into my ears. I turn up the volume and let the music coax out my inner beast, as I mentally map out how I'm going to dominate this match.

Talon always makes fun of this part of my pre-fight routine. He doesn't understand my need to visualize beating the shit out of someone, especially when I don't know who my opponent is yet. Unfortunately, it's just one of the many things I'm not able to explain to him.

Traces of whatever it is that exists inside of me light up throughout my body. The mysterious spark of ability stretches out inside of me like a languid cat, and as much as I revel in this flow of power, I'm careful to keep it in check. If I welcome in too much, it will flood me and turn me into the human version of a Fourth of July sparkler. That would thoroughly fuck up the *I'm just like everyone else* act I'm trying to maintain.

The smell of whatever cleaner they use to battle the

residual odor of sweaty bodies sits heavy but pleasant in the air. I breathe in the clean lemony smell as I methodically stretch and prepare my body for the fight. I don't know what it says about me, but I find the pungent scent of this room comforting. My brain links it with hard work and success. I swear, every gym I've ever worked out in, and every locker room I've ever used has this same citrusy smell.

The growly part of "I'm So Sick" begins to stream into my ears, when the metal door clangs open, and in walks Talon. He looks like he should be walking into a boardroom instead of this concrete, lemon-scented locker room. His suit is custom-made and pristine, at odds with the old, gruff, Viking vibe the rest of him exudes.

He had long hair the first time I met him. The blond locks danced in the wind, and ocean blue eyes stared up at me, as I stood on top of his SUV with a rock in my hand. I was fifteen and homeless, running from a couple of assholes who got pissed that I dared to fight back when their group tried to steal my backpack.

Talon wears his hair buzzed now, his beard shorter, more well-kept. The facial hair does little to conceal his square jaw or sharp nose. I discovered over the years that his blue eyes only ever seem to soften for me. Everyone else gets the ruthlessly cold and calculating side of Talon. Me? I get the protector and friend. At six feet two inches, he's tall enough to hulk over me, and everything about him——from his size to the way he carries himself——oozes, *don't fuck with me*.

"You ready?" he asks, and I nod.

"Good. Take your time. Give a good show. Then fucking annihilate him," he coaches me, the instructions unnecessary.

I grunt in approval at his viciousness, though I can't help but roll my eyes, too. This isn't some choreographed dance, and he knows it. Talon chuckles, reading my thoughts from the expression on my face. The driver that brought me here still stands in the corner of the room. His spine stiffens at the sound of Talon's mirth, as if his laughter equates to a death sentence. For all I know, that could be true.

Outside of training and fighting, I keep my nose out of Talon's business, but he could definitely be the type to deal out laughter with death. I'm not so cavalier about it, but I don't have any qualms about death either. I roll my neck in an attempt to alleviate the anticipation I feel. This always happens to me before a fight. It's not nerves, and even the word *anticipation* doesn't quite capture the true essence of the feeling. It's more a drive to get on with it, a need to attack.

"There's my little warrior, let that bloodlust soak into you, and let's do this," Talon encourages.

He hugs me and gives a playful tug to the end of one of my Dutch braids. I punch him in the side, but I don't put any power behind it, and he laughs. I don't know what it's like to have parents that give a shit about you. I never met my father, and Beth—my egg donor—threw me away, like the garbage she always told me I was.

Talon's the closest I'll ever get to experience how a parent should act. I have no idea why he plucked me from the roof of his car and off the streets of Vegas, but I'm thankful every day for everything he's done for me.

Veering away from the sentimental direction of my thoughts, I clear my mind and slap my game face on. In the world of shady underground deals and cold brutality, where Talon and I live, pretty thoughts and indulgent memories have no place. I refocus and bounce in place to warm my muscles and get loose.

The roar of the crowd reaches us through the thick walls of the room, and it's clear from the noise that someone in the current fight just took a serious hit. The concrete muffles the shouts from the spectators, but it's easy enough to get a sense of what's going on. Talon grows edgy as my match looms closer.

We sit in companionable silence until someone pounds twice on the metal door, indicating it's time. Talon turns to me, his fathomless blue eyes taking my measure. I catch a flash of sadness in his gaze as he seems to find whatever he's looking for and turns away. With a resolute nod, he leads me out of the locker room.

Entrances to a match can vary depending on the venue and scale of the fight. Today, there's not much fanfare other than some lighting and the sound system. The booming resonance of an announcer bellows out my name, *Vinna Aylin*, and I walk into the shadow-soaked room at my introduction.

The spotlight trained on me makes it difficult to gauge how big of a crowd fills the arena. Their shouts of support or disdain wrap around me like a blanket, cocooning me in their aggression. The octagon cage sits in the middle of the cavernous warehouse, bathed in light, and Talon and I stride toward it with confidence.

The door to the cage opens, and I turn to Talon. I wrap my arms around his waist, sneaking in one last hug before I enter. I'm the first to arrive, and I wait for my opponent's entrance into the arena to be announced. Shouts of my name bombard me, but I ignore them as my gaze sweeps over the crowd, assessing the details of the room.

My eyes land on a man watching me with such a quiet intensity that it sets off an alarm in my brain. I'm not sure why this man's acute scrutiny stands out amidst the other bloodthirsty fans who are watching and waiting, but something about him sets me on edge. Based on his tawny complexion and dark hair, I'd guess he's Middle Eastern.

His honey brown eyes are fixed on me, and they shine with a predatory gleam.

The man smiles, but it's all lips and no teeth. There's no flash of fang or reddening of his eyes, which would make it easy to confirm my suspicions. I call them fanged fuckers, but I doubt that's how they refer to themselves. My best guess would be they're some kind of vampire, but none of the ones I've killed ever tried to eat me; for some reason, they just wanted to take me.

Instinctually, I want to group this man in with the other fanged fuckers I've run into over the years, and I trust my gut when it tells me this black-haired, whiskey-eyed spectator represents a threat to me.

The first time one of them attacked me, I was fourteen. It would have been easy to dismiss the speed and strength, or the glowing eyes as some kind of shock-induced hallucination, but I knew better than to try and convince myself that I mistook what I saw. That it was impossible. After all, if not for the impossible things *I* was capable of, that thing would have taken me wherever or to whomever it wanted.

I fight my desire to show this man that I'm the predator and not the prey, but I don't want to tip my hand. If he is what I think he is, it's only a matter of time before the fucker comes for me. Then he'll learn. Then he'll die like all the others.

2

The booming voice of the announcer pulls me away from my thoughts and from the eyes of the man whom I've marked for death. The deep bass of the announcer's voice introduces my opponent, and I hone in and refocus my attention on his entrance.

A large group of men move toward the cage. I can't help the small smile that takes over my face when the entourage splits apart in what has to be a practiced move. Clearly, I was wrong, and this is a choreographed dance after all. I try to rein in my amusement and adopt a more fitting badass demeanor, but now I'm picturing these big, burly dudes breaking into a flash mob.

Tonight's opponent ambles toward the entrance. The word huge comes to mind but doesn't quite encapsulate just how big this motherfucker is. The spotlight emphasizes his muscles and the thick veins that sit almost snake-like under his skin. He either spends ninety percent of his day in the gym, or he's on a first name basis with steroids. My guess would be both.

He enters the cage and looks me over, dismissing me as a threat in about two seconds. He then turns to the crowd and lets loose a ridiculous roar. Oh yeah, there's some definite roid rage going on.

The ref calls us to the center of the ring to give us our instructions. It's the typical no biting, hair pulling, or shots to the junk speech, and I tune him out as I assess the beast of a man across from me. He's colossal, and a hit from him is going to come with some serious damage. If he's fast on top of that, then he'll definitely make me work for the win.

My bloodlust simmers inside of me, and I revel in the potential for a challenge.

I make eye contact with colossus for the first time. He licks his lips and starts air kissing, then flicking his tongue at me. Is this guy serious? I roll my eyes and look around for Talon so I can throw him a *where'd you find this guy?* look.

Talon's usually standing front and center, but I can't seem to find him in the crowd. I do catch a glimpse of a guy who's staring at me with so much tension that it borders on panic. I'm used to seeing this look on people's faces. If they're new to the fights, it can seriously freak people out to see all five foot eight inches of me in the ring with a big scary looking dude like the one I'm about to fight.

I smile and wink at the guy, hoping he'll relax a little, but it doesn't seem to work. He looks like he's seconds away from trying to haul me out of this ring. Oh, ye of little faith. He's about to find out that there's no part of me that's a damsel, and nothing about this match has me distressed.

"I hope you're still smiling when I pin you down and fuck you right here, in front of this crowd," Colossal Douche sneers at me.

He grabs the crotch of his shorts, drawing my attention to the sad excuse for an erection he's sporting. I know Talon told me to take my time and put on a good show. But this piece of shit needs to learn some manners.

The ref finishes his instructions, and the Colossal

Douche and I touch knuckles before separating. The adrenaline coursing through me rubs up against the nameless power that lives inside me, and my power sits up like an overeager puppy, ready and waiting to be called on.

The ref drops his raised hand, signaling for us to start, and I immediately move in. Colossal Douche roars and charges me. He holds his arms out in a useless Frankenstein stance as he stomps closer, aiming to wrap his arms around me. Quick as lightning, I lift my foot up on his thigh and use it as leverage to climb his massive frame like a jungle gym.

His arms squeeze closed, but he only manages to trap one of my legs. I climb high enough up his torso to give myself a clear shot at his unguarded head and face. I punch him *hard* multiple times in quick succession, each hit lands on the sweet spot of his temple. The hits daze him, and his hold on my thigh relaxes.

I drop down to the floor as Colossal Douche takes a few staggering, unsteady steps backward. He teeters but doesn't go down. I stay on the offensive and attack again, searching for a good opening. He swings for me when I get close, but it's wild and doesn't connect.

I grab his arm and use his swing against him, pulling him off balance before slamming my elbow into his forearm. Colossal Douche lumbers forward from the impact, still trying to clear his head. I grab onto his shoulder and pull myself up to knee him in the ribs. He makes a rookie mistake and bends to the side, trying to protect his ribs, which provides me another clear shot at his head. *Dumbass.*

I slam my knee into his face. A loud crunching sound bounces around the chain link enclosure, and I jump back to avoid the explosion of blood and cartilage. He falls backward onto the mat, out cold, and I bounce a little as his massive frame crashes to the ground. The ref rushes to check on him and signals for the medics to take over.

An odd rumble rises from Colossal Douche's entourage, but I ignore it as I pull out my mouth guard. I scan the crowd of cheering fans that remain on their feet until I find the guy who looked so worried before. He stares at me wide-eyed, with a dumbfounded look on his face. I answer his misjudgment with a smug smile.

Someone tosses me a towel, and I wipe my hands of sweat and blood. The ref declares me the winner, and I exit the cage among the flurry of activity from people trying to revive my opponent. I look for the man who set off all my alarm bells earlier, but I don't see him anywhere.

Security escorts me away from all the commotion and back toward the locker room I dressed in earlier. I don't find Talon waiting to congratulate me in his usual position by the door. I don't see him anywhere which sends a trickle of unease through me. The driver-turned-henchman who brought me here stands in Talon's place, so instead, I follow him back to the locker room.

"Where's Talon?" I ask, as soon as the metal door clangs shut behind me.

"He was called away."

I wait for the guy to elaborate, but it appears that's all he's going to give me. I pull loose sweats on over the spandex boy shorts I'm wearing, and I slip on my socks and shoes. I yank a shirt over my black sports bra and grab my bag.

I'm ready to go in minutes, but judging by the impatient tap of the driver's foot and the irritated expression he's wearing, I've somehow taken too long. I make a mental note to ensure that Talon doesn't stick me with this prick again.

I swing the straps of my bag over my shoulder and square up to the driver.

"After you." *Asshole.*

3

I follow my curt escort out a door that exits to the rear of the building. The makeshift parking lot is barely lit, and a solitary black SUV sits parked fifteen feet away from the door. As the driver leads the way to the car, a quick flash of something catches the peripheral of my eye. I freeze and scan my surroundings, alert and ready for an attack. I swear I just saw something run past me, but I don't see anything there now.

I find myself expecting the creepy, dark-haired guy from inside to pop up out of nowhere, but all I see is an expanse of packed dirt and a smattering of small shrubs. Just as I'm about to turn away, I notice a faint shimmer in the air about ten feet in front of me.

"Miss Aylin?" the driver calls to me.

I'm sure I look like a mental case, standing here staring off into empty darkness. *Okay, Vinna, get your shit together.* A weird noise, almost like a grunt, interrupts my inner chastisement, and I find myself moving toward the weird shimmer. As I get closer to the anomaly, power roars through me like a flash flood.

"What the hell?" I mutter.

I look back to find the driver staring at me like I've lost my mind, and I wonder for a second if maybe he's right. Another sound pulls my attention back to what seems like empty space, but something about it feels really fucking off.

I continue walking forward, and my body is overcome with a staticky sensation. It feels like every muscle in my body simultaneously fell asleep and is now in the process of waking up. I take a second to shake out the buzzing in my limbs, and then I step into that shimmer in the air to find complete chaos on the other side.

The outbreak of action all around me, where seconds ago there was nothing, is disorienting. I stand frozen in place as I take in the melee. I'm surrounded by people... fighting. I look around, and recognition sparks through me when I realize that one side of the battle involves the entourage of the guy I just fought.

There are seven of the big burly men against four other middle-aged men I don't recognize. *Five,* I realize, when I spot a guy standing off to the side, separate from the others. He stands there with closed eyes and his lips move like he's talking to himself. *Well, if I am crazy, it looks like I have company.*

One of the men from the entourage sprints with alarming speed, heading right for the solitary guy, a glint of metal flashing in his hands. He bears down freakishly fast on the mumbling man, who doesn't seem to realize that danger is coming for him like a freight train.

My internal power perks up, eager to answer my call. The strange markings that showed up all over my body on my sixteenth birthday begin to tingle in anticipation. I call on the energy in the markings that line the bottom curve of my butt cheeks, and throwing knives become solid in my hands.

I wait a few seconds to see if the chanter will respond to

the threat, but when he doesn't even open his eyes, I spring into action. As the attacker brings up his knife, I throw my own at him. He roars out in pain and then drops to the dirt, blood flowing freely from the dagger that just landed cleanly in his throat.

The mumbling guy's eyes fly open, just as the body of his attacker skids to a stop a few feet away from him. The man's gaze lands on me, but instead of the look of gratitude I expect, his eyes narrow in irritation. He starts walking toward me, the constant movement of his lips never ceasing.

A man's shout of pain fills the night air, pulling my attention from the chanter. I focus on a man who looks to be almost seven feet tall, with long red hair that falls past his shoulders. He pulls a knife from his side, and blood seeps through the seams of his fingers as he applies pressure to the wound. He continues to fight off a man in front of him, oblivious to the threat that creeps up behind him.

"Aydin, watch out!" the chanter yells to his friend.

I run toward the man creeping up like a coward behind the ginger giant. I laugh at the look on his face when I pop up out of nowhere, fucking up his clear shot at the ginger giant's back. A flurry of punches and a quick twist of the neck has the big, burly coward face down in the dirt and out for the count. I turn to check on this Aydin guy and watch, completely gobsmacked, as a ball of fire floats above his hands.

His large frame and the loose auburn strands of his hair are alight with the glow of flames, and the ball of fire he's somehow creating swells between his palms. He throws it, and the man in front of him erupts into flames. The pain-filled screams snap me out of my shocked inaction, just as a whirring sound comes toward me. I reach out and catch the hilt of a knife, stopping it before it's embedded in my chest.

Holy shit, that was close!

I scan the fighters, looking for the dead man who just threw a fucking knife at me. I turn in time to see a dagger sink into the shoulder of the guy who's *still* talking to himself. He lets out a surprised yelp and grimaces against the pain. His mumbling stops, and suddenly two of the big burly fighters *explode* into gigantic fucking grizzly bears.

What in the furry fuck?

4

I don't even try to make sense of what the hell just happened. Instead, I focus on a man from the Colossal Douche's entourage who's trying to surrender. He's on his knees, crying and staring up at an older guy who has a bright ball of who-the-fuck-knows-what, pulsating between his hands.

What the hell?

You don't kill someone who's surrendering. Isn't that like a rule or a code that fighters are supposed to live by? I run past the man on his knees and slam into the magic ball wielding asshole. Thank fuck the glowing orb doesn't connect with me or the man on the ground. I yell at him to run. I don't look to see if he listens, because the guy I just body checked jumps back up, and he's pissed.

He's tall with dark hair and furious green eyes. Something about his face seems familiar, but I don't have time to think much about it before I'm dodging and evading his attack. I don't fight back, because I'm not sure if I should. After all, when I invited *myself* to this party, I took the side of this guy's group. They were outnumbered and fighting big dudes with knives, and it seemed unfair.

Then I went and switched sides by helping the surrendering enemy. Moral of the story: I need to learn to mind my own fucking business. I don't let the angry green-eyed man get in any hits, but he's relentless in his attack, and if I'm honest, I'm enjoying the challenge.

His eyes flit over my shoulder for a fraction of a second, giving away that someone's about to come at me from behind. *Oh come on, green eyes, you should know better than that.* I reach over my shoulder and stroke one of the lines of markings on my back, and a staff solidifies in my hands.

I feel a shift in the air behind me, and I twirl the staff, aiming for the body I know is closing in on my back. The green eyes of the man in front of me widen in shock at the sudden appearance of the weapon in my hand. I make contact with whoever's behind me, just as a third guy comes at me from the side.

It's three against little ol' me now, and I'm no longer questioning which side I should be on. The answer is *mine*. Three against one is bullshit, especially when I saved two of their posse from getting gutted. Bunch of ungrateful assholes.

The three assholes start grunting with exertion as I stop merely defending myself and start attacking. I rotate blows between them and continue to dodge their hits. The tattooed asshole, who joined the fight last, miscalculates a move, and I swing my staff hard toward his unprotected head.

I see the moment the tattooed guy realizes he's about to get seriously fucked up. Something about the sad resignation that bleeds into his expression compels me to let go of the energy that keeps the staff solid. It disappears from my grip just before it would have delivered a crushing blow to his skull. Surprise replaces the resignation on the tattooed guy's face, and he stiffens with shock.

I deliver a brutal kick to his chest, which knocks him out of the fight. I turn to block the fist aimed at my face. It's clear the two remaining assholes I'm still fighting don't give a shit that I just showed their buddy mercy by not bashing his skull in. I'm starting to get seriously pissed, and my power rises with my mounting anger. Orange and fuchsia bolts of energy move over my skin and someone around me swears.

The green-eyed asshole forms another one of those glowing orbs and lobs it at me. It sails unerringly fast toward me, and I have no idea how the hell I'm going to keep it from touching me. Images of that other man going up in flames flash in my mind, and for the first time in a long time, I'm scared.

Right before the orb connects with my shoulder, a blue convex shield explodes out of the markings on my arm. The glowing ball hits the shield, sparks and then fizzles out. I have no idea what the hell just happened, but I repress my astonishment. I'll have to explore this new ability later, when I'm not about to fuck somebody up. I turn back to the green-eyed asshole's stunned face and glare at him.

This fucker just scared the shit out of me...*let's see how he likes it*. He watches tensely as I reach behind my back. Instead of calling on the staff again, I stroke the markings for my sword. I'm not fucking around with these pricks anymore.

He steps back and produces another orb. My whole body lights up with crackling energy in response. My markings start to glow, and I feel the source of my power completely open up, ready to be called on. I clap a hand against the hilt of the sword that flashes solid in my palm, and it splits in two.

A blade now gripped in each hand, I give them an expert whirl and start stalking forward.

5

Someone shouts, "Lachlan, Keegan, stop," but I ignore the voice as I prowl forward. It's time to end this shit and show these assholes what I can really do. The command *stop* bellows out around me again, and for some unknown reason, this time I listen.

The green-eyed asshole does the same, sneaking wary glances my way, but the ball of light disappears from his hands. I back up until I can see all five of the strangers as they gather in front of me. I'm tense and ready for any of them to come at me. Energy still crackles over my skin in a steady warning. The strands of hair that have fallen out of my braids are floating around my face like I'm surrounded by water, instead of pissed-off power.

"Lachlan, why are you attacking her? She's on our side!" Aydin yells at green eyes.

The chanter stands just behind Aydin, and I can feel his caramel brown eyes on me as he brushes back a few wisps of his raven locks from his face. He's not as tall as some of his buddies, and I would place the lot of them in their early to mid-forties. His midnight curls are mostly pulled back, but a few strands have escaped and stick to his day-old inky stubble. His skin matches the caramel tone of his eyes.

"How is she on our side? *She* attacked me!" the guy, apparently named Lachlan, defends.

"Oh, please, I pushed you, I didn't attack you. I didn't even fight back until you three assholes ganged up on me!" I correct him.

They all turn to me like they're surprised I can talk. I don't get the vibe that any of them plan to attack me, and it's obvious I'm in a different league when it comes to fighting. They're all breathing heavy from exertion, and even though they're fit for men their age, they've got nothing on me. I release the energy maintaining the swords' solid form, and they fade from my hands into nothing.

"Holy shit! So that's how you kept from bashing my head in," the tattooed guy marvels out loud. "I'm Evrin, by the way," he offers.

Evrin holds his hand out. I just stare at it—*yeah not a chance buddy*—I've seen what his friends can do with their hands, and I'm not going down from what was supposed to be a friendly handshake.

Evrin's dark brown hair fades from long on the top to very short on the sides. It's super disheveled, either from all the activity or how he styles it. He looks strong like the others, but I wouldn't call him bulky, like the men they were fighting.

His features have a baby-faced quality to them. He looks younger, closer to his thirties than the others in this group. The innocence in his face is at odds with his heavily tattooed body. There's not an inch of skin, aside from his face and ears, that isn't decorated with ink.

"You're welcome," I tell him with a sardonic grin, and his boyish face lights up with a genuine smile.

"Thank you," rumbles out into the night, but it's not the tattooed guy who speaks but Aydin, the ginger giant.

He easily stands a foot taller than me, and he's thickly framed and stacked with muscle. His red, wavy hair hangs just past his shoulders, and I offhandedly wonder why he doesn't tie it back when he fights. It must get in the way. He has a short beard that softens the angles of his jawline, and his dark denim blue eyes bear those crinkly wrinkles people who laugh and smile a lot get. I find it odd when I notice he's not bleeding or favoring the side that I know took a knife earlier.

"Yes, and thank you from me, too," the chanter adds.

I give a small nod to both of them.

"Well, you'll get no thanks from me; you let my shifter get away!" Lachlan huffs.

Shifter?

I guess that explains the sudden appearance of grizzlies in the Nevada desert. First the fanged fuckers, now shifters? Throw in whatever these guys are, and there's a hell of a lot more out there in this world than I ever thought possible. I swat away the shit ton of questions I now have and glare at Lachlan.

"He was surrendering. Who fucking kills someone when they're surrendering?" I ask him, condemnation saturating my tone.

"They're traffickers. We have *orders* to kill them."

"Well... I didn't know that," I snap back, the righteous indignation falling from my voice.

"Of course not, because you have no business being here. Is vigilantism how you get your rocks off?" Lachlan sneers at me, and I snort out a laugh.

"Dude, rein in the asshole if you want any answers from me," I warn him.

Get your rocks off? Okay, grandpa. Seriously, who says

that? When Lachlan remains quiet, I decide that maybe I should explain why I stuck my nose—or knife rather—into their business.

"I fought here tonight. I was leaving when I stumbled into all this shit. One minute I was staring at the empty desert, the next I was watching some guy try to kill your friend." I gesture to the chanter.

Lachlan turns his angry gaze on the chanter. "How'd she get through your barrier, Silva?"

"I don't know. It shouldn't have been possible. I didn't feel any breaches in the magic. She just appeared inside," Silva adds, as he studies me.

"You're the girl that beat the shit out of their alpha," Keegan, the tall tan man with light brown hair and blue eyes, comments.

"Um, sure," I agree, not sure if it's true. Was Colossal Douche the leader of the pack? Suddenly that song by The Shangri-Las gets stuck in my head.

"Does anyone else think it's weird that she looks super familiar?" Aydin asks randomly.

They all look me over more critically, and I fidget, uncomfortable with the intense appraisal.

"Who's in your coven?" Silva asks me, a strange look in his eyes.

I look around the group in confusion...my what? "Am I supposed to know what that means?"

Lachlan scoffs. "She probably doesn't want to tell us so she can't get into trouble with mommy and daddy."

"Annnnd, now I'm done talking to you," I snap.

Aydin laughs and then coughs, trying to cover it up.

"We're paladin. We'll find out anyway. You might as well make it easier on yourself and just tells us," Keegan coaxes, his soft-spoken words matching up with his easygoing surfer vibe.

"Yeah, I didn't understand a fucking word of what you just said."

I glare at him, my irritation growing by the second.

Lachlan snorts. "All casters know what paladin are. Nice try, little girl."

"For fuck's sake! Are you always this much of an arrogant prick? I don't know who the fuck you are, or what a damn caster is, and honestly, I don't care. So, fuck you very much, I'm out of here!"

I find my bag laying abandoned in the dirt, and I sling it over my shoulder. I look around for the black SUV and the driver, but they're both long gone. I laugh, but it's hollow. Yeah, I can't blame him for taking off. I wonder if it was before or after the grizzlies showed up.

I fish my phone out of my bag, and I call Talon. It goes straight to his voicemail.

"Talon, your man left me out here in the middle of bloody nowhere, call me when you get this."

I pull up my Uber app, even though I know what it's going to say before I open it. I'm stuck out in the middle of nowhere. Fuck my life.

"Where are you going?"

"Away from you weirdos."

"You can make weapons out of magic, and we're the weird ones?"

Magic?

A hand comes down on my shoulder. Acting on instinct, I turn and punch whoever's touching me. I use my markings to add extra power to the hit, and Aydin flies back a couple of feet, landing flat on his back with an *oomph*.

"By the moons, you're fast," Silva exclaims, eyeing me warily.

I meet his caramel eyes, raising my eyebrows in unspoken challenge.

"And strong," Keegan adds.

"I don't know you. We're not friends. Don't touch me."

A couple of them put their hands up in an effort to show they're not a threat. Aydin coughs and rubs his chest where I hit him. He gives me a big smile, and his blue eyes light up with excitement.

"Fucking creepers," I mumble under my breath.

6

"Are you serious about not knowing what a caster is?" Evrin questions.

I want to stare at his tattoos, ask why he's covered himself in them. It dawns on me that maybe they're not tattoos at all. They could be like my markings, filled with power and ability. I bite down on my questions when Lachlan gives a rude huff at Evrin's query. I've had enough of this guy.

"I'm done answering your questions. Run along now. It wasn't a pleasure meeting you, and good luck dealing with the dick."

I flip Lachlan the bird over my shoulder as I turn around and start the long walk toward civilization. If Talon calls, he can pick me up on the side of the road.

I ignore the part of me that's screaming to turn around and see if these guys have any answers about why I'm different and can do the things that I can. They called themselves paladin; could I be one of those too?

Lachlan seemed to think I was...what was it...a caster, and Aydin said something about making weapons out of magic. Could that be what's inside of me? I've always called it power or energy for lack of a better word. Referring to it as magic makes me feel like some delusional Hogwarts wannabe.

I scrub a tired hand over my face and adjust the strap of my bag across my body so that it's more secure against my back. Pushing through my exhaustion, I start jogging down the black deserted pavement. I run for about thirty minutes before headlights appear behind me.

I've fallen into the comfortable rhythm of a fast-paced run while all the crazy events of the night play on a loop inside my head. I swerve off the warm blacktop of the road and onto the dirt of the surrounding dry landscape, to allow the vehicle to pass.

A silver SUV slows down next to me, and immediately my defenses are up. The back window whirs as it rolls down, and Aydin's auburn beard and pale skin peek out of the shadows of the back seat.

"Are you seriously going to run all the way back into the city?"

I look over at him and shrug, picking up my pace a little.

"Get in. The least we can do is drop you off at home after you saved most of our lives tonight," Aydin says with a smirk.

I weigh the danger of accepting a ride from these strangers, versus running in the dark out in the middle of nowhere. I'm, like, ninety-seven percent sure I could take these guys, so I decide a ride doesn't sound like such a bad idea.

"Okay fine, but if you guys do anything shady, or if you get too rude and annoying, don't blame me for what happens to you. It's clear whoever said *respect your elders* didn't know you assholes."

Aydin laughs, and I hear a couple more chuckles bounce around the interior of the SUV. The vehicle crawls to a stop, and Aydin unfolds his big ass out of the back seat. I'm worried they expect me to squish back into the small third row, which makes me rethink this ride decision, but thankfully Silva moves back there and gets himself situated.

I'm sandwiched between Aydin and Evrin as they manspread across the back seat. We ride in silence for a bit, and I'm starting to relax, the sounds of the tires against the smooth road beginning to make me sleepy.

"So what's your name?" Evrin asks me, breaking up the quiet atmosphere.

"Vinna Aylin."

As soon as my name leaves my lips, the car comes to a screeching halt. I slam forward and thank fuck for the seatbelt, or I'd be flat against the windshield right now.

"What the hell?" I shout.

"What did you say?" Lachlan growls at me from the driver's seat.

Everyone stares at me like I've grown a second head.

"What, my name?" I ask, confused.

Lachlan gives a terse nod.

"Vinna Aylin," I repeat.

Aydin whispers, "Holy shit," and Lachlan turns to Keegan in the passenger seat. They share a loaded look that I can't decipher.

"Does my name mean something to you guys?" My eyes jump to each of them. "You're all acting super fucking weird right now."

Lachlan turns back around in the driver's seat, and I stare at his back while no one answers my question. The silence in the car has a seriously uncomfortable weight to it, and I feel the sudden need to escape. I move to take my seatbelt off, but the car starts moving again.

Why would my name freak them out so much?

"Can you tell us a bit more about yourself?" Evrin encourages, and I look at him, hesitant and on guard.

"There's not much to tell."

"How old are you?" Silva queries.

"Twenty-two."

"Have you always lived here?" Keegan prods.

"No, I moved a lot when I was little, but I've been in Vegas for the past eight years."

"What's your family like?" Aydin throws out there casually, but the tick in his beard-covered jaw betrays his tone.

The rapid-fire Q and A session stalls while everyone waits for me to answer Aydin. I wrestle with how vague I should be about how I grew up, but my gut tells me to lay it all out there. I go with my gut.

"Until I was fifteen, I was raised by a monster of a woman named Beth. There wasn't a single moment where Beth let me forget how much she despised me. I had a sister. I was five when Laiken was born—."

I choke on the words in my throat as I'm hit with the sudden sadness and grief that always slams into me when I think about Laiken. My heightened emotions send a flash of magenta and orange energy down my arms, and I grit my teeth in an effort to control my emotions and the power.

"You okay?" Aydin asks me, and I notice he and Evrin leaning as far away from me as possible.

I tighten the stranglehold on my emotions and start again.

"I'm fine. Strong emotions feed the power," I offer vaguely. "Beth and Laiken were murdered when I was eighteen. Beth was always mixed up in some shit, and Laiken paid the price. I'd probably be dead too if Beth hadn't done me the favor of kicking me out of the house at fifteen. I've lived on my own ever since."

I decide not to say anything about Talon. These

strangers know enough about me as it is and talking about Talon feels like it should fall into *snitches get stitches* territory.

"That's about all you're going to get out of me until you tell me what's going on."

Veiled looks are passed back and forth at my demand, and just when I think they're not going to say shit, good ol' Evrin breaks the silence again.

"Um...you know you're not human, right...Vinna?"

7

Evrin's question sits like an anvil on my chest. *Not human?* I mean I knew I was different, that I was somehow *other*, but I never really questioned my humanity underneath all the extra I could do.

"So what the fuck am I, then?"

"Well, witch is probably the name you're most familiar with, but we call ourselves casters," Silva tells me.

I look around to gauge if these assholes are fucking with me, but I'm met with dead serious expressions.

"What makes you so sure I am one?" I whisper, not quite willing to believe what they're telling me.

"We all saw you use magic when you fought, and then there's these..." Evrin points to the line of markings that run up the outside of my arm, and dot my ring and middle finger. "I don't recognize these exact runes, but there's no doubt in my mind these are caster runes you've been tattooed with."

"Which should be fucking impossible," Lachlan grumbles, speaking for the first time in a while.

Man, I wish he'd just kept his mouth shut. "What should be fucking impossible?"

"You can't tattoo runes on a caster. It messes with the caster's natural branch of magic. You want us to believe you have no idea about casters and magic, but the magic-infused runes tattooed all over you tell a different story."

"First of all, you fucking tool, why would I lie about the shitty childhood I had. Secondly, my markings or runes—or whatever the fuck you want to call them—aren't tattoos. I didn't do this to myself. I woke up on my sixteenth birthday feeling like I was melting from the inside out, and then these showed up." I pull the neck of my shirt away and point to the *runes* that run across the top of my shoulder to the base of my neck.

"Lachlan, just stop. You're not helping."

To my surprise, Lachlan listens to Aydin and grinds his teeth closed. The car grows quiet again as each of us silently navigates through the smothering tension. Eventually the questions burning holes inside of me win out over my desire to master the silent treatment.

"So give me the *everything I need to know about being a caster* cliff notes," I urge no one in particular.

"Well...we're a race as old as time, with abilities that fall into one of five categories: Offensive magic, Defensive magic, Elemental magic, Spell magic, and Healing magic. There are casters out there with abilities in more than one branch of magic, but it's rare," Keegan tells me as if he's reading from a brochure.

"Our abilities first manifest about the age we reach puberty. It's called a *quickening*, and we come into our full power around twenty-five, and that's called an *awakening*," Evrin explains.

A massive yawn fights to take over, and it's like the action reminds the rest of my body just how tired it should feel. I'm muddled with exhaustion, and I lean my head back against the seat and close my eyes as I run through everything they just told me.

"Vinna, could Beth do the things you can?" Evrin pries.

I snort. "No. Thank fuck. She was normal, well, as normal as a sadist can be."

"Are you sure?" Silva presses.

"Positive. If she had any abilities, she would have used them to hurt me more," I mumble through another yawn.

"What do you know about your father?" someone murmurs, but I don't open my gritty eyes to identify who.

"When I could catch Beth drunk enough to ask about him, she always said he was a fling, that she didn't know who or where he was. But some obvious holes existed in that story. The biggest being that I have a different last name from her. I couldn't tell you where the hell it comes from though because, eventually, I stopped asking questions. It wasn't worth the beatings," I mumble, semi-conscious and borderline incoherent.

* * *

The pain is all I can think about, the burning consumes every cell in my body, and I writhe in a tangle of sheets as I scream into the pillow that's underneath my head. Death breathes expectantly down the back of my neck, and I almost welcome it.

I can't do this. I can't survive this pain, but as much as every fiber of my being believes that, it doesn't release me from this torture. All at once, the burning stops, my breaths hitching as relieved sobs tumble out of my mouth.

I've been clenching my jaw so hard that I'm surprised my teeth haven't shattered. I slowly and cautiously unlock the stiff muscles of my body, taking stock of myself. I'm a sweaty, tangled mess. What the hell just happened? I exhale a shuddering sigh and scrub my hands over my face to try and release more of the coiled tension trapped all over me.

What the fuck?

Small, intricate symbols run up one side and down the other of both my middle fingers.

I turn my trembling hand over and find an eight-pointed star mark sitting under the nail of my ring finger. I scramble to turn on the bedside lamp. Symbols line the outside of my arm, and when I look down, more trace the top of my shoulders.

Panicked, I untangle myself from the bedding and dash into the bathroom. I flick on the light and find my reflection in the full-length mirror hanging from the back of the door. I rip my tank top over my head, and I frantically search to see what other parts of my body the intricate symbols have claimed.

Two rows of symbols now run down the back of my neck to my lower back, and my torso is marked on the sides. The symbols start at the bottom of my armpit and stop at my hip bones. I'm marked from my heel, all the way up the back of my leg, until my thigh meets my butt.

The markings on the back of my legs remind me of the black seam that ran up the back of the old-school stockings that women used to wear. On the underside of each of my butt cheeks, symbols follow the natural curve of the bottom of my glutes and stop just shy of the side of my ass.

I spot three symbols on the helix of each of my ears, a line of markings on the outside of each of my feet, and a crescent moon on each of my middle toes. Everywhere I look, from head to foot, I now bear lines of these symbols, one side of my body a mirror image of the other.

I stare at my reflection in the mirror, examining my naked body and the mysterious markings. I don't know how to even begin to make sense of any of this. I clamp a hand over my mouth in an effort to trap a sob that tries to escape.

What the fuck does any of this mean? I put my back to the

wall of the bathroom and slide down until my butt meets the floor. I rest my forehead against my knees, allowing myself to get lost in my thoughts. I run my fingers over the symbols on my arm. They're not raised at all, which surprises me. The markings feel smooth like they've always existed there.

I stroke my now marred skin absentmindedly. Fuck, first Beth kicks me out and now this? I take a deep breath and release it slowly. Just when I think I couldn't feel any more lost, the world has to slap me in the face with something else. I sigh, story of my fucking life.

8

Someone shakes my shoulder, pulling me from my memory-filled dream, and I grunt in irritation at the contact.

"Vinna, wake up. We're here."

The deep rasp of a man's voice registers in my brain, and I peel my tired eyes open. I shake off the phantom pain in my limbs from the memory of the day I received my marks, or runes, I guess they're called. Evrin watches me, curiosity brimming in his eyes as I blink a few more times to clear my head.

Wait, this isn't my apartment building!

A Spanish style mansion frames Evrin's head, and I shoot upright, my gaze sweeping over the immaculate landscaping and gigantic fountain.

"Where the fuck are we?" I croak, my voice heavy with sleep.

Real smart, Vinna, what could possibly go wrong when you fall asleep in a car full of crazy weirdos? Way to think that through.

"This is where we're staying. We all decided it would be best to do a quick beacon spell. It will confirm for sure if you're a caster, and everything we need for the spell is here," Silva tells me.

Aydin gives an almost imperceptible shake of his head.

"So you guys just up and decided this, and now you expect me to what...go with it?" I ask, incredulous.

"It won't take long, and then we'll take you home. We're leaving tomorrow, so this is the only chance you'll get to find out for sure."

I glance back and forth between Silva's caramel brown eyes and the well-lit stucco monstrosity of a house behind him. My fear of missing out on answers overrides my apprehension at the shadiness of this situation. I climb out of the SUV and follow them through the front door, staying alert and keeping a suspicious eye on my surroundings.

"Keegan, set up in the library. The rest of you go get cleaned up, you have about thirty minutes," Lachlan barks out.

The others split apart, and Aydin gestures for me to follow him. We wind through a few hallways before he shows me to a guest bedroom, pointing out the attached bathroom. Immediately thoughts of a steaming hot shower flit through my head, and I race into the bathroom, Aydin's chuckles rumbling in my wake.

I lock the door, adjust the temperature of the water to just shy of lava-hot, and step into the stream of water. The steam and heat instantly relax me as I scrub the fight and aggression from my skin. The hot water feels so good, but it drains the last of my remaining energy, causing sluggishness to creep in. I crank the knob from red to blue and force myself to stand under the icy bombardment in hopes that it wakes me up a bit.

I towel off and wipe the steam from the mirror. I tilt my head from side to side and stare at my reflection. "Magic," I say out loud, trying to get a feel for the word on my lips and tongue. I have *magic*. Maybe.

I look back and forth between my eyes and take in the seafoam green color that leaks into a darker jade that rims my irises. Long, thick black lashes frame my large eyes, and I have a small straight nose that turns up at the end.

Beth used to taunt me about my *posh* nose, always doing whatever she could to make me feel insecure. But I liked my eyes and my nose, so it didn't bother me. My lips, however, are a whole other story. They've always been big and a constant source of teasing and torture when I was younger. Some people call them bee-stung lips, but Laiken always joked that mine were more wasp attacked.

Thinking about Laiken and her silly jokes sends a bolt of pain through my chest, but I try to shake it off. I lean in closer to the mirror and continue my scrutiny, running my hand over my long, almost black hair. I tilt my head and find the hints of plum that peek through in the right light. It's down to the middle of my back now, cut in layers that under normal circumstances, make it look voluminous and textured. Right now, it just looks matted and tangled.

I may not have known that *magic* was behind the things that I can do, but I've been using it in many ways since it first showed up. Aside from the things my *runes* do, one of my favorite tricks is to use my unique skill set to dry and style my hair. It's the best hairdresser a girl could ask for, and it saves me a crap load of time. Now, if I could just figure out how to magically apply my makeup, I'd be set. I tried it once, but the results were more of a *what not to do*.

I dry my hair until it's straight and shiny, but I don't bother to do much beyond that. I change into my spare workout gear and retrace my steps back out to the front door.

Dropping my bag by the entrance, I sit on the bottom

step of the stairs and wait for someone to come to collect me. This place is massive, and I don't want to get lost. Sure enough, soon Aydin tracks me down and leads me to a huge, fully stocked library.

I look around in awe and fight the desire to have a full-on *Beauty and the Beast* moment, twirl and all. When I'm done fighting off my inner Disney princess, I notice that the others are seated on brown leather couches and chairs arranged in the middle of the lounge area of the room.

"All right, Vinna, we're all set. We just need your blood, and we can get this spell started," Keegan tells me.

"Oh yeah, that doesn't sound ominous at all," I snark. "How much *blood* do you need and from where?"

Keegan gives me a warm smile, but this time I don't match it. "Only a drop. A prick of your finger will do just fine. Then I need you to drip it right in here." He points to a stone bowl that has some other unidentifiable things in it.

I move closer to the bowl that's centered on a big leather ottoman. Everyone is watching me expectantly.

"Aydin, pass me your knife?" Keegan instructs.

"It's fine, I've got it," I tell him.

I call on the runes that give me my throwing knives, and one solidifies in my hand. I use the tip against my middle finger. I extend the cut over the stone bowl, and a couple drops of blood drip in. I release the magic, and the throwing knife evaporates.

"I cannot wait to find out how you do that!" Evrin exclaims.

Keegan starts to add other things to the bowl, and it looks like he's getting ready to bake something instead of performing a spell that could possibly change my future. My stomach growls, and I silently agree that brownies would be better than whatever this spell is supposed to do.

"So what happens now?" I ask.

"Keegan will combine your blood with spell-woven magic. If the spell works using your blood, we'll know you're a caster," Silva explains, and I notice for the first time that he's standing by a set of windows instead of sitting with everyone else.

His ebony curls hang loose, instead of in a ponytail, and it makes him look younger than the mid-forties I pegged him as initially. Aydin growls and turns to scowl at Silva. He looks pissed as he stares daggers at Silva and then Lachlan. The venom in his eyes immediately makes me second guess what's going on. Aydin turns to me, and we watch each other for a beat without speaking.

"This spell will also send out a signal to any blood relatives that you may have," he grumbles. "You deserve to know everything that it does."

Aydin's words take a second to sink in, and when they do, I'm fucking livid.

"Whoa, pump the fucking brakes. You never said anything about finding any relatives! You said this would just tell me if I'm a caster or not!" I seethe at Silva.

"We need to not only confirm what you are, but we need to know where you come from," Silva replies, showing zero remorse over not telling me the whole story.

"I already fucking told you where I come from."

"No, you didn't, because you don't even know," he shouts back at me.

"What the hell are you talking about?"

"If Beth didn't possess magic, then there's no way she could be your biological mother. For a child to obtain magic, *both* parents have to pass it down. We don't know how you ended up with nons, or how you've even survived on your own for this long. It doesn't make any sense. We *need* to know where you come from."

I plop down on the sofa, and the cushion bounces back

against me. All my rage drains away with Silva's revelation. I'm not sure if I should feel relief or rage right now.

What the actual fuck?

Is that why Beth hated me? I've spent most of my life trying to solve that puzzle; is this the missing piece? But if I wasn't hers, then why the hell did she keep me for as long as she did?

"Well, isn't that just fucking perfect," I grumble to myself.

They need to know where I come from, but I seriously doubt that road leads anywhere good. You don't leave a child you care about with someone like Beth. Whoever I come from and wherever they are, they obviously left me on my own for a reason.

9

"Okay, Vinna, I'm going to activate the spell. If it works, you'll feel a small pull on your magic. It won't hurt, and it will be over quickly," Keegan tells me.

I don't respond. I get up and wander over to the bookshelves succumbing to the sudden need to move. They already have my blood and clearly plan to complete this spell regardless of how I feel about it. Pricks. Well, the jokes on them. They can tell me if I'm a caster, but they're leaving tomorrow, so even if they discover someone related to me, it doesn't mean I'll let them find *me* again.

Now that I know about them, I can try to track down some other casters and see if they can teach me more about my magic—that is, if that's even what I am. There's a flash of light inside the bowl Keegan's working over, and a trickle of red smoke wafts up from it. I feel a quick jerk in my chest, but just like Keegan said, it's over almost as soon as it starts.

I run my finger over the spine of a leather-bound book, and I hear a sharp intake of breath.

"Impossible!"

I turn around at Lachlan's pained shout. He leaps over

the back of the couch and slams me into a bookshelf. I'm so shocked that I don't initially react. He has one hand around my throat and the other digging into my shoulder. He shakes me as he screams in my face, asking things that make no sense to me.

Hands appear on Lachlan, trying to pull him off of me, but his hold around my throat is solid. Rage overtakes my shock, and I call on the runes of two short swords. I move one to Lachlan's throat and the other to his dick. The look on Lachlan's face is pained and manic, but I see the trickle of fear that seeps into his face when he registers the blades biting into him.

Everyone goes quiet and steps away from us at my silent threat. Lachlan slowly drops his grip from around my throat. I push against him, and he backs up to keep the knives from cutting him deeper. A trail of blood leaks out around the blade I hold at his neck, but there's not a single ounce of me that cares.

"I don't know what the fuck your damage is, but if you *ever* put your hands on me again, I will fucking end you," I seethe at him, pressing him back even more.

"Vinna, you don't understand—"

"I don't care!" I shout at whoever's trying to defend this asshole. "Keep this fucking mental case away from me!"

Hands wrap around Lachlan's shoulders and pull him free from my blades. I let them take him away, but I hold firmly to my weapons, staring at everyone else in the room and daring them to test me.

Silva moves toward me, and I crouch defensively. He raises his hands in a placating gesture and stops.

"I won't hurt you. I just want to know if you know where Eden is, or Vaughn and Lance?"

Silva's voice breaks with emotion when he says the name Eden. I stare at him, completely confused.

"I don't know who you're talking about," I yell at him.

Silva closes his eyes, seemingly in pain from my declaration. I see Keegan cradling Lachlan's head against his shoulder and speaking in hushed tones with him. It's clear that Lachlan is in pain, but I can't be bothered to care to know why. *I need to get out of here.* I start to back away, easing my way toward the doors that mark the closest exit.

"Vinna, stop," Aydin implores. "I'm sorry that just happened, but please let us explain."

I vacillate between my need to escape this nightmare, and the need to make sense of what the hell's going on right now. I step out of the room.

"Vinna, please!" Silva begs, and I pause.

I stand half in and half out of the room, not sure which way I want to go. Keegan walks Lachlan over to the stone bowl, and he starts chanting. Lachlan mumbles something and runs a finger across his palm where a slash appears. He closes his fist over the bowl and blood trickles in.

Keegan chants some more, and the inside of the bowl flashes again. Lachlan releases a relieved breath and calm washes over me. I don't know where the feeling comes from, but I know it's sure as hell not from me.

"Vinna, come, sit down, and we'll explain," Keegan tells me.

I shake my head, not willing to go anywhere near these paladin or casters or whatever the fuck they are. The best I can offer is to lean against the door frame.

"I'm related to you?" I question, looking at Lachlan like he's shit I just discovered on my shoe.

He solemnly nods, clearly not any happier about this revelation than I am.

"You knew from the minute I told you my name in the car, didn't you?"

"We all suspected, but we couldn't be sure until we completed the spell," Keegan explains.

I stare at Lachlan with more scrutiny than I previously had. His hair is dark like mine and styled in a very *McDreamy* kind of way. His eyes are a darker green, more emerald to my sea foam. We share the same high cheekbones and oval face, his the masculine version of mine. He's all chiseled jaw and manly edges with the faintest hint of stubble on his face. I choke a little on my sudden thought.

"Are you my father?" I croak out, my breaths becoming rapid and shallow.

"No, I'm your uncle."

"Where are they...my...uh...my...parents?" I finally manage to get out while trying to keep from free-falling into full-blown hyperventilation.

"We were hoping you could tell us that," Silva confesses.

"I told you, I've only ever known Beth."

I'm losing the battle with my runaway breaths. Evrin hops up and strides toward me. I'm bent over at the waist, but I hold out a short sword at his approach.

"Don't...come...near...me," I warn him between frantic breaths.

"I just want to help you," he soothes.

"I don't care; I don't want any of you to come near me," I huff out, labored and slow.

I look up at Evrin to make sure he listens, and I see the hurt on his face. I move my gaze down to his chest and watch it rise and fall with his calm, normal breathing. I focus on that, trying to match my own inhale and exhale with his.

It takes time, but my panic gradually recedes, and my lungs inflate rhythmically as I get myself back under control.

"If you're my uncle, are you from my mother's side or my father's?" I ask, staring at the ground.

"Your father's."

"What's his name?" I whisper, tracing the pattern of the carpet with my eyes.

"Vaughn Aylin...we're identical twins," Lachlan laments, his voice breaking at the admission.

This revelation shakes me. This is what my father looks like. I stare at Lachlan, going back over the pieces of myself in his face.

"I don't know how you came to be, but I know that Vaughn would've never willingly walked away from his child," Lachlan tells me.

I think he means for his words to comfort me, but they don't counteract the holes in the story of my existence. I have my father's last name. Either he knew about me, or Beth knew more about him than she admitted.

"Do you know who my mother is?" I ask Lachlan, feeling more and more empty as the seconds tick by.

"No."

"Are you sure Beth was a non?" Silva asks me.

"What the hell is a non?"

"It's what we call humans or anyone who's not supernatural," Silva clarifies.

"Yeah, I'd say about ninety-eight percent sure. So where is...uh...Vaughn?" There's no way I can call him my *dad* or *father*. It feels too fucking weird.

"None of us knows," Keegan answers. "Another coven of paladin requested help with a nest of lamia they were assigned to purge. The other coven required more protective magic, so the elders assigned Vaughn. No one ever returned from that mission. The entire coven of paladin, and the lamia they were supposed to exterminate vanished.

"It's been over twenty-three years, and we've never

stopped looking. We've done everything possible to try and find them, but at every turn, we've hit nothing but dead-ends and walls." Keegan looks to Lachlan with sadness in his eyes.

"And now, here you are, Vinna, another piece in a seemingly impossible puzzle to solve," Silva adds, and he sounds surprisingly hostile.

I can connect most of the dots now. What happened to the people they love, it makes it easier to understand the frustration and sadness that's palpable and suffocating in this room. What I don't get is the anger and hostility that's directed at me. Why am I being attacked over something I wasn't even alive for?

"What is a lamia?"

"They're basically vampires," Aydin tells me.

"So the fanged fuckers are lamia," I mumble to myself.

Five heads snap to me.

"What did you say?" Lachlan asks me.

"I always called them the fanged fuckers. I could never make one of them tell me what they called themselves."

10

"You've come in contact with lamia?" Aydin asks, his look of shock matching the expression on everyone else's faces.

"Um...yeah," I answer cautiously, not sure why this seems to be an issue.

"By the moon, how have you survived this long on your own?"

Evrin's question seems rhetorical, so I don't bother to reply. Instead, I focus on the soreness weighing down my limbs and the scratchiness of my eyelids. Every blink feels like sandpaper roughly smoothing and reshaping my eyeballs.

"Well, that ends now. We pack up what we can of her things tonight and arrange to have the rest shipped. Silva, stop and get some boxes, the rest of us will take Vinna to start packing," Lachlan orders.

"Whoa, what the fuck are you on about? I'm not moving in here with you," I gesture from the house to the paladin with one of the short swords in my hand.

"That's correct because we don't live here. We're only

here on assignment. You'll be moving with us to Maine. The town of Solace to be exact," Lachlan arrogantly informs me.

What an asshole.

"Yeah, thanks but no thanks. That's going to be a hard pass for me," I tell him as I push off from the wall next to the door frame so I can leave.

"Lachlan is your family, and he's claiming you; you *have* to go with him," Keegan tells me.

"I'm not some sweater in the lost and found or a dog at the pound; you cannot *claim* me."

"Vinna, you're a caster, and as a caster, you're considered underage and claimed by your parents or a guardian until your awakening," Evrin explains to me with soft, sympathetic brown eyes.

"You can run, but we will find you. If you don't come willingly, we'll get the elders involved. If you fight them, they will bind your magic until you learn to listen. You can make this easy on yourself, or you can make this difficult, but either way, the outcome will remain the same," Lachlan threatens.

I release the magic of the two short swords I'm holding and reach behind me. I call on the runes for my big ass sword and draw it over my shoulder like I'm pulling it from a sheath on my back.

"Do what you've got to do, asshole. But keep in mind, it's hard to tattle to some magic-binding elders when you're dead." My voice is saccharine, but my eyes blaze with the promise of pain.

I'm so tired and pissed off right now. I don't care if I am related to this fucker. Who the hell does he think he is?

"By the bleeding stars, Lachlan, your Dictator Aylin routine isn't fucking helping things!" Aydin yells at him. All five of them start shouting at each other, and I take advantage of the distraction and step out of the library. I let my sword dissipate as I retrace my steps to the front door. I grab my bag and bolt. Let the *hide and seek* begin, motherfuckers.

* * *

I SPOT a familiar auburn-bearded giant in the crowd. He's wearing a baseball cap, but it does nothing to hide every other prominent feature that Aydin has. It's like these paladin fuckers *want* me to spot them from a mile away.

After I snuck out, I spent the first two nights in random motels. I thought for sure there was no way they'd find me, but I was wrong. I'm pretty sure they put some kind of magical LoJack on me, but I can't figure out how to find it, let alone get rid of it.

It either has to do with Lachlan and I being related or with the blood I gave them for the beacon spell. Caster lesson number one: don't give your blood to any fucker for a spell. It seems, if I keep on the move, they can't track me as well, but as soon as I stop for too long to eat or sleep, these assholes start to close in on me. So I changed the game from *hide and seek* to *catch me if you can*.

I pick up my pace as I weave through the pedestrian traffic on the Las Vegas Strip. It's night time, and the lights are blazing, the booze is flowing, and the streets are packed with people here to have a good time. I sneak a glance behind me and chuckle at the sight of Aydin being accosted by a group of drunk women, who look like they're here for a bachelorette party. Either that or they really like dicks and find them to be the perfect accessories—we're talking light-up headbands, necklaces, rings, straws—these ladies are dicked-out.

I take advantage of their sexual harassment of Aydin and dash toward the closest resort. I navigate my way through the casino, past all the shops, and out the back into a parking garage. I sprint toward the exit and hang left, trying to give myself as much of a lead as possible. I don't hear anyone behind me but better to be safe than sorry.

I run behind the hotel and round a corner that will take me up the side and eventually spit me back out on the Strip. The smell of the alley full of dumpsters hits me, and I pull my shirt up over my nose. I move past the last can of stench when several things fall from the sky to land ten feet in front of me.

Did these idiots just jump from the roof? I skid to a stop as I try to gauge how far it is from the roof of the hotels surrounding me to the ground. I glance around and discover it's not the paladin in front of me but something else.

"Hello there, little caster. You've certainly been a hard one to pin down." The lamia smiles, flashing just enough fang to leave no doubt as to what he is.

He's slightly taller than I am and possesses an angelic beauty, just like all the others I've encountered. I've never seen a female or even a fat fanged fucker. Either lamia are super picky about who can be in their club, or being a lamia makes you stone-cold gorgeous.

I scan the four lamia surrounding me, all of them have brown hair and various shades of alabaster skin. Each of them wears a confident smirk, and I can see the dismissal in their eyes. It's okay though; underestimation always works in my favor.

"Aww, I'm sorry. If I had known you were looking for me, I would have sorted out your death wish sooner," I wink at him and watch amusement flicker over his face.

I call on the runes for my short swords, and they flash

solid in my hands. The amusement blinks out of the lamia's expression and is replaced by intense indignation.

"Now, now, little caster, don't be like that. Be a good girl. I promise we don't bite...much."

The four lamia titter at the lame joke as they close in on me.

"Could you be any more unoriginal? Really, you don't bite *much* is the best you could come up with? How disappointing. I'd tell you to work on your lines, but you'll be dead soon."

The lamia furthest to the left spontaneously combusts into flames. The unexpected inferno makes everyone freeze, and I hear heavy footsteps pound against the pavement behind me. I recognize the cadence of Aydin's giant stride, and he saunters up to me, fireballs alight in his palms as he takes in the scene.

"Well, look at you, Little Badass, how did you know I was itching for a good ashing?" Aydin remarks, excitement and anticipation sparkling in his gaze.

"I'm an excellent gift giver. It's one of my many shining qualities," I deadpan.

"Why are we just standing around? Let's do this." Aydin's fireballs begin to grow, and I watch, envious.

"You really need to teach me how to do that."

"Come home with us, and I will," Aydin tells me with a wink.

Before anyone else can so much as move, Aydin throws a ball at another lamia. It misses and explodes against a wall, and the magic fizzles out. I lose track of what he does after that as two of the lamia descend on me in a flash. I twist and dodge their sharp claws as I slash and stab with my swords to try and create an opening.

Based on the fireballs Aydin's throwing, I deduce that's

one way to take them out. I've always had to remove their heads. Before my runes and magic armory showed up, I would force my power into the fanged fuckers. It would turn them to ash immediately, but I could never quite master how I did it.

Claws skate across my back, and my magic surges inside of me. I twist and slam my short sword down, and the blade takes a forearm and hand clean off. I follow through with my other sword, and the lamia's head tumbles from his body. I twirl around and catch the chatty lamia with a blade to the stomach.

"Faron's coming for you. Your free days are numbered. My sire will own you soon enough."

My blade slices through his neck, cutting off any more bullshit threats.

I turn to see if Aydin needs help, and find him leaning against the hotel wall. He stands there, his arms crossed, one foot on the pavement, the other on the stucco of the wall. He looks like he doesn't have a care in the world.

"Well done, Little Badass, you went right for the kill each time, no hesitation."

I roll my eyes. "Yeah, I've been doing this since I was fourteen, but I'm glad I could entertain you."

Aydin rubs the back of his neck and takes me in. "You're this fucking powerful, and you don't even have your full magic yet," he shakes his head and snorts. "Are you going to keep running, or can we move past that and go the fuck home?"

I stare at him, not sure what the answer is. It's clear by now that running is only delaying the inevitable. I may hate how this whole situation played out, but I've lived most of my life wishing I had answers. The road to understanding is laid out in front of me, but it's paved with an asshole of an uncle and his half hostile coven of paladin.

I start walking toward the bright lights and bustle of the Vegas Strip.

"Where are you going?"

"My apartment. You going to come help me pack or what?"

11

I push the button to call the elevator. I usually take the stairs, but after the night I've had, I'm dead on my feet. The doors open, and I drag myself in. My floor lights up with a ding, and moments later, I'm stumbling into the apartment. There's a black duffel bag on the kitchen table, and I walk over to it and unzip the top. There's a note inside:

Little Warrior,

Here's your cut. Sorry I couldn't stay, but business calls. I'll be out of contact. I'll call when I'm back.

Talon

I huff out a sigh and look around. I've lived here for five years now, but it still doesn't feel like home. When Talon offered me the deal to train and fight for him, he did it on the steps of this building. It wasn't a difficult proposition to accept. Not a lot of options existed for girls in my circumstances, and working my ass off was infinitely better than selling my ass.

When I agreed, he walked me up to this apartment, and I've lived here ever since. It was fully furnished when I moved in: towels, linens, dishes; it had everything, which worked for me because I didn't have shit. The only things

I've added over the years are clothes, books, and some hiding spots for money. I chuckle to myself; after five years of staying here, I still don't really have shit.

"What's so funny?" Aydin asks me, as he lumbers through the doorway.

"Nothing."

I groan and scrub my tired face with my hands. I drop the duffel bag of money by my hiding spot in the bookcase. A knock pounds on the door. I run my hands through my hair and stare at the door like the harbinger of doom that it is.

I open the door silently and wave the four tired looking paladin in. Judging by their haggard expressions, they haven't gotten much rest, and their age is showing. They take in where I live and look at me like they expect me to bolt any second. I trudge over to the living room, and they trickle in after me. We all stare awkwardly at each other and around the room, no one eager to break the silence.

"Nice place," Evrin offers, always the one to lose the silent standoff.

For someone who looks like a tatted up badass, he seems awfully nice. It's that, or he can't stand awkward silences.

"It's not mine," I monotone.

"Uhh...you live with someone?" he pries, scrambling for something to say.

"No."

I know I'm confusing him, but I don't care, so I don't elaborate.

"Look, I know this probably feels overwhelming and confusing, and a little out of nowhere—"

"Oh, you *know*? Is that how you felt when all of this happened to you?" I snark at Keegan, unable to rein in my inner grumpy bitch.

He turns to Lachlan, who just watches me.

"We aren't going to leave you behind. Like it or not, you are now a part of this coven, and it's not safe for you to be on your own," Lachlan tells me, his voice a smooth calm I haven't heard him use until now.

"So *ask* me then."

Lachlan looks confused.

"Ask you what?" he finally relents.

"Ask me to come with you. Don't dictate or command like you would a pet. Ask me, like you would a person you actually gave a shit about."

My voice betrays me and breaks a little as I finish. I look away and tighten my stranglehold on my emotions. When I feel under control, I look back into two green, fathomless pools of emotion I couldn't even begin to decipher.

"Vinna, will you come with us?" Lachlan caves, his tone even and emotionless.

I guess that's the best I can hope for from the prick. I release a big sigh but don't bother to answer him. I just turn around and start pulling two rows of books from their shelves and set them on the floor.

"These are the only things in here that are mine. I have a couple of duffel bags, but I'll need some boxes for some of my other things."

Silva stands up and walks out the door. I'm about to follow him and tell him that he won't find anywhere around here that sells boxes this late at night, but he walks back in with a stack of boxes. I shake my head. Maybe box making is one of his magical abilities. Who am I to judge? I mean, I use magic to style my hair.

"We can spread out, each of us packing a different room," Keegan directs and reaches for a box.

"That's not necessary. I don't own a lot. These books and some stuff in the bathroom and bedroom," I explain. I grab a box that Silva taped together and walk to the bedroom.

"Silva, I'll probably only need three," I yell over my shoulder.

I assign Keegan my closet and Evrin my dresser. Mostly I just wanted to see how uncomfortable the tattooed hard ass would be when he has to pack my underwear. Lachlan's texting on his phone, so I turn to Aydin with a shrug.

"I don't have anything for you to do. Nothing else in here is mine other than the clothes."

"And there's not many of those either," Keegan grumbles from the closet.

He's right. I don't own a lot of clothes. I hate shopping, and most of what I do have is workout clothes because that's how I spend the majority of my time. I leave them to it and head to the bathroom to pack it up. Twenty minutes later, all my possessions sit in three boxes stacked by the door.

"You weren't joking when you said you didn't have a lot to pack," Silva comments looking at the small stack.

I shrug. I can tell that my meager collection of belongings bothers them. I keep catching looks of sympathy and dismay being exchanged back and forth, but it is what it is.

"So where the fuck are you dragging me off to?" I walk over to the black duffel bag that's sitting by the bookshelf and open it.

"We live in a town called Solace. It's in northern Maine, a couple of hours west of Presque Isle," Keegan starts, as I pull out the bottom shelf of the bookcase.

"It was founded in 1635 after the first witch trials began in North America. It's predominantly a caster community, although a few shifter packs live there too. It's spelled so nons can't find it, which allows us to stay safe and secluded."

"Don't the locals think that's weird?" I ask as I start to transfer stacks of money from the bottom of the bookshelf into the duffel bag. "I mean they would know there's a town there but can't find it on a map or GPS?"

"It's spelled to keep nons away entirely, so they don't even know it exists," Keegan explains, sounding distracted. "Anyway, inside Solace, our coven has about 25 acres with all sorts of fun things to do: lakes, ATVs, camping, swimming, and there's a stable on the property next to ours, so there are horses."

I place the full black duffel bag by the boxes and grab the empty one I set aside earlier.

"I'm still listening, just talk louder, I need to get my stash in the back," I tell Keegan.

I walk back to the bedroom, and everyone follows me.

"Uhhh...we...um...recently tore down the old house and rebuilt one that works better for us. We all live there, including Silva's two nephews."

I pull out the two bottom drawers of my dresser and nod at Keegan, encouraging him to continue talking. I pull more stacks of cash from the dresser and begin filling the second duffel bag.

"You rob a bank, kid?" Aydin finally asks me.

I chuckle, shaking my head. They've all been watching me empty my hidey-holes with wide eyes, and I wondered how long it would take before someone asked me what the hell I was doing.

"Nope, I earned this fair and square...well...maybe not exactly square. This is what I earned from my fights." I nod at the duffel bag as I keep piling stacks in. "I couldn't put it in a bank, so...yeah." I pop the drawers back into the dresser and zip up the duffel. I look up, and they stare at me like I've done something crazy.

"What?"

"How much is in there?" Aydin asks, and Evrin slaps him on the back of the head like he did something naughty.

"What, you know you want to know," Aydin scowls at Evrin and rubs the back of his head.

"About 200,000, give or take," I shrug. I haven't counted what I made from last night's fight yet, so I'm not one hundred percent sure.

Aydin whistles. "It's a good thing we aren't flying commercial. They'd never allow those bags on the plane."

"It looks like fighting's worked out well for you," Silva comments, though I can't tell if he's judging me or impressed with my haul.

"Yeah, I can hold my own," I tell him, and I can't help the smirk that sneaks across my face.

"I can't wait to train with you, Little Badass," Aydin exclaims with enthusiasm, rubbing his hands together in anticipation.

I feel a tingle of excitement myself at the prospect of training and using magic. "I'm all set," I announce, looking back over everything. I pull out my phone and place it next to the keys I left on the kitchen table. I set the note I wrote for Talon in the same place and take one last look around.

This place wasn't mine, and it never quite felt like home, but I was protected and nurtured here, all the same. Gratitude and a twinge of sadness fill me as I close the door on this chapter of my life.

12

Something tugs at my insides, coaxing me from the nothingness of deep sleep. A quiet but consistent hum sounds all around me, and I groggily try to figure out what the noise is. I settle on *I don't care,* as I snuggle into the side of whoever's holding me and breathe out a contented sigh.

What the fuck? Where am I, and who the hell am I snuggled up against? A jolt of panic shoots through me, adrenaline slamming into me like a tsunami. My heart thunders and a charge laps across my body, making magic crackle over my skin. Voices whisper around me, and something makes a chill run down my spine at the hushed tones.

I sit up in a flash, trying to get away from the arm draped around me. Another set of arms wrap around me from behind, and I almost taste the rising panic as I call on my magic. I send a jolt into anyone who has their hands on me, and it's answered by a satisfying, pained shout. I run my hands over the runes on my sides, calling on the short swords. A squeal sounds off from somewhere around me, and I'm thrown forward, smashing into something hard. I shake it off as I reach for a door handle and scramble to escape.

"Vinna, wake up!" a familiar voice shouts, but I dismiss it as my feet sink into something cool, and I begin to run.

Air whipping past my face and the cool ground pounding against my feet pull me fully conscious. I'm in a grass-covered field, quickly approaching a line of dense trees. I hear footfalls behind me, and I push myself harder. If I can just make it to the trees, I can lose them. *Wait*...who am I trying to lose?

"Vinna, stop!" a voice behind me bellows, confusing me even more.

"You're safe. We're in Maine," someone else yells, and I stop in my tracks.

I spin around to find Aydin and Silva running toward me, though they're still about fifteen feet away.

"Holy shit, what just happened?" Aydin pants, stopping in front of me.

"Where am I?" I ask, my voice gravelly from sleep.

"We just passed into the boundaries of Solace," Silva reassures me.

"By the moon, you're fast!" Aydin declares as he bends over and tries to calm his breathing.

"Yeah, and you need to work on your cardio."

The stoic Silva shocks the hell out of me when he busts out laughing. I stare at him in wide-eyed surprise, and Aydin cracks up as he points to the expression on my face.

Evrin pulls Keegan up off the ground as we walk closer to the two Range Rovers that are stopped on the side of the road. Looks like Keegan took my jolt of magic. I feel kind of bad, but I was half asleep and didn't really know what I was doing. We can be *even* now for his part in ganging up on me in the fight with the shifters. Evrin looks me over from a distance.

"How'd you get her to stop?"

"She woke up and stopped herself," Silva tells Evrin with a shrug.

"You okay?" Evrin asks me.

"Yeah, sorry, I felt something weird and...well...freaked out." I run my hand through my sleep mussed, and now windblown, hair.

"Shit, that's on us," Lachlan admits, and I look at him confused. "We just passed through the boundary. It would have pulled on your magic. We're used to the sensation, but you've never experienced it before. It can feel alarming."

Realization dawns on the faces of the paladin around me.

"I didn't even think about that," Evrin admits sheepishly, and the others agree.

Aydin lets out an excited squeal, and I look at him like the mental case he clearly is. I didn't know a grown man could sound like that.

"I am just so excited to see all of the things you can do. It has me giggling like a kid on Christmas morning! A staff, a sword, throwing knives, baby swords...what else do you carry in that magical arsenal of yours?" Aydin wonders, his blue eyes bright and eager.

"Wouldn't you like to know," I reply evasively, and Aydin giggles.

"Little Badass, you live up to your new nickname more and more as I get to know you."

A smile lights up Aydin's face, and the girlish giggle coming out of this auburn-haired, seven-foot-tall giant, is contagious. I'm trying so hard not to laugh, but I can't seem to help it.

"Do you know how to use all of those weapons?" Lachlan probes with feigned nonchalance.

"Yes."

"Who trained you?" he presses.

"YouTube."

Aydin and Lachlan scoff and laugh like I've just told the best joke. Laugh it up, bitches. They'll be choking on those chuckles when they realize that endless hours of videos can teach you to do practically anything. With my ability to mimic the things I see, I've developed quite a diverse range of skills.

We pull off the road we've been on and head deeper into the forested landscape. We drive through a valley, and there are trees and hills all around us. An occasional house pops up in the distance, but for the most part, everything seems to be spread out. It's incredibly green and beautiful, and I can see why someone would name this place *Solace*.

"In about ten minutes, we'll pass through another barrier," Aydin informs me. "The wards start about ten acres from the house. You might feel a rush or a pull on your magic. It can feel different depending on the type of magic you have, and we won't know that until you have your reading."

"My reading?" I repeat, and I can't help but feel like I'm drowning in a sea of unknown. For every answer I get, a thousand more questions arise, and it feels never-ending.

"It's a ritual that identifies the kind of magic you possess and determines the level of strength you'll exhibit when wielding it," Keegan clarifies.

"What kind of magic do each of you have?"

"I have Elemental magic." Aydin holds up a tiny ball of fire as proof. "Lachlan has Offensive magic."

I snort and try to swallow my laugh. Everything I discovered about my uncle thus far has been offensive, so it's only right that his magic is too.

"Evrin has Healing magic, Keegan has Spell magic, and

Silva has Defensive magic," Aydin finishes ticking off his fingers.

A gate swings opens on its own as we approach it. We drive through the stone pillars, and I admire the intricate details of the black iron gate when a warm sensation envelops me, and the runes on my body all start to tingle.

"Something is happening," I announce and stare at my runes.

"Don't worry, we're approaching the barrier, it'll be over in a minute," Lachlan says dismissing my concern.

Without any additional warning, the runes on my body start to glow...*well shit*, here we go.

"What the..." someone exclaims, and the SUV suddenly stops.

I stare at the glowing runes and start to feel the now familiar sensation of magic building inside of me. I fling open the door and scramble out of the SUV. My runes feel like they're heating up. It's not painful, just odd. The sensation building within me plateaus, and I hold my breath and wait to see what the fuck is going to happen.

"Do you feel that?" Aydin asks.

Everyone nods and mumbles affirmation. I stare at them, waiting for someone to fill me in.

"Vinna, can you—"

Before Lachlan can finish his question, magic surges out of me in a massive pulse. It exits with such force that it blows everyone off their feet. The Range Rovers rock side to side, both of their alarms breaking out into shrill wails. A combination of bright orange and deep pink magic blankets everything it touches as it spreads out and away from me. The magic wave hits an invisible barrier and then shoots up to dome above us.

"Are you okay?" Aydin questions, the first to make it back on his feet.

I nod absently, unable to speak because it's taking everything in me right now to keep from collapsing and blacking out. I feel like I have been running nonstop for days, every ounce of energy sucked from me. My muscles feel like jelly and quiver like they've been overused. Whatever the hell just happened has completely drained me.

The others get up and dust themselves off. I can tell that none of them have any idea what the hell just happened, so I don't even bother asking. I take deep, slow breaths and focus on not showing any signs that something is wrong with me.

"Can you tell what she did, Silva?" Lachlan asks as he sweeps blades of grass off his pants.

"She strengthened it," Silva states, looking at me shocked, and they all turn and look at me in the same way.

"What? It's not like I have a clue what the fuck just happened," I defend. "What did I strengthen?"

"The barrier around the house. It keeps out unwanted entities and anything that means harm."

"Oh...cool," I say casually and climb back into the car alone.

I put my head back against the seat, exhausted and overwhelmed. Listen, magic, can we go a solid twenty-four hours without you doing something no one has ever seen before? Let's not give Lachlan any more reason to want to burn me at the stake.

The paladin are huddled together in some kind of deep discussion. They throw the occasional look my way, but other than that, it's all serious and brooding faces, with an exasperated arm flail every now and again.

Happy for the reprieve, I rest in hopes it will help get my energy reserves back to normal levels. Aydin, Lachlan, and Keegan eventually pile back into the car. Everyone is silent as we continue on.

13

We crest a hill, and Keegan announces, "Home sweet home."

I raise my head up and peek out the front window. We are driving toward what looks like a hotel. I lean forward and stare slack-jawed.

"That's not a house, that's a damn resort!"

Laughter titters around me, and I'm not sure what's funny. The *house* is palatial. The outside is grey stone, broken up by huge trimmed windows and dark wood doors and accents. I can see three stories, and to the left of the main house is a square courtyard surrounded by six garage doors.

We park at the front door, and everyone piles out.

"Vaughn originally set up the wards. I've just been reinforcing them. I didn't see a point in redoing perfectly good wards," Silva tells Lachlan.

Oh goody, we're still discussing the cluster fuck that is me and my magic.

"I wonder if her magic recognized his?" Aydin hypothesizes.

"Yeah, but how did she strengthen the original wards?

It's unreal the juice that she pumped into them, I wish you guys could feel it like I can," Silva remarks.

"Oh, we felt it," Keegan tells him, and they all turn to examine me again.

"Can you stop staring at me like I'm a freak puzzle you're trying to solve?"

They all look away and start unloading my boxes and their luggage. I take in the gorgeous landscape and beautiful façade of the monster mansion. Silva starts humming the tune to "Super Freak," and I snort, unable to hide my amusement at his newfound sense of humor.

"Where are the boys?" Evrin asks Silva, as we all move toward the front door.

"Last I heard, they were camping."

"How do you call this a house?" I ask rhetorically. "This is the kind of place that has a name like *Chateau be Jealous of All My Money*."

I look around in complete astonishment. Aydin and Evrin guffaw with laughter.

"I'll get a plaque made," Lachlan deadpans, and I see the faintest hint of a smile before the asshole in him scares it away.

We walk into what Lachlan refers to as the *foyer*. Dark wood floors with white marble, are interspersed together to create a beautiful geometric pattern. To the right, a set of dark wood stairs lead up to the next floor. The ceilings are incredibly high, and I glance up to find a masculine iron and glass chandelier.

Lachlan points out a pair of arched doors to the right that he announces lead to his office, and I follow him into an open and spacious living room. Natural light pours into the room from two-story high windows, and it makes everything appear bright and inviting.

The space is comfortable and lush, but not so nice that

you're afraid to touch anything. Lachlan leads me into the kitchen, which opens to the living room on one side and the dining room on the other. A gargantuan island easily fits the five tall chairs tucked into one side of it. Aydin opens a cabinet, which turns out to be a fridge, and hands me a bottle of water.

Out of nowhere, three elderly women pop out of a door, and I squeak out a surprised noise.

"Vinna, I want to introduce you to Roberta—who everyone calls Birdie—Adelaide, and Lila. They manage the house, and if you're in need of anything, track one of them down."

The three women appear related. They all have beautiful white-gray hair, cut in different but complementary short styles and similar facial features. They're all about a couple inches shorter than I am, and they have lightly lined faces with strong looking arms and hands. They seem like they've laughed a lot in life and aren't afraid of hard work.

Each of them gazes at me with such warm affection, and I'm not sure what to think about it. I offer a small smile and an awkward wave in greeting. Birdie walks over, and before I can do anything to prevent it, she snatches me up in a firm hug. I stiffen automatically, and I know she notices.

"Sorry, I'm just not used to affection," I tell her and give her an awkward man-pat on her back. She pulls back, holding my shoulders, and a sheen of tears glistens in her eyes.

"Don't worry, love, we'll get you used to hugs in no time."

She moves her hands to my cheeks and cradles my face. "Have you ever seen a more beautiful young woman?" Birdie beams and looks to the guys for confirmation.

They don't answer her, but she's not bothered and answers herself.

"No, I think not. Oh, the boys are going to love you," she

proclaims, as she looks back toward the other two women who nod their heads in agreement.

I'm not sure if she's referring to *the boys*—which is the title that the paladin seem to use for Silva's nephews—or boys in general. Birdie gets right in my face, her soft blue eyes demanding my undivided attention.

"We couldn't be any more excited that you're here. My sisters and I have been all aflutter since Lachlan called and told us about you."

I stare at this woman before me, seeming so comforting, so loving in a way that feels safe and genuine, and I shock the hell out of myself when I start crying.

"There, there, my love, what is this?" Birdie soothes.

Her sisters step toward us, and they wrap me up in a group hug, each of them stroking my hair in turn. It feels so foreign and yet, so soothing, and apparently, the only response I can give is to cry harder.

"Well crap, sisters. You broke her. She's been tough as graphene until now, but one minute with you three and this happens," Aydin teases.

Since I haven't made enough of a fool out of myself, I cry a little longer before hiccupping out an apology. I pull back, wiping my face.

"I think I'm just tired, and no one's ever told me that before, it felt so nice to hear. I didn't know this was going to happen," I try to explain, gesturing to my tear-tracked face as I work to wipe away the wetness.

Birdie looks at me confused, her gaze darkening further when her eyes run over the bruises on my neck.

"What do you mean, love? I'm sure all these boys have told you how happy they are you're here," Lila asks me.

I laugh humorlessly. "No, no one other than you three—and Aydin—are the slightest bit happy I'm here," I dispute, wiping the rest of my face dry as I take in the rest of the kitchen.

"Well, no wonder," Adelaide mumbles. Her gaze fixes on something behind me, her eyes transforming from soft and loving to hard and punishing in an instant. "You go on and finish your tour with Aydin. We're just going to have a quick chat with your uncle and the other boys." Adelaide smiles, but it looks more fierce than friendly.

Aydin drags me away and out of the kitchen. We walk through the dining room, with a massive table centered in the middle, and exit into a hallway before he speaks.

"Oooh, Little Badass, you just sicced *the sisters* on all of them. It is not going to be pretty, and there will be casualties."

After a quick walk through the rest of the main floor where I'm told Lachlan and Keegan reside, Aydin shows me the second floor where the rest of the paladin coven lives, and then we climb up to the third floor.

"The boys stay over there," Aydin explains, pointing to the left of the staircase where we stand.

I figure at some point someone will tell me their names, but for now, I guess referring to them as *the boys* will have to do. We walk over to a door on the right, and Aydin motions for me to open it.

"This is your room."

The door swings open, and I freeze, completely shocked. Aydin chuckles and rubs my back in what I'm sure he means as a comforting gesture, but I stiffen all the same.

"Sorry, Vinna, I keep forgetting that you don't like to be touched."

I ignore the incorrect observation, not bothering to enlighten him. It's not that I don't like to be touched, I'm honestly just not used to it. Beth never touched me unless it was to punish me, and since I've been on my own, I focused only on training and fighting. I'm affectionate with Talon now, but it took time for him to earn my trust.

My eyes flit all over the room, not sure where they want to land. To my right, a beautiful cream colored limestone fireplace takes up most of the wall. Across from the fireplace is a humongous, black four-poster bed with a tall arched headboard that sits on top of a colorful rug in gray, purple, pink, and blue hues. The bed is covered in grayish purple bedding, with different textured pillows in the same color, stylishly placed at the head of the bed. The wall that the headboard sits against is the same gray stone that's on the outside of the house, and it makes the room feel old and warm.

A collection of small canvases hang above the headboard, and they artfully come together to create a picture of a pixelated peony. Tall windows brighten the room, and another set of doors lead out to a private balcony.

My hands come up to my mouth as I turn to the left to see a sitting area with a cream colored couch complete with two matching chairs centered around another colorful rug. They face a huge TV mounted to the upper part of the wall, with built-in black bookshelves below it. I gawk at everything, rendered speechless.

"Welcome home, Little Badass."

A knock sounds at the door, and Evrin sticks his head in with a shy smile.

"We brought your things up," he tells me and pushes open the door. He whistles as he enters the room, and Silva follows in behind him.

"Wow, the sisters really put in work," Silva declares, looking around as impressed as I am.

They drop off the boxes, and we all stand around awkwardly, staring at each other.

"Anyway, we'll leave you to get settled," Aydin finally declares.

Evrin and Silva move to leave, but Evrin stops so abruptly that Silva slams into his back.

"I'm glad you're here, Vinna," Evrin tells me, and I regard him for a couple beats.

"Thank you, Evrin," I whisper.

He continues his exit from the room, but Silva hesitates.

"I am sorry about what happened after the beacon spell," Silva tells me. "I know things have gotten off to a horrible start, but they'll get better."

I offer him a small smile that ends up feeling more like a grimace. The term *horrible start* feels a little tame for how things have gone. It's tempting to believe him; it would be nice to be wanted here, but I can't help feeling like Birdie, Adelaide, and Lila forced this apology out of him.

Maybe I'm wrong, and I should give them the benefit of the doubt. Or perhaps I'm so desperate for a connection and guidance, that as bad as things started, it really doesn't matter. I give an awkward wave goodbye as the three paladin leave.

As soon as the door clicks shut, I twirl around and squeal. *At least there's this.* I run my hands over all the different textures in the room, inspecting the details. I walk through the frosted glass double doors just past the sitting area, and I stumble to a stop. Is this a spa or the bathroom? Vases of fresh flowers sit atop a long black vanity with two sinks and a distinct area to lounge while putting on makeup and getting ready.

Across from the vanity is a crazy huge shower, and I spot several showerheads positioned throughout the ceiling. At the end of the long room is a behemoth-sized soaking tub with an insanely tall window above it.

"Hello, beautiful. You and I will be getting acquainted very soon," I promise the tub.

I walk back into the bedroom and run my hands over the soft sofa and pillows. I slip out of my shoes and run my toes through the velvety fibers of the rug. I climb into the mountain of pillows on the bed and lie there, trying to process what in the hell I'm doing here.

14

Delicious smells beckon me forward as I reach the bottom of the stairs. I'm not sure what time it is since I don't currently have a phone or own a watch. Apparently they don't believe in clocks in this house either, because I have yet to find one. I follow my nose toward the kitchen, which I find filled with the rumbling sounds of deep laughter and animated conversation.

I passed out yesterday afternoon, and I just woke up maybe ten minutes ago in full starvation mode. I take the back way into the kitchen and find the paladin sitting at the island, enjoying a delicious looking spread laid out before them. My mouth waters, but I hesitate to interject myself on their happy breakfast. I'm about to turn around and sneak away when Birdie stops me mid-pivot.

"There you are, love, I wondered when I'd get to see that gorgeous face of yours again. Where are you going?"

I pivot back toward her which means I just full-on twirled and now look like an idiot. I don't answer her, and I can't seem to make my feet move forward either. Birdie gives me a sympathetic look and walks toward me.

"Here we are, love, you just sit right here, and let's get

some food in your belly. Do you like eggs benedict?"

I sit in the chair Birdie points to.

"I'm not sure. I've never had it," I manage to say as I run my hands over the rich wood of the dining room table.

"Well, let me fix you up a plate. You just eat what you like and leave what you don't, okay?"

Birdie flits away, and I sit silently, staring at my hands. It's not lost on me that the happy conversation I heard before I walked in was apparently killed off by my arrival. Each of the paladin now sits silently at the kitchen island.

Birdie sets a heaping plate of food in front of me, and my taste buds are frenzied with excitement. I look up at her with a small smile and mumble thank you. I take my first bite, close my eyes, and moan in pure ecstasy. I open my eyes and notice Birdie still standing there, watching me.

"This is the best thing I've ever eaten," I confess to her as I shovel in another bite.

Birdie's face lights up, but she also looks a little sad. I'm not sure what to think of that, so I just focus on the fantastic food in front of me. Each bite is a bliss-filled experience, and before I know it, the plate sits empty.

Birdie must see my disappointed expression when I look down at my empty plate, because she steals it away and replaces it with a new full one. I give her an elated grin as I dig into my second helping.

I can feel eyes on me, but I can't even be bothered to care or feel embarrassed; the food is that good. I finish my second serving and have a long debate with myself about licking the remaining sauce off the plate. I decide showing even more of my inner heathen this soon could be a bad move, so I resist the call of the sauce and stand with my plate in hand.

"Where do you think you're going, my love?" Birdie asks me, as I carry my plate toward the sink.

This feels like a trick question, and I hesitate.

"I was going to wash my plate," I tell her, and it comes out like I'm asking a question.

"Oh no, love, that's my job," she tells me cheerfully and reaches for the dish in my hand.

I pull it away out of her reach. "You cooked, and I don't mind cleaning up after myself," I explain to her.

Birdie just smiles at me and pats my cheek. The next thing I know, my hand is plate-less, and Birdie is humming away at the sink. I stand there open-mouthed and baffled, trying to figure out how that just happened. I suspect magic was somehow involved, and I conclude that I'll need to step up my game for that sneaky, plate-stealing Birdie.

"Vinna," Aydin calls my name, pulling me from my plans for a dishwashing counterattack. I turn my attention to him.

"I need to go get some things in town today. You want to come with and check things out?"

"Is it shopping? Because if it is, I'll pass. I hate shopping," I tell him.

"A small amount of shopping may be involved, but you won't hate it," Aydin assures me.

"Challenge accepted," I mumble, and Aydin's resounding laugh echoes around the kitchen.

"Bring your money. I'm going to get a bank account set up for you," he shouts to me as I head toward the stairs to get dressed. I give him a thumbs-up over my shoulder.

* * *

Aydin parallel parks his fancy sports car that I don't know the name of, in front of a brick building with ivy growing up the sides and encroaching on the front. As I tilt my head in consideration of the sight, I discover that I'm slightly obsessed with the look of the deep green plant taking over the sun faded brick. It completely encapsulates what I envisioned buildings on the east coast to look like.

We walk up to the door, and Aydin presses a buzzer. A man's bored voice comes through the speaker, asking if we have an appointment. Aydin doesn't answer one way or the other. He merely announces *Aydin Calix* into the speaker and steps back to wait. A couple of seconds later, the door gives a buzz, and I follow Aydin through.

He guides me into a posh sitting room and tells me to take a seat. I'm scanning the room, searching for clues as to what this place is and what we're doing here when a gorgeous blonde woman comes out of nowhere and greets Aydin with an open-mouthed kiss. I'm a little surprised, but I try not to gawk at the public display. Eventually, they separate, and I spot Aydin's blush covered cheeks.

"Staysha, this is Vinna Aylin. Vinna, meet Staysha," Aydin offers in introduction after taking a moment to compose himself.

Staysha's eyes widen in shock when Aydin tells her my name.

"Lachlan?" she asks, aghast.

"Vaughn," Aydin replies.

She stares at him, her eyes burning with questions. He gives her a subtle shake of his head, which causes a professional mask to shutter over her features.

"What are you two looking for today?" Staysha inquires, smoothly transitioning into business mode.

"Vinna needs some clothes, so we're here to get her set up."

My head snaps to Aydin at his statement.

"Wait, I thought we were here for you?" I question, feeling duped.

Aydin's smirk would make the Cheshire Cat jealous, and I shoot him a murderous glare.

"Any particular occasion, season, or style?" Staysha queries, unfazed by our exchange.

"She needs anything and everything that you can think of," Aydin supplies, and I hold back a groan.

I feel like that response is too general, but it seems it's enough information for Staysha because she just nods her head and makes a couple of notes on a tablet.

"Vinna, do you have any brands or styles of clothing that you gravitate toward?"

I pause, trying to gauge how to answer her question best.

"I like to be comfortable and casual most of the time, but I'm not afraid to peacock when it's time to show off."

Aydin laughs, "What does that even mean?"

"You know, flash my pretty feathers when the time is right?" I explain, realizing I sound like an idiot as the words leave my mouth. I look at Staysha for help.

"You know the assets that you're working with and don't mind playing to your strengths when the occasion warrants it," Staysha clarifies, giving me a kind and knowing smile.

"Exactly," I agree, the satisfaction of being understood replacing the embarrassment coursing through me.

We spend the next hour or so perusing an online catalog, marking the things that I like and styles I'm willing to try. Staysha takes a lot of notes, and after a short time, I feel confident that she understands my personal taste. She takes my measurements and notes my shoe size before she tells us she has everything that she needs.

"See, that wasn't so bad, was it?" Aydin teases as he opens the car door for me.

"I can't lie, that was the least painful shopping trip I've ever experienced."

"It will be even easier in the future, now that she has

your sizes and knows what you like. You'll only need to call and whatever you need is delivered right to our door," Aydin explains.

"Who gets the bill?" I inquire, trying to figure out how I go about paying for things.

"You don't have to worry about that," he dodges.

"Aydin, I have money. I can pay my own way."

"I know, and I don't care," he huffs. "Do you want to stop and get a phone next, or go set up a bank account?"

I roll my eyes at the obvious evasive maneuvers and implement some of my own.

"So all of these people are casters?" I ask, pointing at the random people going about their business in town.

"Yep, throw in a smattering of shifters, and that's Solace for you," Aydin confirms as he starts his car and pulls out onto the road.

I didn't really have any preconceived notions or imaginings of what this place would look like, but I can't help feeling a little surprised by how normal it all seems. It's not a one street, one stoplight small town, or a bustling city. It's something snuggled quaintly in the middle.

People are walking to different shops, heading in groups to restaurants, grocery shopping, all perfectly normal things. I do notice a couple of stores for spell ingredients and other unusual items, but those are the only things that strike me as unusual.

We drive past The Academy, which I find out is a prestigious school for casters. It looks regal and old, but the campus is empty, and the school looks lonely without any students. Aydin informs me that classes start next month, and a weird look crosses his face as he relays that tidbit of information. *Maybe he thinks I didn't graduate* I think to myself as I try to interpret why Aydin's acting strangely as he talks to me about school.

We tackle the bank next. I'm impressed when the man setting up my account doesn't even blink twice at the two duffle bags full of cash I set on his desk. He just took the money to be deposited, handed me a debit card, and off we went.

After stopping off at a couple more places, I began to pick up on the veneration and esteem that everyone seems to treat Aydin with. I've noticed most people used the word *paladin* like a title, and it reminds me that I have no idea what it means.

"So where do paladin fit in the supernatural food chain?" I finally query after leaving the phone store where people seemed to fall all over themselves to help Aydin.

He chuckles. "We're not separate entities, Vinna. We're still casters."

I look at him confused. "But you guys always call yourselves paladin, not casters?"

"Well, because technically, that's what we are now, what we've earned the right to be called. Paladin are like an elite police force for casters. We are the top tier of warriors and guardians. The word *paladin* references what we do, and when someone uses it as a title, it's a respectful way of acknowledging our rank amongst casters. It's like saying *officer* or something along those lines."

"Gotcha, that makes sense," I acknowledge, watching the scenery of the town flash past the car window. "How do you become a paladin?"

"There's a lot that goes into it, but for starters, to even qualify, you need to have either powerful magic in one of the branches, or moderate magic in more than one branch. Then there is rigorous physical training and years of skills testing before you can earn a place as a paladin," Aydin explains, and his pride in his accomplishments overflows as he speaks. "Speaking of which, it looks like we'll be headed out soon on another case. Lachlan is finalizing the details, but we shouldn't be gone more than four days."

I wait a couple of seconds to see if Aydin will offer any more details about what they're going to do, but he's quiet. Figuring it's a *need to know* type situation, I don't press for more information. Besides, it might be nice to have the mega-mansion to myself. Lachlan has a library in his office I've been dying to raid, but his grumpy ass is always in there.

We park in front of a nondescript little white building, and I'm ushered inside and greeted by a man at a desk. He shakes my hand and quickly covers the look of delight on his face when he spots Aydin behind me. They engage in some small talk, the details of which are lost on me, and I find myself once again searching the room for clues as to what this place is.

"What can I help you with Paladin Calix?" the man asks.

I smile because I'm now in the *paladin* loop and know what the heck it means.

"We are in the market for a car," he explains to the man.

"For fuck's sake, Aydin!" I screech and move to get up.

"Hear me out," Aydin begs. "You need to be able to get around here. You'll have classes to get to. Eventually, you'll have friends you want to hang out with and places that you'll want to go. We live far enough out of town that you'll have to drive."

Classes I'll have to go to? What the hell? I shove this new information aside and focus on the argument I need to win.

"There are garages full of cars at your mega-mansion, why can't I just drive one of those?"

"All of those cars have owners, and they will want their car available to them when they need it."

I glower at him for a minute, a plan formulating in my head. Aydin takes my silence as compliance and gives me a victorious smile before continuing.

"I want something top of the line, four-wheel drive, all the bells and whistles," he states.

The man starts typing away, and after a couple of minutes, he flicks on the large TV mounted on the wall behind him. On it are two SUVs. He starts showing Aydin the features of each vehicle, comparing the pros and cons of both. I wait patiently until he turns his attention to me. Aydin finally asks my opinion, and I offer him a tight, sweet smile.

"This"—I point to the screen—"is not happening."

He frowns and opens his mouth to say something, but I cut him off.

"That is a ninety thousand dollar car!" I exclaim. I know that because the numbers at the bottom of the screen change as they add and remove features. It doesn't take a genius to figure out that's the price tag.

"No way in *hell* that is happening," I say again, pointing to the screen, so there is no doubt about what I'm referring to. "If I need a car, fine I won't argue, but I can't rationalize spending that much money on a car. I'd be afraid to touch it!"

Aydin and the car man both laugh at the last part of my rant.

"You need a car that can handle the weather up here. There will be snow, ice, rain, and animals that you'll need to be able to navigate. I would feel better if I knew you were in a safe and reliable vehicle. These are the best, and I want you protected by the best," Aydin proclaims.

"Aydin, that SUV is an overly extravagant, unnecessary purchase. I don't need bulletproof windows or armor plating."

"What's your point?" Aydin deadpans.

"There has to be some sort of compromise here," I insist. "There has to be a vehicle that checks all your boxes but doesn't cost ninety thousand dollars...and isn't a fucking tank," I throw in for good measure.

We both look back at the gentleman behind the desk who immediately starts typing away. After arguing about several options, we both finally agree on a Jeep Wrangler. Aydin adds more upgrades than I think are necessary, but I stop fighting him.

In the end, it still looks kind of tank-ish, featuring a matte black finish complete with rims, winches, and a bunch of other things Aydin said I had to have *just in case*. It looks so masculine and, well...badass, that I can't deny I'm really fucking excited to drive it.

When we both finally agree on what's on the screen, Aydin hands over a card to pay, and that's when I execute my plan. I snatch Aydin's card and replace it with my own. My *sleight of hand* apparently needs a lot of work, because Aydin catches me in action and scowls at me.

"Give it back, Vinna!" He growls, and I narrow my eyes in challenge at him.

I look over to the man who watches our exchange with a glint in his eyes.

"What are you waiting for? Run the card," I urge him.

He starts to reach for it, but when Aydin shouts, "Don't you dare, Neil!" Neil stops.

Aydin grabs my card and throws it behind us. I take the bait and scamper to retrieve it. I'm faster than Aydin anticipated, and he hasn't managed to pull another card out of his wallet before I'm back. Taking a page from Aydin's playbook, I snatch the open wallet from his hands, run for the door, and chuck the offending card-carrying leather as far as I can.

I don't see where it lands before arms wrap around me from behind, pulling me in from the open doorway. I can't help the victorious laugh that escapes me as I'm pulled back into the small building sans wallet. Aydin searches my hands and quickly realizes what I've done.

"You little shit!" He grunts incredulously, but I see the smile in his narrowed eyes.

Aydin looks at me, then at Neil, and through the glass of the door. I can see the wheels turning as he contemplates his next move. He knows if he goes outside to get his wallet, I'll force Neil to run my card. A spark flashes in his eyes, and he lunges for me, throwing me over his shoulder.

"Give me my card, Vinna!" Aydin demands as he starts searching my pockets for the original card I snatched.

I'm laughing so hard, but *shit,* Aydin's going to find it if I don't do something quick. I flip over his shoulder landing behind him. I swing around and launch myself on his back and put him in a chokehold. Aydin maneuvers out of it like I'm merely giving him a hug, and we start wrestling.

I'm slightly aware of how utterly ridiculous we must look right now. I'm trying not to do any damage to Neil's office, which is proving more and more difficult. I get Aydin in a great position for an arm bar, but there's just not enough room to follow through without putting a hole in a wall. I release my hold, and we're all over each other again, both looking for the opportunity to gain the upper hand.

It's time for the big guns, or rather the big knives, I think to myself, as I flip out of Aydin's grasp and call on the runes on my ribs. A long dagger forms in my hand, and I point it at the advancing giant. Aydin stops a few inches shy of the point of the blade and glares at me.

"That's cheating!" he pouts.

"I know...jealous?" I tease.

Aydin laughs. "Yes, I am, actually!"

I laugh at his admission. "I had to. If we keep it up, I'll not only be paying for my new Jeep but a new office for Neil too." I chuckle and give Aydin a wink.

We both look over to Neil, and he's shaking with laughter and wiping tears from his eyes. "I could watch that all day," Neil admits and falls into another fit of laughter.

I pull out my card and hand it over to the giggling Neil, keeping my blade trained on Aydin.

"As soon as that blade's gone, you're going to get it, Little Badass."

Aydin's playful threat hangs in the room as Neil runs my card. He hands it back to me with a huge, beaming smile.

"You're going to make a fine paladin if you can best this one already," Neil points at Aydin.

I open my mouth to tell him I can't be a paladin, as I'm late to the game, but Aydin's voice cuts me off.

"She'll be the best we've ever seen."

I turn back to Aydin, surprised at the admission. He winks at me, his smile growing even bigger. Neil hands me the receipt, and I let go of the magic keeping the dagger solid in my hand.

Neil lets out a surprised gasp. He quickly covers his shock over my disappearing knife trick and extends his hand for me to shake. Aydin throws me over his shoulder again before I can shake it. He spins in place, making me dizzy, and I'm squealing with laughter. Aydin shakes Neil's hand and thanks him before carrying me out of the door.

"Thank you, Neil," I shout before the door closes.

A laugh-filled "You're welcome" is shouted back.

"You better hope no one stole my wallet. Now, where did you throw it?" Aydin grumbles.

I use my foot to point since I'm still thrown over his shoulder and laugh at the grumpy mumbling coming from Aydin as he vows, "This isn't over."

15

I wake up to the sun streaming through the windows, making my bed nice and warm. I stretch and let out the obligatory *screech*. I should get up, but this is the most comfortable bed I have ever slept in, and I don't want to seem ungrateful by abandoning it so soon.

I lay in the embrace of the perfect mattress and pillows, noticing the exposed beams on the ceiling for the first time. I groan and reluctantly pull myself out of my covers, giving the bed an appreciative pat for the awesome sleep it gave me. I straighten the bedding and arrange all the pretty pillows exactly how they were the first time I walked into this room.

Lila greets me merrily when I walk into the kitchen. She hands me a warm omelet, and I stare at it, wondering how she knew to have it ready. I chalk it up to the sisters' sneaky magic and proceed to straight-up inhale everything on the plate.

I get up, intent on cleaning my dish, but Lila snatches it away as quick as lightning and starts scrubbing it. I gape at her.

"Birdie warned me about you," she laughs over her

shoulder.

I shake my head at her. "This means war, Lila." My attempt at sounding formidable falls flat when she giggles at me. "Seriously, I can fend for myself while the coven is gone, you don't have to wait on me," I tell her again, but it's obvious my declaration falls on deaf ears.

Lachlan and the coven left on another case a couple of days ago. I get that the sisters cook and clean when the paladin are here, but it's just me right now, and being waited on and served feels awkward. The sisters won't let me help with anything, and I've already been lectured twice for trying to eat cereal for every meal.

"I like it, dear," she states dismissively. "My sisters and I have been with the Aylin family for a very long time, and we love what we do, so don't you go feeling bad about it or trying to put us out of a job."

Lila gives me a *don't mess with me look* and snaps me on the butt with the drying towel in her hands. Like the true badass I am, I squeak and scamper away.

"Go be lazy!" she orders with a chuckle.

I rub my butt cheek and salute her as I head outside to follow orders. I've spent the last two days lounging by the pool and reading. I've been raiding the library in Lachlan's office where I discovered a ton of books about casters and magic, and I've been completely engrossed.

Today, I decide to do some exploring outside. I walk for hours around the property, making it familiar and getting my bearings. I spot an inviting little path, and I decide to follow it. I walk for a while, running my hands over the trunks of trees and listening to the birds chatter back and forth when I stumble into a clearing that overlooks a big lake.

The clearing is covered in soft grass with little white flowers sprinkled throughout, and it's so idyllic it looks like it belongs in a painting. The soft grass begs me to take my shoes off and run my toes through the lush green blades, so I do just that.

The grass is cool, and a breeze sneaks by, bringing the smell of rain and something floral with it. There's a rocky drop off before it meets the dark blue lake, and I sit and watch patches of sun sneak through the clouds to kiss the lake until it sparkles. I brush my hand over the top of the grass, tilting my face back and relishing in the sun, and then the shade when clouds float by, blocking the rays and diminishing the heat.

I'm not sure how long I sit peacefully before the first raindrop hits my skin. I open my eyes and inspect the sky, seeing some darker, more ominous clouds in the distance. I pull myself from the tranquility I'm surrounded by and start heading back toward the house.

The light sprinkle of rain turns into a downpour, and I'm grateful that Lila warned me to take something warm with me when I headed out. I pull my hoodie on, flipping the hood up over my head in an attempt to keep my face and hair somewhat dry.

My stomach growls, and I pick up my pace. The thought of some yummy food and dry clothes motivates me to move quicker. I'm thinking about how I can bottle the smell of fresh rain when I hear the sound of heavy footfall pounding behind me.

Before I can so much as look for the source, something slams into me from behind. My legs fly out from underneath me, and I hit the ground hard, landing on my side. Rocks and other debris dig into my skin as I fight to regain the breath that was just knocked from my body. A hand grabs my shoulder and flips me onto my back. My lungs finally inflate, and I gasp in air, trying to get my brain to focus on defense and not on what's hurting.

"This is private property. What the fuck are you doing skulking around?"

A tanned, masculine face glowers at me, while simultaneously ripping my hood back from my face, taking some of my hair with it. I wince in pain and watch shock fill the hazel eyes of the man pinning me down. He gawks at me, taking in my features, and I feel his grip on me loosen.

I take advantage of his distracted hesitation and punch him in the throat. He falls forward and clutches his neck.

With serious effort, I roll us over and switch our places. The man gasps for air, his hands at his throat, and his eyes tightly shut. I'm not sure how long I have before he recovers from my hit so I waste no time in doing what I can to incapacitate him.

I hit him several times in the face and drop my knee onto his side. I try to knee him a second time, but two huge arms wrap around me from behind. I'm lifted off of the guy who tackled me and thrown at least five feet away.

I roll as I land and come up in a crouch. I call on the runes for several small throwing knives and palm them in both of my hands as I study the newest threat.

My mind stutters for a second as I stare into the same face I was just hitting. No, not the same, I realize as I look to the man still groaning on the ground. These two must be twins. This one's hair is pulled back into a knot, but the same pissed off expression crosses his face.

They've got to be at least six foot five, and they're sporting lean, defined muscles. They have a golden tone to their skin, strong angled jaws, and full lips. Their noses can join mine in the posh club, and long obsidian lashes surround their hazel eyes. I would wipe my drool from my chin over how hot these guys are, if these assholes hadn't just picked a fight.

The one still standing forms a ball of magic in his hands, but he just holds it there and glares at me.

"Who the hell are you, and what are you doing here?" he snarls.

"I live here," I snap back irritated.

"Bullshit, try again," he sneers at me, feeding more magic into the ball hovering between his palms. Orange and fuchsia-tinted magic crackles over my skin in response to his threat, and I see a sliver of uncertainty on his face before he masks it.

"My Uncle Lachlan owns this house."

"Funny that, as our uncle is in his coven. I'd think we'd know if Lachlan had a niece."

The arrogance wafts off him, but his statement helps something click, *the boys!* These two must be Silva's nephews. With everyone referring to them as *the boys*, I pictured younger... well...boys. That assumption could not have been more wrong. *The boys* are two super-hot, fully grown *men*. I relax my aggressive stance slightly, hoping his body language will mirror mine.

"You should probably call your uncle so he can fill you in on what's happened while you *boys* were off camping."

Confusion seeps into his features, and he reaches for something. My instincts take over, and my hand frees itself of a throwing knife. I watch as the blade flies past his cheek, mere centimeters away, and thuds into the trunk of the tree behind him. The magic ball he holds bursts, and he jerks his head back to look at the knife in the tree.

As his head pivots, a couple strands of hair come away loose from his scalp. The nick in his hair won't be noticeable, but we both know how close that knife just came to his head. He looks back at me alarmed.

"What the fuck? I was just reaching for my phone!" he yells at me, and I almost feel bad for scaring him...almost.

I stand up all the way, hoping he sees how nonthreatening I am now, and he reaches for his phone again, his movements slower this time. I watch him carefully as he puts the phone to his ear, his wary eyes fixed on me.

"Hey, Sil, we just found a random girl sneaking around the property. She's saying that she's Lachlan's niece, know anything about that?"

He smirks at me, thinking he's caught me in a lie, but I wait and watch his face fall as he gets clued in. He shoots another glance at me then looks away turning to the side.

"Shit, yeah, um, Bastien kind of just attacked her."

Yelling squawks out from the phone, and he pulls it away from his ear.

"We didn't know who she was; he just saw someone in a black hood roaming around in the woods, and he took off. You know how he is, attack first, ask questions later." He pauses. "Our phones were dead, we just charged them, and I haven't checked any of my messages yet."

Twin two looks over at me, and I can see him scan me from head to toe.

"I can't tell, she mostly just looks wet and muddy, but Bastien tackled her pretty hard."

Seeing that this lovely misunderstanding is getting cleared up, I start walking toward the house. My stomach grumbles angrily, making it clear it didn't appreciate this delay.

I brush a finger over the runes on the helix of my ear to increase my hearing. I can now hear the phone conversation as if I were standing next to twin two.

"Fuck. I'm sorry, Uncle Silva, we didn't know. Tell Lachlan to stop freaking out. We'll fix this. Yeah, I have to call Ryker anyway. Bastien's going to need it."

Why would Lachlan be freaking out? I thought he'd be all high-fives and baking brownies for anyone who came at me.

This mentality of attack first and ask questions later obviously runs in the family, or I guess I should say coven since they're not all blood-related. Twin two is quiet, listening to whatever Silva is saying on the other end of the phone.

"Because she kicked his ass. He's all bloody, and his left eye is swollen shut. I think he passed out though; he's not groaning and rocking around on the ground anymore."

Twin two sucks in a breath.

"It's not funny, Silva, it was fucking mental! One minute he's tackling her, and the next she's on top of him, beating the ever-loving shit out of him. I pulled her off, and next thing I know, she pulls a bunch of knives from her ass. Like literally from her ass!" he exclaims. "She threw one at my head. Thank the moon she missed!"

"I didn't miss!" I yell back at him and make my way up the back steps into the house. I disengage my runes and walk into the kitchen. Adelaide covers her mouth in shock when she sees the state I'm in.

"Don't worry. I'm fine. Just had a run-in with *the boys*. Would you mind if I take some lunch upstairs? I'm starving, but I need to get cleaned up."

Like the gem she is, Adelaide quickly puts together a huge bowl of spaghetti and meatballs. I groan, it smells so good. I thank her and head up to my room, shoving unladylike bites into my mouth as I climb the stairs. I move straight into the bathroom and set my bowl of pasta on the vanity. I start to strip out of my wet and muddy clothes while I simultaneously shovel food into my mouth.

I lean toward the mirror to check out my new injuries. I have small scrapes on the left side of my face from my temple to my cheek, and some bruises are forming on my hand. I'm going to have some nasty bruises on my side from my impact with the ground.

Guess they can join the ones I already have from

Lachlan choking me, and the claw marks the lamia gave me. At the rate I'm getting hit with random attacks, I'll be one big giant bruise soon. I mumble to myself irritably as I turn on the water in the shower to just below scalding. I hop in and scrub all the mud and crap off me then relax under the hot spray, letting it work the adrenaline and soreness from my muscles.

After about an hour in the gloriously hot shower, I convince myself to get out. I dry off and finish the last couple bites of cold spaghetti. I use my magic to dry my hair and throw it up in a messy bun. I pull on some workout leggings, a sports bra, and an oversized sleeveless tank with big, comfy armholes.

I decide to hide out in the gym for a while. If twin one is as hurt as twin two said, they might not be too happy about it. Laying low sounds like a solid plan. I grab my phone and see that I missed a couple of calls from Aydin. I text him back.

Vinna: Sorry I was in the shower when you called. Everything okay?

Aydin: You tell me? Silva filled me in on what happened with the boys, you okay?

Vinna: First of all, they are not boys, they are fully grown men! That nickname is incredibly misleading. And secondly, yep, I'm good. Can't say the same about twin one though ;)

Aydin: LMFAO, Valen gave us a rundown of what happened...he had it coming. I'll call you later, glad you're okay.

I sneak out of my door, ignoring the voices I hear coming from the rooms *the boys* occupy. I gingerly make my way down, breathing a sigh of relief when I make it unaccosted. I sneak to the sink and wash my spaghetti bowl before anyone comes along to stop me. Victorious, I congratulate myself that no one snatched it away from me. Sisters: twelve, Vinna: one.

16

Hours later, I'm still in the gym, working through several combinations on the punching bag and jamming to Trapt's "Headstrong." I love working the bags, and I always save them for last, like they're my workout dessert. I'm sweaty and buzzing with adrenaline as I move into punch-kick combos. Some sweat threatens to trickle into my eye, and I pull up the bottom of my loose tank top and wipe at my face. That's when I notice I've got company.

Four hulking figures stand by the door whispering to each other like they're playing telephone. I run my finger over the runes on my ear so I can hear what they're saying.

"Why is there a hot chick raging in your gym?"

The question belongs to a tall guy with buzzed black hair, mocha skin, and stunning gray eyes. He has a square jaw, thick neck, and if the rest of his body is as cut as his arms, then he is all hard angles and delectably chiseled muscles. He has a very hot jock vibe about him.

"Knox, seriously, do you ever pay attention? That is Lachlan's long-lost niece."

"You're telling me *she's* the one who did that to your face and ribs?"

The owner of that question is shorter than the others. He's still taller than the average guy, but shorter than the group surrounding him. He's blond with hair almost to his shoulders. His nose and jaw are angled, but his lips are plump and soft looking. He has a defined runner's build, and I would suspect he's fast and agile.

His eyes are a dramatic bright blue that reminds me of Laiken's. She had pretty blue eyes just a touch lighter than this guy's. Melancholy blooms in me as I picture her, and I embrace it like the old friends we are.

"She's faster and stronger than she looks," one of the twins defends.

The twins are standing shoulder to shoulder, their wavy hair past their collarbones. It's the color of the most decadent dark chocolate, and my fingers twitch with the need to run my fingers through it. I figured one of them would be just as bruised as me, but neither one of them looks worse off after our run in.

According to Aydin, one of them is named Valen, but I haven't the foggiest clue which one. They stop whispering when they realize I'm no longer punishing a punching bag but watching them instead. I disengage my runes, and my hearing goes back to normal.

"Ready for round two?" I ask, only half joking while scowling at the twins. I'm not sure which one of them tackled me, so they both get a crusty look.

"Um, yeah, I'm really sorry about that," one of the twins steps forward looking adorably bashful. "I feel shitty about what happened."

"You don't look like you feel shitty about what happened," I say gesturing to where injuries should be visible on one of them.

He chuckles and points a thumb at the blond guy.

"That's because Ryker fixed me up. You broke some ribs and my cheek," he murmurs, rubbing a hand against the latter.

"Well, don't go around tackling unsuspecting women and maybe that won't happen to you again."

I use the bottom of my tank top to wipe more sweat from my face. When I pull it down, I watch as each of their gazes sweep back up my body, and I fight a smirk. There are worse things than getting checked out by a bunch of stone chiseled eye-candy.

"You guys need something?" I ask.

"We brought Ryker to fix you up, and we thought we should introduce ourselves in a way that didn't involve throwing punches," one of the twins explains, finishing with a smile.

Holy shit! I thought they were hot when they wore angry or confused expressions, but a smile with full lips, straight white teeth, and a cheeky twinkle in the eye makes them worship worthy. I force myself to blink and start talking my libido down.

"I'm Bastien, the asshole who tackled you," the twin smiling at me explains.

"I'm Valen, the better looking and less aggressive twin."

"I'm Knox."

"And I'm Ryker." The blond with pillow lips takes a hesitant step forward. He holds his arms out non-threateningly like he's approaching a wild animal. When I don't move to bolt or hurt him, he continues to get closer. He stops about a foot away from me and pauses.

"Can I touch you?" he asks.

His tone resonates in me, and goosebumps rise up on my whole body.

"That's a loaded question," I reply, my voice sounding a bit breathier than I want.

What the hell is going on? I'm drooling like a teething baby all over these strangers, and I have no idea where that's coming from. *Your vagina, Vinna, it's coming from your vagina.* I wave off the unhelpful thought.

"It's just to heal you," Ryker explains, with a small chuckle.

"Oh, you don't have to do that. I'm fine."

I sidestep him and head toward the door. I grab my phone on the way out, squeezing past the others still grouped at the entrance of the gym. My arm just lightly grazes Valen, and it sends chills through my whole body.

I'm beyond grateful and a little surprised that I make it through the door without suddenly stopping and trying to lick one of these guys. I make it as far as the stairs on the second floor before they all catch up with me. *Well...fuck!*

"Why won't you let him heal you?" Bastien—I think—asks me. He keeps pace with me as I increase my speed. Damn shorter legs.

"Because I'm not really hurt."

"But you have scratches and bruises."

"Yeah, just scratches and bruises, no big deal. They'll be gone in a week."

I step through my bedroom door and turn to close it, thinking they've stopped on the other side, but they brush past me and pile into my room.

"Well, why don't you come on in fellas, don't mind me."

"Don't mind if we do," a twin—I have no idea which one—smiles at me. Throwing in a wink for good measure, he shuts the door behind him.

Fuck. Shower, I need a cold shower ASAP.

"Will you guys leave, I... uh...need to clean up."

"Let me heal you, and we'll leave," Ryker counters.

"Why is this such a big deal?"

"You're a caster. It's what we do. We use magic to make our lives better."

"I'll remember that for next time," I say, opening the door and motioning for them to leave. I look up, and they're all just staring at me.

Ryker steps toward me, and the earnestness in his eyes makes me pause. I'm not even sure why I am fighting this so hard, other than it's something they want me to do, and I'm being stubborn.

"Tell me how it works?" I ask hesitantly.

Ryker steps closer and a flutter sweeps through my body.

"It may not even work," I tell him nervously. "When I was fighting with the paladin, Lachlan tried to throw a couple of shiny orb thingies at me. They didn't work the way he wanted them to. Which was good for me in the end, but... my point is...don't get too excited about your magic working," I proceed to ramble like an idiot.

"There are so many things about that statement I want to know about. Starting with why you were fighting your uncle's coven?" Knox asks me.

"That's a super long story."

"I've got time," Knox smiles.

My brain stutters and then freezes as I stare at that smile. Luckily Ryker rescues me.

"Let's focus on the healing first, and then we can move on to the interrogation."

I move past Ryker and the twins, but now I don't know where to go. I spin around, stuck in between the side of my bed and the sitting area. I swallow as Ryker closes the distance between us, an excited light in his eyes.

"All I have to do is touch the areas that are injured and then use my magic to heal them," he tells me casually, making it sound perfectly normal. "Can I see your side?" he asks, gesturing to my ribs.

I nod, not trusting my voice with his close proximity. Ryker takes the bottom of my tank top and raises it up over my head. I wasn't expecting him to take it all the way off, but he does, and the intimacy of it makes my breath hitch. I'm trying to ignore my body's reaction to him, and I have to consciously slow my lungs as he leans in and looks closer at my side. He turns me just a fraction and looks at my back.

"Where did these come from? They look older."

"Which ones?" I twist around to see where he's pointing. I turn around, my back now facing the other boys and more than one of them hisses.

"Holy shit. What happened to you?"

I twirl back around and take in the shocked and angry looks.

I point to my side and then the scratches on my face. "This is from whichever one of you is Bastien." I point at the twins. "This is from some lamia." I point at the gouges on the upper part of my back. "And this"—I gesture to the rest of the bruises on my back and neck—"is from Lachlan. The asshole blindsided me when he realized we were related."

"He attacked you? Why?" Ryker asks quietly.

I look up into his bright blue eyes. "Your guess is as good as mine. He clearly has problems," I reply just as quietly, and I have to look away from the intensity in Ryker's gaze.

He continues to look me over, running the back of his hand over the slight bruise on my knuckles. I look around, and everyone is watching Ryker examine me with ferocious intensity. Knox keeps leaning in closer, and the twins are absently running their thumbs over their bottom lips. The synchronicity of it is mesmerizing. One of them busts me staring and smiles.

"Why didn't Evrin heal you?" Ryker asks me, his eyes growing stormy as he looks over the marks on my neck.

I shrug my shoulders, not sure of an answer. Why *didn't* Evrin heal me? They told me he had Healing magic. I didn't give much thought to what that meant, and he never offered. Ryker bends over and strokes the runes on my side, causing me to shiver. I look down at him as he looks up at me, neither of us saying anything. Slowly, he does it again and breaks eye contact to watch goosebumps trail his touch.

"What are these?" he asks, his breath caressing my skin.

"I guess they're runes, at least that's what the paladin said."

The other guys get closer, running their eyes over my visible runes.

"They're hot," Knox declares, and I can't help but laugh.

"Thanks."

"Ready?" Ryker asks me.

I nod anxiously and wonder if this will actually work. Ryker places a large hand on my left side and another on my right hip. The air in the room charges, and his palm heats up against my skin. After a couple of minutes, it cools down, and Ryker pulls his hand from my side. I look down, and the skin is unblemished, no bruises or scrapes in sight.

I look up into his eyes in awe. "Holy shit, that's incredible," I stammer.

He rewards me with a gorgeous smile. "Next time you won't fight me so hard," he teases.

Ryker takes his time and thoroughly heals all the marks and bruises on my neck and back. When he places his hand between my underwear and the sensitive skin of my hip and lower abdomen to heal a bruise, I almost lose all my self-control and start rubbing all over him like a needy cat.

The atmosphere in the room is intense. No one speaks or moves as we all watch Ryker put his hands all over me.

"Now your face," he directs, tilting my chin back with one hand and putting the other on the scrapes on my cheek.

His touch on my face feels intimate and sensual. The way he positions his hands makes me feel like he's going to kiss me. I stare unabashedly into his blue eyes, and I feel his hand on my scrapes heat up.

In less time than my side and back required, his hands cool. He grips my chin, and his gaze morphs from something clinical to something curious and sultry. He lightly runs his thumb vertically down my lower lip. The pressure pulls my lips apart and opens them for the briefest of seconds before he steps back and away from me.

There is a sudden void where the heat and mass of his body once was, and my instincts urge me to pull him back into me. I look over to find the eyes of one of the twins, and heat banks in his gaze. I close my eyes to try to calm the overwhelming arousal and need that is inexplicably crashing through me, but I can feel the echo of Ryker's hands on me, and the tiniest whimper escapes my lips. *What the hell is going on right now?*

"Did you do something else to me?" I accuse, my eyes landing back on Ryker who's now sitting in a chair.

He looks at me unsettled. "What do you mean?"

I study his face, my eyes flicking back and forth between his ocean dipped irises, taking in the genuine confusion I see there.

"Nothing, I just feel...weird. My body is reacting weirdly," I finish vaguely.

Ryker moves to get up, I'm assuming to come to see what in the hell I'm rambling about, and I panic. If he comes near me again right now, I'm done for. I will climb him like a tree, with no hesitation or apology.

"Never mind."

I dash into the bathroom and close the frosted doors

behind me. I start the shower and hear someone shout to come downstairs when I'm done. I look myself over in the mirror, marveling at my now injury-free body.

Holy shit, what just happened? I strip down and step into the warm stream of water. How am I going to be around these guys when *that's* how my mind and body reacts?

I scrub my hands over my face and notice that Ryker forgot to heal my knuckles, but there is no way in hell I am going to call him back and ask him. I consider that this could have something to do with magic, but I don't know enough about any of it to tell one way or another.

I'm certainly not going to ask them why I'm suddenly so hot and bothered. I turn the water cold, hoping the icy bite will cure me of the heat I feel coursing through every inch of me. After fifteen teeth chattering minutes under the spray, I give up and get out.

I dry off, and for my own sanity, I decide to ghost their invitation to hang. I grab a book on Elemental magic and choose to hide out in the safety of my room instead. I climb into the cloud that is my bed and fall asleep reading about fire incantations while trying not to recall every detail of these men and exactly what it felt like to have Ryker's hands all over me.

17

I step off the stairs and hear male voices in the kitchen, so I tap the runes on my ear to spy. They're talking about their classes that are going to be starting again soon, and grumbling about the end of their lazy summer. None of that has anything to do with me, so I turn the runes off and head toward the kitchen. I woke up early for breakfast and then escaped outside to walk around all morning.

I crept back into the house at lunchtime, and I've been in my room all afternoon, reading about magic and basically hiding. Unfortunately, hunger has forced me to the kitchen where *the boys* are currently congregated. I guess there goes my plan to avoid them like the plague until I can convince my body parts to behave.

"There she is," Knox announces as I hesitantly round the corner and spot them all gathered around the kitchen island.

I curse my empty and demanding stomach as I cautiously approach the group. When I get closer, Knox puts an arm around my shoulder and tucks me into his side. His contact surprises me, and as usual, I tense up. He either doesn't notice or doesn't care, because his arm stays draped around me. After a couple of seconds, I decide that it doesn't bother me, and I start to relax.

"All right, what are we ordering?"

Four sets of eyes turn to me.

"A yacht," I randomly guess, completely clueless as to what they are asking me.

"No, pizza. What do you want on your pizza?" Knox clarifies, giving me an amused smile.

"Ahhh, you should really be more specific next time. Um, I'm good with anything as long as there's no fish, olives, or mushrooms."

I internally congratulate myself for formulating a coherent answer in the wake of Knox's perfect smile.

"Sweet, let's do two of the usual. One without mushrooms for the lady, two BBQ chicken, and a meatball and artichoke in case Sabin can make it," one of the twins declares.

When there are no objections, he calls to place the order.

I'm a little confused as to why I'm being included in this process, but I'm starving, and pizza sounds amazing.

"Why a yacht?" the other twin asks me.

"Well, you've got a plane, the mega-mansion, and all the cars, I just figured it was the next logical purchase."

He chuckles and shakes his head. "I'll tell Silva to get on it. Until then, we'll have to slum it and ask Evrin or Aydin to use one of their boats."

I smile at the smart ass twin and raise my hand like I'm holding a drink. "Here's to slumming it." I toast and laugh when they all mirror me.

"To slumming it," choruses around the kitchen.

"Okay, so remind me which one of you is Valen and which is Bastien," I ask.

"I'm Valen."

"And I'm Bastien."

I glance back and forth between the two looking for markers that will help me identify them separately. They are both in t-shirts and sweats, and their hair is pulled back into knots on the back of their heads. The only difference I can physically spot is that Bastien has a touch more green around his pupil than Valen does. I cling to that difference, hoping it will help me correctly identify them in the future.

"Sabin is the last member of our boy band. He's going to try and come by later, but he's been caught up doing some family stuff," Valen tells me, and I nod. All of their eyes are back on me, and it takes me a minute to realize what they want.

"I'm Vinna," I tell them, realizing that I never told them my name last night.

They nod at me, and I see Bastien silently mouth my name to get a taste for it.

"So, Vinna, tell us about yourself," Ryker says.

"Yeah, we're all dying to know," Knox adds, his thumb rubbing absently on my shoulder.

Ryker swats his arm, but Knox just chuckles and brushes him off.

"It's kind of a long story," I say dismissively, slinking out from under Knox's arm and claiming one of the seats at the island.

"Oh no you don't, you tried that evasive maneuver last night and then left us hanging. We've got time," Bastien calls me out.

I stare at the extra green in his hazel eyes and get lost for a moment.

"I don't really know where to start," I admit. I think back for a second and decide to start with the magic. "I've had these weird abilities since I was about twelve, but I never knew why. They'd show up off and on, usually when I was in trouble or super emotional, but what would happen was always unpredictable.

"I ran into my first lamia at fourteen, and since then, my abilities have become more reliable. At sixteen, the runes showed up, and four days ago, I learned that all of this means I'm a caster. I have no idea who my parents are, and no idea why I was given to a woman who had no business caring for another living thing. To the paladin's dismay, I come with more questions than answers, and I guess that about sums me up."

I shrug.

"Well, now I feel like an even bigger asshole for hurting you," Bastien laments.

"You should," I tease and offer him a warm smile so he knows I'm not holding a grudge. "You weren't the first and probably won't be the last, so no worries," I offer in jest, but it seems to make everyone in the room stiffen instead of lightening the mood like I was aiming for.

Ryker takes the seat next to me and motions to the runes that flow from my shoulder down my arm. "So these... they're not tattoos?"

"Nope, they were my magic's sweet sixteen present."

Ryker and Knox both lean in for a closer examination, and my heart speeds up. Knox takes my hand, flipping it over, and then brings it closer to his face so he can get a better look at the runes on my fingers.

"Are they just on your arms and torso?" Valen inquires.

"No, they're all over my body."

He runs his gaze all over me, and for some reason, it makes me shiver. Knox starts tracing the runes on my hand with his finger. His feather-light touch sends a whirling sensation throughout me, and the intensity of it builds with each caress. I focus on the unusual feeling, trying to figure out what's going on when it dawns on me that it has something to do with my magic.

I scramble away, worried my magic is going to do something spazzy. I try to cover my panicked retreat by making it seem like I was just heading to the fridge to get a drink.

"You guys want anything?" I offer, trying and failing at coming off casual.

I pass around sodas and then resettle myself between Bastien and Valen. They don't seem to be as touchy as the other two. Knox starts to chuckle, and I look over to him.

"We scare you away?" he teases.

"I'm not used to people touching me. Well, in a non-threatening way, I mean. Try to punch me, and I'm in my comfort zone, but hugs and cuddles aren't exactly in my wheelhouse," I blurt awkwardly. His joking smile disappears.

"Sorry," he offers.

"No, I like it," I rush and then realize how that sounds. "I mean, the sisters have been hugging me a lot, being affectionate to help me get used to it. So it would probably help if you touch me, too." I stop, repeating my words in my head, and I cringe.

Knox gets a mischievous glint in his eyes.

"This is not coming out right," I groan and cover my face with my hands. Man, I am so glad I'm not a blusher. Easy laughter makes its way around the group, and I find I'm laughing awkwardly with them.

"What I mean is, be who you are. If you do anything that I am uncomfortable with, I'll tell you," I finally manage to clarify.

"So what are the runes for, do you know?" Ryker asks, thankfully bringing everyone's attention back to the previous subject.

"They all do different things. Some create weapons or

enhance skills that I have." I let my voice trail off, not sure if I should get more specific than that.

"Is that how you know how to fight?" Bastien asks.

"Yes and no. I've trained and worked hard, so that's part of it. I've been fighting for a living for years now, so that's another part, but I think something about my magic definitely helps me. Fighting seems to come naturally to me. If I see something, somehow I'm able to do it, and my runes all seem to exist to help protect me in some way."

"What did Lachlan say about them? Does he recognize anything?" Valen inquires.

"He just said I shouldn't have them. I think he still thinks they're tattoos, even though I explained they're not. None of his coven know what to make of them—or me for that matter." I circle a finger over my head. "Like I said, I'm a big mystery."

The doorbell rings, and Knox heads off to answer it.

"Well, at least you can feel a little better about Vinna kicking your ass," Valen offers his brother.

Bastien snorts and runs a hand over his formerly broken cheek and then winks at me. Knox returns with a stack of pizza boxes, and each of us grabs one to help lighten the load. Valen waves us downstairs, and I follow the boys to the theater room, pizza box and drink in hand. I create a little nest for myself in the corner of the gigantic bed-like sofa that takes up most of the room.

Bastien and Valen sit on either side of me, and Ryker and Knox take up space on the other side of the couch. After a heated debate, we all finally agree to watch *The Rock*. The consensus is that Nicolas Cage is annoying, but Sean Connery's awesomeness cancels it out.

I've never seen it before, but twenty minutes in, I have to agree with their opinions about the actors. The guys laugh and heckle when I start rooting for the soldiers who are technically the bad guys in the movie.

"What?" I protest, throwing crumpled napkins at all of them. "They're pissed that the government screwed them and their friends over. I'm with them," I explain, booing loudly as each of the soldiers are bested and killed off. The movie ends, and before number two can get started, I run out for a quick pee break.

When I get back, *World War Z* is queued up to play, and I crawl back toward my nest to find that Valen is lying in my spot. I catch Ryker and Knox watching me out of the corner of their eyes, clearly waiting to see what I'm going to do about it. I grab a slice of pizza and then plop my butt heavily on top of Valen's chest. I hear him grunt and then feel his chest vibrating with laughter.

"Oh, I'm sorry," I say innocently, "I didn't see you there in *my* spot."

"Technically, it's my spot. I always sit here when we watch movies. I just let you borrow it for the first movie because I'm a nice guy," Valen baits me.

"Well, keep that nice guy shit up and give me *my* spot back. I had a sweet pillow nest going."

Valen stretches out and snuggles deeper into said pillow nest. "I know, thank you for getting *my spot* nice and comfy for me."

I look around to the others, and judging by their amused smiles, they're not going to be any help. I'm growing more aware that I've put myself in a bit of a precarious situation. I don't know Valen, and now I've gone and sat on him, which is probably crossing some kind of normal social boundary.

I'm perched on him awkwardly, now debating what to do. Valen laughs again like he can sense my internal dilemma, and I bristle. Well, here's to being a stubborn bitch, I muse as I lay down on top of him and wiggle around until my back is to his chest. I try to be as annoying as possible and wedge myself half on top of Valen and half against the back cushions of the sofa.

He doesn't seem to object to my purposefully making things as uncomfortable as I can for him and adds further insult to injury by grabbing my hand and taking a bite of the pizza slice I'm holding.

"What kind of man-animal...first my spot, then my fucking pizza?"

I feel him laughing, the vibration and movement warm against my back. It feels nice, and I'm so focused on that, I forget to be incredulous. Someone presses play, and the movie starts, but I'm wrapped up in my head and can't pay attention. Is it normal for things to feel this easy and comfortable with people I just met? Do I really even care if this is not normal if it involves cuddling that doesn't freak me out?

I've never had many friends. I'm not socially awkward by any means, but as much as Beth moved us around, it was hard to make and keep friends. It feels nice joking around and sharing the same space. *They're the ones who keep initiating things* I tell myself, getting a little more comfortable when Valen wraps an arm around my waist.

Now, if I can just get my attraction and my body's reactions under control. Screaming draws my attention back to the screen, and I check back in to the movie, where people are scrambling to get away from the fastest zombies I've ever seen.

* * *

I wake up confused, not sure where I am. *I really need to stop waking up like this.* I take in my surroundings. The last thing I remember is watching movies. I realize I'm still in the theater room, but it's completely dark.

I move slightly and feel a hand around my waist twitch. Apparently, I'm still lying on Valen, but at some point, I've moved from my back and am now tangled chest to chest around him. My head is resting on his chest, and my knee is hiked up over his hips. He has an arm wrapped around my waist, and the other is gripping my wrist which is resting dangerously low on his stomach.

He's breathing slow and even, completely asleep. I slip my wrist free from Valen's grip and place my arm on the other side of his chest. I lift the weight of my torso off of him and slowly try to slide off without waking him up. I hover above him, getting my leg to the other side of his body when I feel two hands grab my hips and bring them down on top of him.

I freeze for a moment, heat rushing to where our hips are now connected, but I think he's still asleep. I wait for a minute, and when nothing else happens, I continue to slide myself off. I've barely moved when Valen grinds himself up into my straddling thighs.

His hardness connects with me perfectly, and an involuntary moan escapes my lips. He does it again, and I do everything I can not to make any more noise. I watch as his eyes open lazily taking in our position.

"Hey," he greets me, his voice deep and gravelly from sleep.

"Hey. Sorry, I was trying to move without waking you up, but you're not making it easy," I explain, pointing to where he's holding on to my hips. Valen chuckles sleepily and easily lifts me up and off of him.

"Don't be sorry. I like waking up to a beautiful female on top of me." He winks and stretches out.

I chuckle and offer him my hand. He takes it and pulls himself up. I should look away when he adjusts himself, but my raging hormones have apparently fried my brain, so I just gawk. Eventually, I look up to find Valen smirking at me.

"Sorry," I mumble contritely and then mentally execute a facepalm for getting caught staring at his dick.

I start to walk away before I do anything crazy like jump him. Valen chuckles and follows me up the stairs. I reach our level first and turn around to tell him goodnight. He pulls his eyes up quickly to my face, and I realize he was looking at my ass.

"Not sorry," he mocks, with an innocent shrug of his shoulders. I shake my head smiling, and he chuckles as we head to our rooms.

"Goodnight," I whisper-shout over my shoulder.

"If you're in the mood for more cuddling, you know where I am," Valen calls back before he walks through his bedroom door, leaving it open a crack behind him.

I pause, my hand on my doorknob. Holy hell, it's all I can do not to follow him into his room. I put my forehead against the cold wood of my door and breathe. The coolness feels amazing against my fevered skin, and I again find myself wondering if something is messing with me.

Why is being around these guys with magic turning me into a lusty hot mess? I walk into my bedroom and strip out of my pants and bra. I crawl into my amazingly comfy bed, and I'm unconscious before I can make any sense of what's going on with me.

18

Pounding on my door shocks me awake. I rush to the door and swing it open, adrenaline slamming through my veins.

"What? What's wrong?" I demand, sweeping sleep-mussed hair out of my face.

"Good morning, Bruiser," Bastien teases.

"Why are you beating down the door?"

Bastien smiles sweetly at me. "Because when I knocked on the door softly, you didn't answer."

"For fuck's sake," I moan as I try to slam the door on him.

I turn and crawl back into bed. Seconds later, my covers are ripped away, and I groan an objection. "What about slamming the door in your face gave you the impression that you were invited in?" I mumble into my pillow. I hear two sets of chuckles but don't lift my head to see who the other laugh belongs to.

"Come on, Bruiser, wake up. We're all waiting for you to go out and play."

"What are you, seven? I'm not interested in babysitting today. Thanks anyway."

I reach for my phone, and the light of the clock blinds me.

"Bastien, it's not even eight yet. What the fuck's with the early morning harassment?"

"We got woken up early, and if we can't sleep in, then you can't sleep in. Didn't Lachlan tell you the rules of the house?"

Without warning, I grab the pillow next to me and fling it at Bastien's head. He catches it, the quick fucker. Bastien holds it and does a belly flop onto my bed, bouncing me around.

I register that I'm only in a tank and undies, but I elect not to care. I start playfully kicking Bastien in the side, trying to force him off my bed. I look over and discover a guy I don't know is looking through the books on my bookshelf.

"Uh, who are you?"

He looks up bashfully. "I'm Sabin."

Sabin's voice is a smooth baritone, and just like the other guys, he's sex on a stick. He has a trendy crew cut that's combed to the side. It looks medium brown and wet, or maybe he has product in it. He has masculine eyebrows over gorgeous forest green eyes.

His nose is straight and a defined cupid's bow slopes into luscious lips. His ears are gauged with small black plugs. My attention is drawn to a full sleeve of tattoos on his left arm. I can make out trees and what looks like a full moon, but I'd have to get closer to take in all the details. Sabin smiles at my obvious inspection of him, revealing a set of dimples.

Everything about Sabin screams heartbreaker. *Great*, let's just add one more temptation to the overfilled plate that is my libido. I look away from him and notice that while I was distracted by sexy motherfucker number five, Bastien has grabbed my ankle and is now pulling me off the bed.

I feint a kick with my free leg toward his crotch, and he

lets go of me to protect himself. I get my feet under me and launch myself onto Bastien's back. I hook an arm around his neck and start to administer an epic noogie.

Bastien starts laughing and screaming "my hair, my hair" in a high-pitched overly feminine voice. I'm laughing so hard I can't hang on when he grabs my knee and swings me around to his front. Satisfaction with my new position sweeps through me, and my rational side clutches its pearls at the scandalous thought.

Bastien plants a raspberry on my neck, which makes me squeal and wiggle to get away from him. He lets me drop to my feet, laughing, and Sabin is staring at us with an unidentifiable look on his face. The saucy side I never knew I had is apparently out and proud, because I wink at Sabin as I walk to the bathroom.

"Don't tell Lachlan that I've relocated a chunk of his library," I tell Sabin as I close the doors to my bathroom behind me.

"Don't shower, Bruiser. We're going to play outside, so wear a swimsuit. The skimpier, the better."

I roll my eyes and then laugh. It looks like Bastien's saucy side is out to play too. I clean up and use my magic to remove all the unwanted hair on my body before I put on a bright purple bikini. It has a crochet racerback and crochet details on the sides of the bottoms. Over that, I throw on a white V-neck tee and some jean shorts.

I slip into some old beat up black chucks, and I put a towel and some flip flops in a canvas crossbody bag. Lastly, I put on some aviators and head out. I make my bed, giving it the necessary appreciation for my awesome sleep before I rush down the stairs. Birdie bids me good morning and hands me a smoothie and a breakfast sandwich. I give her a quick side hug and sit at the island to quickly chow down.

"The boys are in the garage," she tells me with a playful

glare after I win the battle to clean my cup. She still snagged my plate, so it's not a total win, but I'm making progress.

I walk through and find the guys in the middle set of garages amongst a ton of *toys*. I spot jet skis, snowmobiles, camping equipment, ski and snowboarding equipment and a plethora of other things I can't identify. They are loading up several ATVs with a couple of bags and a cooler.

A bottle of sunscreen is tossed to me, and I start to spray it all over. I catch Knox watching me, and I pause. When I don't resume whatever it was that had him so enthralled, Knox looks up and realizes he's been caught ogling. He just smiles at me with no shame. I shake my head and mouth *pervert* to him, which brings a chuckle from him and Ryker, who was apparently watching our exchange.

"You guys need any help?"

"Nope, I think we're just about set," Valen tells me.

I step back and try to get out of the way, while I watch the organized chaos of their preparations. Bastien hands out walkie-talkies, and they all test that they're working. The group suddenly starts playing roshambo, declaring best two out of three.

The final match is between Knox and Valen. Valen walks away victorious, and Knox wails dramatically. I'm laughing and getting ready to ask them what that was all about when Valen crooks a finger at me and tells me I'm riding with him.

"Did you just rock-paper-scissors for me?"

"Well, not for you exactly, just to see who you'd ride with." Valen smirks at me.

"Maybe I want to drive myself."

"Do you?"

I stare at him for a beat.

"I have no idea how to drive one of these things," I admit.

Valen shrugs. "I can teach you. Either way is cool with

me; it'll be your arms around me or my arms around you," he finishes with a faux dreamy look on his face, and I laugh.

I climb on behind him and position my bag so it's slung across my back. Valen starts to pull his hair back into a knot, and I follow suit. I secure my hair up into a messy bun and try not to drool over the rippling muscles moving along his back and arms.

"Do I hold on to you?" I ask, unsure if he was joking or if that's legit.

"Yes, please. Nice and tight, wouldn't want you to fall off."

He looks over at the other boys, and I catch a couple of playful glares thrown his way. We take off with a burst of speed that steals a squeal from my lips and has me tightening my grip around him. The wind whips Valen's laugh back to me, and my own laughter joins it.

We head down a trail through the woods that's the perfect size for these four wheelers. It's a gorgeous sunny day with boastful blue skies and not a cloud in sight. It's hot out even though it's only 8:30 in the morning. We speed through the trees, and the air rushing by feels incredible.

I'm having so much fun that I have a perma-smile stretched across my face. I feel like I've laughed and smiled more in the past couple of days being here than maybe I have in my whole life. Something about all of this feels so natural and right. It's like I can feel layers of sadness and loneliness peel away with each smile and laugh.

My life up to this point has required me to be so serious and vigilant, always looking for the next thing to come at me. But right now, with these guys, it feels like I can let go, be silly, laugh, and tease. I look behind me, each of the guys on their own ATV trailing in a line like baby ducks. I face forward just in time to see us plow through a little stream.

The cool water splashes up at me from both sides, and I laugh.

I feel the vibrations from Valen's back in my chest before the sound of his laughter reaches my ears. Between the vibration of his laughter and the coldness of the water, goosebumps rise up on my body and my nipples harden against his back. I wonder if he'll notice, and I find myself scooting back a little, separating my chest from his back so that I don't make him feel uncomfortable. He hits the brakes suddenly, forcing me back up against him and someone behind us shouts their irritation.

Several more times over the hour that we're driving, Valen seems to brake for no apparent reason. I start to suspect there are titillating motivations behind his actions, and it's cracking me up.

The trees around us grow fewer and farther apart as we approach a clearing and a lake. There's a big tree with branches hanging over the water, and I can spot a couple of ropes tied high up in the branches and hanging lazily down.

I climb off the ATV, feeling a twinge in my muscles from riding in the same position for a while. I catch the shit-eating grin across Valen's face, and it confirms my suspicions.

"Why are you all such pervs?" I ask with a laugh, slapping the back of my hand against his abs. "You all act like you've never been around a girl before. Bunch of Neanderthals."

"What did he do?" Bastien asks, walking over to us.

"He's been embracing his inner creeper," I joke as the others surround us. When I don't offer any more details, they all look over to Valen and wait for him to supply some.

Valen looks a little sheepish as he brushes the strands of escaped hair out of his face.

"I may have used my brakes more times than were necessary."

I hear a couple sounds of understanding, but Ryker looks at him still confused.

"Newton's first law of motion, bro," is all Valen tells Ryker, and then he seems to get it. Sabin kind of growls at Valen, and the noise surprises me.

"Way to keep it classy and respectful," Sabin throws out, and it washes any trace of humor from Valen's face.

"Whoa, what just happened?" I ask, looking between Sabin and Valen. "I'm not upset, I was just busting Valen's balls," I tell Sabin. "I realized what he was doing, and it didn't bother me. It's just silly fun."

Sabin looks at me.

"Vinna, we all just met you; none of us knows you well enough to navigate what could be a fine line between silly fun and making you uncomfortable. None of us should be crossing into that territory this quickly."

"Sabin, I appreciate that you're looking out for me, but I told the guys yesterday that they can be touchy-feely with me, and if anything makes me uncomfortable, I'll tell them. It may sound weird because, you're right, we all just met each other, but I like the dynamic so far. I like the joking and silliness... and the affection," I finish awkwardly.

"From what the guys tell me, you've been through a lot in a very short amount of time. We should be helping you feel safe and secure, not pushing boundaries. Caster females deserve to be protected and respected," Sabin declares.

It sounds like he just recited a slogan of some sort, and I'm not sure what to say. I just told him I could handle myself, but he's decided I'm wrong. *I can protect myself just fine, you presumptuous fucker.*

"Sabin, you can turn your dad mode off," I suggest, a little irritated.

I hear Knox snicker and then cough to cover it up.

"I can't speak for other *caster females,* but I can speak for myself, just like I can protect myself. I don't need anyone to do that for me."

I look around the group and continue.

"How they've been treating me, it makes me feel like I belong, like I'm part of the group. I like it; it makes me feel safe and secure, and with everything I've been dealing with, I need that more than anything. I'm comfortable with what's happening. Like I said before, if I have an issue with something, I'll speak up, I promise."

Sabin doesn't say anything else, but I can tell he still doesn't really agree with me. That's fine. He'll get to know me more and realize that I mean what I say. I smile at him and squeeze Valen on his shoulder. Bastien breaks the silence with a loud clap and starts tossing out instructions to the other guys about what to unload.

"Do we want to swim before or after food?" Bastien asks the group.

"I vote for both."

"I'm with Vinna, I vote for both," Knox agrees.

The rest of the boys all make affirming noises and start stripping off shirts and shoes, and I find myself completely absorbed in watching them do it. I giggle to myself. See, I fit right in...I'm a perv too.

"Whatchya smiling about, Bruiser?"

"Wouldn't you love to know," I challenge, batting my lashes coquettishly at Bastien.

I mentally file away the image of these half-naked examples of perfection, to be reviewed at a later, more private time. I kick off my shoes and take my bag off. I start to unbutton my shorts when Bastien grabs me and throws me over his shoulder. He starts running toward the water.

"Bastien, no, let me take my clothes off first!" I squeal.

He ignores me and wades thigh deep before he throws me in. He is one strong fucker, because it feels like I fly ten feet before I hit the water. My air time gives me plenty of opportunities to take in a big deep breath before I'm submerged.

I hold my breath, getting my bearings, and swim stealthily back toward Bastien. I hear a surprised yelp when I grab his foot and yank on it. He loses his balance and falls back into the water. I break the surface laughing and rush away from him.

I run out of the water and take off my now sopping clothes. I find the t-shirt that Bastien was wearing and lay it flat in the grass. I put my wet shirt and shorts on top of it, giggling at what his reaction will be when he realizes what I've done. Ryker and Sabin both watch what I'm doing, and I wink at them conspiratorially.

The twins and Knox are all splashing each other but suddenly stop when I'm walking toward the water.

"What? Are you waiting for a *Baywatch* moment?" I jest. "Because I'm not going to slow-mo run for you. Especially you, Valen, you've had enough boob action today."

They all start laughing, and I even wrench a chuckle from Sabin before he shakes his head like he's mentally chastising himself. I wade back into the water with Sabin and Ryker behind me. I look back and catch Ryker focusing on my lower half.

"Not you too, Ryker?"

He looks up, and a blush spreads across his cheeks and neck. "I swear I was just looking at your runes."

Ryker holds his hands up in a gesture of innocence. Sabin passes me, mumbling something, and I turn to watch his hot, grumpy ass dive into the water. I feel Ryker's chest against my back, and he leans in, his mouth next to my ear.

"I guess it's lucky for me that you have runes on your ass."

I gasp in fake outrage and swat Ryker's ass as he walks by me laughing.

"Uh oh, Vinna has opened the ass slapping door," he announces to the other guys. "She just swatted my butt, so hers is fair game now."

I put my hands over my butt cheeks and laugh, sinking into the water.

"I don't make the rules, Vinna, I just follow them," Ryker adds, faux innocence dripping from his words.

19

The day is getting even hotter, and the water feels nice against the punishing warmth. We swim around for hours, playing chicken and racing each other. I take out all of the guys in chicken, and I can tell that they were seriously trying hard to win. When it comes to racing, the twins stomp us all, no contest.

I start to shiver in the water, and my teeth are chattering so I climb out to dry off and get warmed up. The guys are still playing, and I start rummaging, hungry, through the packs and cooler to set out the picnic. I get everything accessible and call them in to eat. We all crowd onto the blanket and start digging in.

I take a bite of a sandwich and moan. It's delicious.

"Did one of you guys make this or do I have the sisters to thank?"

"The sisters," they all admit in unison.

"I swear, every time I eat something they've made, it's the best thing I've ever eaten. *Every single time;* how is that possible?"

The guys chuckle.

"I'm going to have to start doing two-a-days in the gym just to counteract their good cooking," I say absently.

"Just start using your magic more, that burns a ton of calories," Knox tells me.

"Oh, I didn't know that. Aside from fighting and my runes, I'm not sure what other things my magic can even do. I don't know how to use it except for little things here and there," I admit.

"Has Lachlan put in a request for you to have your reading?" Sabin queries.

"Yeah, some guy in Europe is coming to do it, said he'd be here in a couple of weeks."

"Tearson is doing your reading?" Ryker asks, surprise and something akin to reverence in his voice.

"I don't know the guy's name. Lachlan just said that he was in Europe," I reply before shoving another bite of sandwich in my mouth.

Ryker stares at me a bit longer with curiosity before he remembers the food in his hand.

"So what's with the *caster females are all delicate flowers* mentality that some people seem to have?" I ask.

The curiosity has been bubbling inside of me since Sabin's lecture this morning. So far, no one other than him has really treated me like that.

The paladin can't seem to decide how they feel about me, but the other guys seemed fine to treat me like one of them.

"Well, it stems from a couple of things, I guess. One is that there are far fewer female casters than there are male casters—"

"Why is that?" I interject.

"Unfortunately, female casters have taken the biggest hit when it comes to things like inquisitions, witch trials, and any of the other innumerable events where women were killed for being different or more powerful. Because of that, casters in general almost died out. So when female casters were born, they were fiercely protected and hidden in an effort to keep our race alive," Sabin explains solemnly.

"The current situation isn't so dire; the ratio is now probably one female for every six or so male casters. However, that mentality of protect, shelter, and revere has now become embedded in our culture," Ryker adds.

"Not to mention that females are now used to males and covens fighting over them and bending over backward to keep them happy. There's a certain expectation from females about how they should be treated and what their value is."

"The *delicate flower syndrome* isn't just perpetuated by male casters," Bastien explains. "You're lucky because Lachlan is the kind of caster that will support any decisions you make when it comes to your magic or the mates that you choose."

I scoff at what is clearly a delusional assessment of Lachlan being supportive or letting me make any decisions. So far, that has not been my experience.

"Many female casters are more controlled. If not by their families, then by the elders. The stronger the magic in a female, the more the elders will try to match her up with a strong or prominent coven of male casters. There's a lot of politics and matchmaking that goes on," Bastien continues.

"What do you mean by mates?" I query.

"Female casters take more than one mate," Valen answers cautiously.

"What the fuck?" I ask, with a high pitched squeak. I clear my throat and try again, aiming for less spastic. "I mean, excuse me?"

"No one's explained this to you?" Ryker asks me, surprised.

"Uhhh, no."

"Well, because of the skewed ratio of females to males, it became customary for female casters to bond with multiple mates. This allows multiple bloodlines to continue on and not die out. Casters are polyandrous. We all thought you knew," Valen fills in.

Holy shit! Maybe my theory that magic has something to do with my sudden attraction to multiple men isn't so farfetched. *Fuck yes,* I don't have to feel wrong for wanting them...all of them. Well, maybe not Sabin—oh who am I kidding, I'd pounce on him, too. I'd just duct tape his mouth so I could stare at him without having to listen to him say rude, antiquated, sexist shit.

"So how does it work? You said there is a lot of match-making and other things that go into it. Does that mean you date? Like, does a female caster date a group or does she date multiple individuals until she collects all the ones she wants...like a bouquet of males?"

I chuckle at the visual.

"I suppose there's no real *one way* that bonds are made. Typically, a coven that is already formed will start looking for a compatible mate. We start piecing together our covens as teenagers. We all grow up together for the most part, and we naturally start to form relationships with casters that have skills that complement our own."

Sabin gestures to the guys all around him.

"We grew up as friends, but after our readings, when we knew we all wanted to be paladin, we were approved to come together to form a coven. Mates can work similarly. We grow up knowing the females in our community. The elders usually have an idea of the pairings that they want and will facilitate a coven's interaction with appropriate females."

"Plus, different areas around the world have different

elders, and they all interact with each other and help set up matches that way, too," Knox tells me.

I cringe. Well, that sounds like a creepy meat market. It all seems so clinical to me. A bunch of elders gathered together and trading people like baseball cards.

"Does that mean you guys are paired up already?" I blurt, feeling annoyed and a little panicked.

I want to slap my hand against my forehead. I've known this group for like *a day*. Yeah, I want to pounce like a hungry raptor on each and every one of them, but that's just sexual attraction. I don't want to get married, or bind, or whatever the fuck it's called.

I sure as hell am not ready to be having little magic babies. Casters make the females sound like fragile broodmares. Professional baby maker is not exactly what I envision for my future.

"We've been pushed in the direction of a couple of females, but they didn't fit with us the way we wanted. We've all decided we'd rather not bind than settle," Bastien answers.

He looks like he wants to say more but doesn't, and I catch him exchange a look that I can't interpret with Valen.

Bastien's revelation sends a shit-ton of relief coursing through me. The onslaught of that specific emotion creates a solid argument that some part of me does want a claim on these guys, and that freaks me out. It's too soon for me to feel that way.

We seem to click, but I don't know them well enough to envision anything long term, and I don't want to mistake sexual attraction with long-term compatibility. When I look up, they're all caught up in some kind of silent conversation amongst themselves. Sabin seems to get surlier as it progresses, and I'm getting more confused.

I'm clearly out of the loop, which seems to be the story

of my life these days. I decide this discussion has gotten way too serious, so I stand up—a mischievous grin stretched wide across my face.

"Last one in the water has to do *everything* I say for the day!" I shout, sprinting toward the water before I even finish the sentence.

I hear a scuffle behind me, and once I'm in the water, I turn around to catch them battling and manhandling each other as they all rush toward the lake. I'm laughing so hard as I watch Bastien pick Knox up and fireman carry him, in a last ditch effort not to be the last one to touch the water. It works, and Bastien gets his feet wet before Knox can escape the hold.

"Noooooo!" Knox screams and shakes his fists at the sky like he's acting out a dramatic scene from a movie.

Laugh-tears are streaming down my face, and I'm holding onto my side, which now has a stitch in it. Valen scoops me up in his arms and starts carrying me out of the water.

"To the rope swings we go!"

20

I'm riding piggyback on Knox, urging him to go faster. We run through the garage, into the house, and I can feel and hear his laughter as we slide into the kitchen and slam right into Evrin.

"You're back!" I squeak in surprise.

Knox doesn't put me down, and Evrin gives me an awkward high five in greeting. I haven't talked to any of the paladin, other than Aydin, since they left, and I'm not sure what the dynamic will be like now that they're back.

"Well, you all look as thick as thieves," I hear Aydin bellow as he rounds the corner into the living room. I jump off Knox's back and start slow motion running toward Aydin.

"What are you doing?" he asks me with a chuckle.

"They always do this in the movies when there's a reunion. I'm just recreating cinematic gold," I tell him.

Aydin laughs and starts mirroring my ridiculous slow-motion run. We meet in the middle, and he picks me up and twirls me. Rumbling laughter spills over to us from the kitchen at our antics.

I turn to the guys. "Guess you got your slo-mo run after all," I tease, and they laugh even harder.

"We could have used some of your skills on this assignment, Little Badass," Aydin tells me as he sets me back down on my feet.

"Feel free to take me next time then," I reply, not missing a beat but shocked that he'd want to include me in what they do.

"Looks like you've forgiven the boys for their attack," he observes and shoots an exaggerated glare over my shoulder. I look behind me, and the twins are looking everywhere but at Aydin and fidgeting.

"I still think we should punish them," Silva declares, as he walks over and gives the twins a bear-hug. He hugs the rest of the guys and looks over at me. "What do you think, Vinna?"

I bring the tips of my fingers together, adopting a nefarious pose. "Tell me more," I cackle evilly, and Silva laughs.

"You kids go get cleaned up. We're going to eat in about an hour," Lachlan—the party pooper—swoops in, breaking up the fun. He also hugs all of the guys, and it's painfully awkward when he doesn't acknowledge me at all. Yep, he's still anti-me. Good to know.

I shake my head, refortifying some of the defenses I let drop while the paladin were gone.

I leap onto Knox's back, trying not to let Lachlan's and Silva's slight get to me. He catches me like I weigh nothing.

"To my room, trusty steed," I order, and Knox does a lap around the kitchen island before running through the living room.

* * *

I dry myself off from the long shower I just indulged in, when I walk into my closet and freeze.

"What the fuck?" I shout in shock and look around confused.

My closet is completely and inexplicably filled with clothes. I pull open my underwear drawer, and it's full of new underwear, the different styles labeled and separated. I start pulling all of the drawers open and find new bras, new swimsuits, new skimpy things to sleep in. I roll my eyes at that drawer. *I'll stick with tank tops and t-shirts, thank you very much.*

"Are you okay? What's wrong?" Valen, Sabin, and Ryker all ask in unison as they tumble into my closet.

Aydin comes running in not far behind the guys, asking the same questions. I just sweep my arm toward all the clothes in the closet. The guys still look confused, but Aydin quickly realizes what's going on.

"Um, did magic fairies break into my closet and replace everything?"

Now clued into what I'm distressed about, the guys look around and huff in amusement.

"These are the things we ordered the other day, remember?" Aydin explains.

"Holy shit, Aydin, this is a little overboard, don't you think?"

I pull out a light pink lace bustier and matching panties from a drawer.

"Why do I need these?" I ask him, waving the scandalous set in front of him.

Aydin blushes and quickly looks away. "I did tell her to get everything she thought a female should have." Aydin chuckles awkwardly.

"Holy crap, I don't even know what to do with all of

this," I whisper overwhelmed and run my fingers through my wet hair in exasperation.

I spin around taking it all in. I spot the rack of new shoes and boots, all of them are flats and totally awesome. Things are arranged by season, and inside each seasonal section, outfits have already been put together.

"Do you like it? Will this work for you?" Aydin asks, sounding a little insecure.

I realize that my shocked ranting is sounding extremely ungrateful, and I mentally slap myself. "I'm sorry. I sound like a complete ungrateful bitch. What's not to like? It's incredible!" I tell him and genuinely mean it. "Thank you, Aydin." I hold my arm out, and we bump knuckles.

"Anything for you, Little Badass," Aydin declares and disappears out of the doorway.

"I can't believe this," I say to the guys in awe.

"He's taking care of you, Vinna, that's all," Sabin tells me, with a satisfied smile and leaves.

Ryker and Valen watch me while I stare at everything, dumbfounded. I run my hands over some of the clothes closest to me and marvel. I catch my reflection in the mirror on the far wall. I'm in a towel that's covering the important bits but not by much. My wet hair is dripping down my back and shoulders, and Ryker is watching the trails of water as they make their way down my body.

He looks up, and something happens inside me. I meet his bright blue eyes in the mirror, and the memory of his hands on me flashes through my mind, making me feel instantly flushed. We watch each other, and it's like Ryker's having the same flash of memory. I turn around to face him, and Valen surprises me by stepping determinedly toward me. I feel pulled to both of them in a way I can't understand or explain, but I'm okay with that.

I sandwich myself between them as they press in against

me. Valen traces a finger along the runes on my shoulder, and I shudder with weighted anticipation. A palpable lust fills the room, and my breaths quicken as it soaks into my skin. Valen cups my cheek in his big hand and runs a thumb across my lips.

Ryker grabs my hips and nuzzles up against me. His long blond locks tickle my cheek and shoulder, and his arousal fits nicely against my ass. I close my eyes and revel in the feel of them. I reach back, wrapping the palm of my hand around the back of Ryker's neck, pulling him into me even more. His breathing hitches and then his lips connect with the runes on my shoulder. I tilt my head giving him better access.

I open my eyes and get sucked into Valen's molten hazel gaze. His thumb still rests on my lips, and I lightly lick the pad of it when he makes another sweeping gesture. I don't know who the self-assured wanton woman is that just slipped into my skin—but I like where she's going with this —as Valen groans, and his eyes blaze even brighter. I tilt my head back, inviting him to bring his full lips down to mine, and Ryker nips at the speeding pulse in my neck.

I want them both so badly, and I don't care if it's magic or me or anything else that's fueling this, because it feels so fucking right. Something clicks together inside of me, but I can't focus on what. I watch Valen's lips draw closer, and Ryker's hands start pulling up the hem of my towel.

"The showers are free, guys. You can hop in and get cleaned up," Sabin shouts, and his heavy footsteps clomp toward us from my room.

His voice shatters the moment, and both Ryker and Valen withdraw from me. I glare at their speedy retreat. Sabin walks into the closet, oblivious to his unwanted intrusion. Is he really that dense or that intent on getting in the way?

I let out a frustrated huff and watch Sabin coldly. He doesn't say anything, but it's clear he's not going to leave until Ryker and Valen do. Ryker relents first and walks out. I feel like something in me goes with him.

Valen moves in behind me, skimming my back with his chest, and runs his hands up my arms. He leans down, his lips achingly close to the shell of my ear.

"I can think of a couple uses for these," he tells me, running his index finger over the pink lace lingerie still clutched in my hand.

Valen places a lingering kiss on my neck and then leaves. Their absence tugs on me, and I feel unfinished and empty in a way that's crushing and painful. I look at Sabin, and his disapproving and judgmental mien makes me snap.

"What? Are you still of the delusion that my vagina makes me too fragile and feeble minded to make decisions for my fucking self?"

I can't help the disdain that takes over my face as I bark out the question. Sabin's attitude is starting to get old. At first, it felt protective, but right now it feels controlling, and I've had enough. I like the look of shock that sweeps over Sabin's face at my accusatory words.

"No, I don't think that because you are female you can't make decisions for yourself. I just think you don't really know what you're getting into."

"Is that why you've taken on the role of Captain Cockblock? You won't allow them to touch me or interact with me the way they want, and now you think you get to make *my* decisions, too? Someone thinks very fucking highly of themselves."

"You have no idea about how our world works or where you'll fit into it. I have every right to be protective of them and of you," Sabin defends.

"If that's really the issue, then enlighten me, Sabin. Tell

me what I need to know so I can make more informed decisions, but stop trying to control me."

He sweeps his hand through his hair and sighs.

"All of you are pushing too far, too fast."

"And again, I ask, who the hell are you to make that decision for me or for them?"

"I'm a member of their coven. Someone who cares about them. You've been a caster for all of a week, and you've known them for less than half of that."

"Fuck you, Sabin, and your misguided protection. It's sex, not torture. We're having fun and getting to know each other. Get over yourself and whatever *god* complex you're obviously suffering from," I fume at him.

Sabin steps toward me, and I can't tell if it's heat or anger in his eyes.

"You think all of this is so simple and innocent, but the reality is you don't know anything. You don't know what your magic does or what direction it will force you in. You might not end up being compatible with the coven. What happens then? All of you are playing with fire, and I'm trying to keep everything from burning to the fucking ground!"

"I'm not the villain here. I know you don't know me and clearly don't like me, but I'm not trying to fuck with your coven or hurt anyone."

"I'm not trying to make you feel like a villain, and I don't dislike you."

I scoff at the declaration. "Oh yeah, you're just overflowing with acceptance and support."

He takes another step toward me, but my glare stops him in his tracks. He looks torn or maybe regretful, I'm not sure, but I just want him to leave. I'm so tired of people trying to convince me that I'm not good enough, or trying to make me feel wrong or less than simply because I exist.

"I'll stay the fuck away from all of you; now get the fuck out of my room."

Sabin hesitates. "Vinna, that's not—"

"Leave!" I shout, and I feel pieces of me fracturing.

Sabin stares at me, and I meet his gaze with venom. The door clicks shut behind his exit, and I slide to the ground, putting my head in my hands. He's a dick, but he's right; I don't know anything, not really. I don't know how to be a caster or why I'm so fucking different. I don't know what's happening to me and why I feel the way that I do about practical strangers. I don't know shit about where I come from, and I sure as hell don't know where I'm going.

21

I find everyone around the huge table outside. It's been a week of mostly avoiding everyone who lives in this monster-mansion of emotional torture. I've ignored the knocks on my door, and I've been doing my best to sneak around unnoticed. That is until today when Lila made me promise to come down for a BBQ. To add to my misery, none of the sisters are even here.

Keegan is manning the grill, and I give him my best attempt at a smile as I make my way over to where everyone is sitting. The paladin are talking about the last case they had, and it seems like there's a Q-and-A session going on between them and the guys.

Surprise-filled eyes watch me as I make my way down the patio stairs. I take a seat at the long wrought iron table and try to follow the conversation. I'm completely zoned out when a tap on my shoulder pulls me from my confused thoughts. I look over, and everyone is staring at me.

"What?" I snap a little more harshly than I mean to.

"You okay?" Aydin asks me.

"Yeah," I say unconvincingly, even to my own ears.

He looks at me curiously, but I don't answer the questions in his eyes.

"Any update on when the Reader will be here?" I ask monotone.

"He should be here next week," Lachlan answers, just as short and terse.

Ryker asks Lachlan if it's Tearson who's coming, but I don't focus on what they are saying beyond that. After I catch a couple more curious looks aimed at me, I decide I need to try harder to snap out of my pissed off funk.

"So when do I get to start kicking your ass, I mean training?" Aydin asks playfully.

I take a minute to think about his question. Maybe this is exactly what I need right now. I'm used to training hard and fighting harder, and I miss it.

"Whenever you're ready to be humbled, I'm good to go. Should we start tomorrow morning?"

"I can't do the morning, but I could do late afternoon," Aydin replies.

"I'm watching this," Bastian declares, giving me an excited smile. I try to match it but fall short, and Bastien's smile dims.

"I think we all want to see what Vinna can do. Be prepared for an audience, you two," Lachlan tells us, and I try not to frown at what sounds like more of a threat than an effort at comradery.

I've watched my uncle this past week, and he's completely different with *the boys* than he is with me. He's invested and warm with them, and their dynamic is easy and seamless. It shows me the guy that the sisters insist he is.

But watching him with them doesn't give me hope that someday he'll turn the warmth of his smile my way. It just crushes me in a vice of cold indifference, pulverizing any longing I have to be worthy of his affection.

It's as if I can see everything I've ever wanted through a window, but as soon as I manage to get inside, everything's rotted and wilted to nothing. Things will never be for me like they are for them. I will never have what they have, and it makes me rethink what I'm doing here.

I came to learn about magic and what I can do. Instead, I'm trying to untangle myself from useless attraction and mooning over why my uncle doesn't care about me. I've been here for only a couple of weeks, and I feel more confused and lost than I ever have before.

I stay quiet throughout dinner. I answer a few questions and make a couple of comments, but aside from that, I tune the others out and try to focus on the setting sun, instead of the biting jealousy and loneliness I feel.

I give myself a mental slap to rein in the pity party I'm currently attending. I'm not here for this; who cares if any of them like me? It's time to get what I came for and get the fuck out of here. Let the Reader come and tell me all about what I'm working with. And if these paladin won't teach me, I'll find someone who will.

I push in my chair and retreat inside before anyone can stop me. I flick the lock on my bedroom door behind me, and I grab my phone to call Talon. It goes right to his voicemail, just like every other call has. I stare at my phone for a moment, missing him, missing his protection and the easy way we were around each other.

I grab one of the books I stole from Lachlan's office and slip under my covers. The binding creaks as I open it, and the smell of old paper wafts up to my nose. A tentative knock sounds on my door.

"Vinna, can we talk?" Sabin asks.

I don't answer. I have no desire to hear anything he has to say. I roll to my side giving the door—and him—my back, and I delve into the fine print about offensive magic. The doorknob jiggles, and I stare at the lock to make sure it holds.

"Is she still ignoring us?" Valen questions, and Sabin mumbles a response. "What the fuck did you say to her?" Valen demands.

Their argument grows muffled, and I can't make it out as they move away from my room. Other voices join them before a door closes, and their voices are cut off. I could use my runes and listen to what they're saying, but I don't have it in me to care right now. I fluff my pillow and turn the page of the old book, refocusing on what I'm doing here.

* * *

Aydin's back hits the mat again after I catch him with a low kick that sweeps his legs out from underneath him. I back up so he can get on his feet and engage again, but he stays on the mats breathing hard, drenched in sweat.

Looking at him now, I'm sure he regrets the massive amount of shit talking he did before we got started hours ago. There was excited anticipation floating around before. Bets were made, egos were stroked, and my bloodlust was itching to be fed. But it didn't take long to realize that Aydin was no match for me and what I can do.

I started to hold back after our second match, not finishing moves or being half as aggressive as I'd normally be. I like Aydin, and I figured breaking him wouldn't be the solid foundation to a lasting friendship. It's been fucking torture for me to hold back. I was counting on a serious fight to help release the shit storm of feelings I have swarming inside of me, but I'll have to figure out another way to deal with all of that once Aydin's decided he's had enough.

Aydin pats the floor twice, indicating that he's done, and I relax my stance and put my hands down.

"You were getting better that time. You almost caught me with that knee."

"I'm pretty sure you were two feet away from me before I got my foot off the floor," Aydin chuckles and grabs his side. He raises an arm silently indicating that he needs healing.

Evrin comes over, and before he can even ask where Aydin is hurting, Aydin starts pointing to all of his injuries. Watching others use their magic is something I don't think will ever get old, and I become completely engrossed in watching Evrin heal Aydin.

"You're incredible, Vinna. I've never seen anything like what you can do," Evrin tells me as he heals Aydin's ribs.

"Right, and she's totally holding back too," Aydin tells Evrin, and I can't help but smile at the pride in his voice.

"We finished?" I ask Aydin, desperate to be done so I can move on to something else that will help me quench the bloodlust and aggression I'm still battling. It has me feeling anxious and twitchy, and I need to run my body into the ground to help relieve it.

"Oh, we're done. I can admit when I'm out of my league. I mean really, you're not even sweaty or winded," Aydin laughs and offers me a fist bump.

I give him my knuckles and thank him for the *warm-up*, which has him bellowing with laughter and earns some snickers from Evrin. I tuck earbuds into my ears and nod at Keegan and Silva as they leave the gym. I pull up my playlist and select "I Hate Everything About You" by Three Days Grace. By the time the chorus hits, I'm running full out like my life is on the line.

Over an hour later, Breaking Benjamin's "I Will Not

Bow" is filling my head, and I turn the treadmill off and climb down. I use the hem of my tank top to wipe sweat off the back of my neck as I try to ignore the aggressive itch still skittering inside of me. I immediately become aware that the guys are waiting throughout the gym, watching me and making it clear that I'm not leaving this room without acknowledging them.

I move to the pull up bar refusing to give into their demanding presence. I grip it and easily muscle my chin up and over. I'm on my third set of twenty-five when a pair of arms clamps around my waist and pulls me away from the bar. I consider for a minute getting out of his hold, but maybe it's best to get this over with.

I reluctantly pluck out my earbuds and tell Knox to put me down. He lets me intimately slide down the front of his body. Irritated that I'm completely turned on by the contact, I try to get as much sweat on him as possible before stepping away.

My traitorous body immediately rebels against the separation and starts to crave him. Knox sighs like he's fighting the same battle. The sound pulls at me as it fans my own dissatisfaction. I want to lick his creamy, coffee-toned skin and find out if it tastes as good as it looks.

I run my gaze appreciatively up his thick muscled body until I land on his stormy gray eyes. Maybe sex is the answer. I can't fight to get the rage and aggression out of me, so maybe angry sex will do it. Sabin's voice shatters my thoughts and drenches me in cold reality.

"We were going to wait until you were done, but at this rate, we'll be here all day. By the moons, are you even mortal?" Sabin asks.

I meet his awkward chuckle with an unamused glare. Sabin releases a defeated huff.

"This isn't what I wanted. I didn't mean for you to stop talking to everyone, to avoid us, to turn cold."

I study him for a long moment.

"This is exactly what you wanted. You didn't want them to get attached or for me to push things. I've backed off."

Sabin tries to respond, but Knox cuts him off. "I know Sabin talked to you about how *he* felt, but the rest of us don't agree with him. Sabin's opinion shouldn't be the only one that matters here."

"I get that, but if he's giving me a warning, who the hell am I to dismiss him? He's part of your coven. You're all connected. Despite what some people think, that does matter to me," I tell Knox, and narrow my eyes at Sabin.

Sabin runs both hands through his ash brown hair. His tattoos ripple over the muscles in his arm. "I feel like I've fucked everything up, and I don't know how to fix it. I'm sorry."

I don't know if he's apologizing to me, the guys, or both, but as far as I'm concerned, it's pointless.

"Like you said, I am new to this world. I have no idea where I'm going or what my magic can do. I have no business dragging you guys into all my uncertain variables. I'm doing what you asked. Deal with it."

"You said that to her?" Valen snaps at Sabin.

He doesn't wait for him to answer before turning back to me. "Vinna, you are paladin, not only is it in your blood, but I just watched you crush one of the best fighters the paladin have like it was nothing. I don't need a Reader to tell me that you're one of us," Valen declares.

"Well, I guess we'll find out in a week when the Reader comes. Then Sabin can decide if I'm worthy."

"I'm going to fucking throttle you, Sabin. I can't believe you said that shit to her," Bastien seethes at his friend. I try to leave, not interested in getting any more in the middle than I already am, but Bastien steps in my way.

"Bruiser, I know what's going on with you right now isn't just about us. I heard about all the shit that's been going down with Lachlan and the coven. I've watched you withdraw more and more every time Lachlan shows interest or affection to one of us but ignores you. It has to be fucking with you. By the stars, it's pissing all of us off for you. Please don't keep us from being there for you. We care, and it's killing us to watch you suffer in silence."

I look up into Bastien's hazel eyes, and everything inside of me wants to break and rage simultaneously. We stare at each other, and he watches as I dam up the sorrow that wants to pour out of me and harden my resolve. Bastien lets out a resigned sigh and interlaces his fingers behind his head, frustrated.

Valen moves closer to Bastien, in response to his twin's distress. His chocolate waves sway with the movement, and the pair of them are so achingly beautiful I have to look away. I find no reprieve because my eyes land on Ryker, and I can feel the sadness that radiates from his sky-blue gaze.

His full lips part in preparation for whatever he's going to say, but I have to get the hell out of here. I walk out against their protests. They just don't get it. I want them, even though I shouldn't, but at what cost? I either divide their coven or lose track of what I'm doing here. A set of keys sits solitary on the kitchen counter. I walk past them and then stop and retrace my steps. I snatch them up and silence the tinkling sound they make, in a closed fist. The jagged edges press against my skin, and I see them for the sign they are, freedom.

22

I lean against the brick wall of the bar and try to decide where I should go next. My gym rat attire and absence of an ID have me standing outside instead of inside like I was wanting. I probably should have thought through grabbing my wallet before I stole a car and drove into town.

I'm not really sure what I'm even doing here. I don't even drink. I'm not opposed to it; I've just never done it. Clubs and bars aren't really my scene, but it called to me when I spotted the neon lights in the distance.

I'm still riled up and itching with aggression, and I thought I could just sit inside and quietly wait for a good bar fight. I tried to explain this to the bouncer, but he just looked at me like I had lost my mind and told me to leave. I debated for a second if the bouncer would fight me if I just stayed right where I was, but he didn't seem like someone who'd be the kind of challenge I need right now.

Two men pile out of the entrance of the bar, bringing some of the noise from inside with them. They lean against the wall a couple feet down from me and light cigarettes.

"Who are you going to bet on?" the lumberjack looking dude asks his friend who's a dead ringer for Liev Schreiber.

"Torrez, obviously. The guy's a mountain. I don't care what the pumas say; there's no way McClain is going to beat him."

"What about Stevens? I've seen him train. I think he's got a shot," lumberjack replies.

Liev snorts. "Please, Torrez can fight all night back to back and still not lose. He's done it before."

"You think anyone else will challenge him?"

"I will," I announce and push away from the brick wall.

The two men look me over as I settle in next to them.

"Get real, little witch. You could use every ounce of power in that tight body of yours, and you'd still get torn apart," Liev tells me, and his lips purse with amusement.

I give him a sweet look from under my lashes. "Maybe or maybe not. Let's find out. What have you got to lose?" I ask innocently.

The two men chuckle and send each other looks that question my sanity, and debate if that matters to them. I wait patiently. If they refuse me, I'm just going to follow them, but they don't need to know that.

Liev shrugs and flicks his cigarette. He kicks off the wall and walks over to a shiny black Harley. He lifts a helmet from the seat and holds it out to me. I jingle the keys in my hand and smile at him.

"I'll follow you."

I slam the door of the white Range Rover and walk toward the two men who are climbing off their motorcycles. We're at some type of fairgrounds, and music and shouts stream out from a small arena that looks like it was designed for a rodeo. Rows of bleacher-style seats surround an enclosed oval of packed dirt. Tall lights illuminate everything, and snarls fill the night as I follow my escorts up the stairs that lead to the seats.

Just as we enter the walkway, everyone jumps up out of their seats, screaming and shouting at whoever is in the middle of the arena. Bodies block my view, and I follow the lumberjack as he elbows his way through the aggravated crowd.

"They must have started early, fuck, I could have made some money off this fight. Just look at McClain," Liev shouts behind him to the lumberjack, and his words float back to me too.

An empty stretch of bleachers opens up, and I step up on the seat so I can see over the men who are crowding the barrier. A gray wolf, the size of a horse, shakes his head violently, the tiger sized mountain lion between his jaws yowls and claws to get free. The wolf thrashes again, and a loud crack echoes over the dirt. The mountain lion goes limp, its head wobbling as the wolf gives one last shake before releasing the lifeless body to drop, heavy, to the ground.

I watch wide-eyed as the wolf saunters through an open gate and disappears. The crowd is a mix of elation and bitter disappointment. They start to settle and get ready for the next match.

"I warned you, little witch, you're out of your league," Liev tells me. "That's the Silas pack beta, and no one beats him aside from the alpha himself."

Men drag the limp mountain lion out of the arena, and a guy follows behind them kicking dirt over the streaks of blood.

Lumberjack leans down to me. "He'll heal, can you say the same?" He gestures at the open gate they just dragged the mountain lion through.

"Nope, I'm pretty sure if I get broken in half, I'm going to stay that way," I admit.

The reality of that doesn't have me rethinking my decision but instead excites me on a level that's definitely not normal. I scan the faces of the crowd that I now know is predominantly shifter, and I offhandedly wonder if any of them are grizzlies. I know jack-shit about shifters and their culture, but I could definitely be down to hang with this crowd for fight night.

A man covered in only shorts walks out into the empty arena. The crowd around me stands and starts shouting and cheering. Torrez looks to be about six feet tall, and he has a black beard and a mohawk of long dreads. He's Latino, and his dark brown eyes are shrewd and ready.

Two more men walk into the arena. One is also clad only in shorts and the other looks to be the referee. The crowd is quieter for Torrez's opponent Stevens, but he's still greeted with shouts of excitement and support. Stevens is smaller than Torrez and not nearly as built. He has muddy brown hair and freckles everywhere. They don't look evenly matched, but I'm the last person who would underestimate someone based on that.

"This fight will be wolf only as was agreed by both contenders previously. Begin."

With no more pomp or circumstance, the referee runs back out of the way, and I watch as both men strip out of their shorts and ripple into wolves. It happens in seconds, one second they're men, and the next, wolves. They slam into each other in a flurry of fangs and fur. Their feral growls simultaneously pull goosebumps from my skin and call to my basest nature.

Torrez and Stevens looked mismatched as men, but as wolves, they're closer in size. The gray wolf is taller and fuller than his red and brown opponent but not by much. Stevens bites into Torrez's shoulder, but he's forced to release his hold when Torrez almost rips off his ear. They circle and then slam back into each other, and before I can process how it happened, Torrez has Stevens by the neck, and he's shaking him. The fight is over in a matter of minutes, and now it's my turn.

23

"I fucking told you Stevens couldn't do it," Liev slaps lumberjack on the back, a huge grin on his face.

They rib each other back and forth, and a few shifters around us get in on the teasing and shit talking. A deep voice calls for any other challengers, and I'm up and over the barrier before the announcer finishes his sentence. Jeering and catcalls take over the arena, and small plumes of dust accentuate each step I take toward Torrez and the ref.

I stop a couple of feet away, and Torrez's nostrils flare. His eyes narrow slightly, and he scoffs.

"Lost, little witch?" he asks.

"Nope, I know exactly where I am, and exactly what I'm here to do."

"And what's that, princess?"

"Fuck up your undefeated record, of course."

Torrez laughs a full, deep, and rounded belly laugh, and snickers move like *the wave* throughout the bleachers.

"Well, aren't you cute. Stupid as fuck and delusional, but really fucking cute," Torrez gives me an appraising look and licks his lips. His nostrils flare again, and I have no idea what he's sniffing for. Fear maybe? Or attraction? *Sniff away, wolf-man, you're not going to find either.*

"Oh, come on now, Torrez, you know it's not the size of the dog in the fight, but the size of the fight in the dog."

"True, but you're confusing your witch for bitch, you're no shifter. Why do you want to make me mess up that perfect face?"

His shit talking game is on point, and I can't help but appreciate it. I smirk, and he scents the air again. Can shifters smell emotion? If they can, then he has to know that I need this fight more than I need my next breath. My unsatisfied bloodlust is tearing me apart, and this is the only way to excise all the rage and hurt festering inside of me.

"In or out, wolf?" I ask, stone-faced. If he's not interested, then I'll find someone else to pick a fight with.

Torrez rakes his dark brown eyes over me one more time and shrugs. "In, witch."

I'm pretty sure these shifters expect me to have a problem with their use of the word *witch*, but I couldn't care less: caster, witch, freak, it's all the same to me.

The ref steps forward. "What are your terms? Shifter form, magic, what's allowed and what's not?" He looks at both of us.

"Wolf or man, I have no problem with either."

"She can use whatever magic she has. She's gonna need it."

The ref nods and announces the terms to the crowd, even though I'm pretty sure they have super hearing and already know what the deal is. The ref raises both his hands, and I stretch out my neck while I keep my eyes fixed on Torrez. My magic sparks awake inside of me, and the tingle of bloodlust floods my limbs.

The ref drops his hands, and Torrez is inches away from me in a blink. *Fuck, he's fast!* He's still a man when he tackles me at the waist and tries to muscle me onto my back. I slam my elbow where his neck meets his shoulder, twice, before my back hits the dirt. I use Torrez's momentum against him, and I kick him off of me instead of letting myself get pinned.

I use the runes on my legs to give myself extra power, and he flies five feet away from me before he hits the ground. I flip back up, and I land a roundhouse kick to his head before he can get all the way up on his feet. He grabs my foot as he falls back to the dirt and yanks me off balance.

Fuck, he's strong too. I stumble but somehow manage to stay on my feet. Torrez rolls away from me and pops back up. He lets out a deep growl and wipes a trickle of blood from his bottom lip. His eyes flare with promises of pain, and the tip of his hands elongate with claws.

He slashes out at me, and I dodge and weave out of his reach. He lunges in frustration, and I spin clipping my elbow against his cheek. Claws sink into my side as he falters, and we both step away from each other to recover. Torrez shakes his head in an effort to clear it, and I look down at my shredded shirt, my black sports bra peeking through the rips in the fabric.

I rip off the tattered garment and use it to swipe at the blood slowly dripping down my side. Wolf whistles and howls sound off around the arena. I look up, and Torrez steps out of his shorts. He stands there for a minute like somehow his dick is going to send me running.

I smile. "Cold?"

My smirk falls when Torrez morphs into his massive gray wolf. He apparently doesn't find my dick joke as funny as I did, because he growls at me and then charges.

"Vinna!"

My head snaps in the direction of Ryker's voice. What the fuck is he doing here? The weight of a truck slams into me, and teeth sink into my shoulder. I call on my runes for power, and I start punching the wolf in the face. His weight forces me to my back. When my spine touches the packed dirt of the arena, Torrez releases my shoulder and goes for my neck.

Fangs flash toward my face. I grip the snarling jaws and fight to keep them from closing around my head and neck. Saliva drips down on me, and claw-covered paws dig into my torso. I push Torrez's wolf jaws apart, calling on every ounce of power and strength my runes can give me.

The bottom of his mouth snaps, and a ripping and cracking sound fills my ears. Torrez yelps in pain and scrambles away from me. The bottom of his muzzle hangs loose, and canine cries leak out of his open maw. Torrez lies on his side panting, and the wolf blinks out, leaving a man in its wake.

The ref rushes to him, and I slowly get up, wincing as the movement tugs at my wounds. I'm bleeding steadily from the bite wound on my shoulder and the gouges on my side. I'm covered in varying depths of oozing scratches, and my fingers are torn up and bloody from my efforts to keep fangs out of my face.

I'm sore and gloriously drained. Man, that was a good fucking fight. The ref calls to men standing just outside of the arena. They jog to him and help Torrez stand up. They sling his arms around their necks and half carry him toward the exit.

The ref approaches me. "Torrez is too injured to continue. You've won."

I give him a nod and watch as Torrez is assisted out of the arena. "Is he going to be ok?"

"His jaw is severely broken. It will heal, painfully, but he'll be fine in a couple of weeks. Would you like me to call a healer for you?"

I look out into the mumbling crowd and find Ryker. I'm

not at all shocked to see Knox, Bastien, Valen, and Sabin standing at his side. *Fucking magical LoJack*.

"No, thanks for the offer. I'll be fine."

The ref looks at me quizzically for a minute, before giving me an accepting nod and walking off in the direction that they took Torrez. I walk over to my shredded shirt and snatch it up off the ground. I scan the crowd one last time until I find lumberjack and Liev. I take in their shocked faces and give them a wink.

Five furious faces take me in as I casually make my way to the guys.

"What the fuck are you doing here?" Bastien scolds me.

"What does it look like I'm doing here?"

"It looks like you're being torn to shreds," Sabin snaps.

"Hop down from your high horse, Sabin. It's fucking up your view, because that's what winning looks like."

I gesture over my shoulder to the blood-spattered ring. Knox snorts out a laugh, but he coughs it out when four pairs of angry eyes turn on him.

"Don't encourage her, Knox," Valen chastises.

"Why not? She's right, she won, and I think it's hilarious when she calls Sabin out on his shit."

I smile at him, and he winks at me. Knox is so gung-ho for battle and glory, and I seriously love it. Nothing seems to faze him at all. He should be crowned the king of rolling with the punches.

"Did Lachlan tell you guys where to find me?" I ask, curious as to why Lachlan sent them instead of one of the paladin to collect me.

"No, I doubt he even knows you're gone," Bastien tells me.

"Well, what the hell are you doing here then? You guys come to fights, and you've never told me about it?"

"No, we tracked my car here."

I stare at Ryker confused.

"You stole my car. I went to leave tonight, and it was missing. When we pulled up here, it was obvious who had taken it and what you were up to. How'd you even find this place?"

"Fate," I say with a smile.

Knox snorts again, and Bastien starts to chuckle with him. Valen rubs a hand over his face in exasperation. Something about this situation suddenly seems funny to me, and I start to snicker. I suspect I'm a little slap-happy from the adrenaline rush I'm currently coming down from.

"Well, as much fun as it is to watch the three of you giggle at each other, we should go. I don't like how some of these shifters are looking at her," Sabin declares.

I look up, taking in the faces all around us. I meet a lot of intense stares, but none of them feel threatening. Valen grabs my bloody hand, and I wince at the pain that shoots through my shoulder. I sway ever so slightly before my feet start cooperating, and I'm led out into the parking lot. I stop at the back of the white Range Rover I stole earlier, and I direct Sabin to the wheel well I hid the keys in.

Ryker pulls up the back door. "Vinna, sit before you pass out from blood loss."

I do as I'm told. Ryker starts gently wiping away blood, in search of its source, and his hands warm up when he begins to heal me. My pants have long tears in them, I'm guessing from claws, and one strap of my sports bra is hanging by a thread. My shirt is a lost cause, and judging by the amount of *wipe away the blood and then heal the source* that's going on right now, my body doesn't look much better than my clothing.

Oh well, it was worth it.

The guys all watch with the same intensity they had the first time Ryker healed me, and it sends shivers up my spine.

Ryker tears away the mangled strap of my sports bra, to give himself better access to the bite on my shoulder. The motion sends a zing straight to my clit, and I have to force myself to stop thinking about how hot it is to have Ryker tearing off my clothes.

"Fuck, I know I did this to you, and I'm so sorry. I just saw that big ass wolf charging you, and I freaked out."

For a minute, I thought Ryker was apologizing for getting me wet, and it takes me a second to process what he said. He starts to heal the bite, and relief from the pain floods me.

"Yeah, distractions during a fight are never a good thing. Try to remember that for next time," I tease.

"There won't be—"

"Don't even finish that sentence, Bastien. I promise you're not going to like what happens if you do."

"Bruiser—"

"No, I'm serious. You get no say in what I do. You haven't earned that privilege, and let's get one thing straight right now. There will always be a next time because it's part of who I am. I was made for this, and if you can't handle that, then fuck off."

Bastien and I glare at each other, both of us breathing heavy with anger. Ryker cups my cheeks and forces my eyes from Bastien's stormy gaze, to his warm expression.

"We get it. It took us by surprise to see you out there, and none of us like seeing you hurt. Which is why some of us are saying some dumb shit right now, but I promise you we get it. You get hurt all you want, and I swear I'll always be here to heal it."

His thumbs stroke both of my cheeks. His earnest gaze reaches into me and forces me to see him and what he could mean to me if I let it happen. I lean into his palm ever so slightly and close my eyes. I don't let myself stay there for long, and I definitely don't allow myself to hope that I will ever be able to keep this. But I take a couple of seconds and let myself get lost in this fleeting moment.

"Alright, let's rinse off as much blood as we can, and get a move on."

Valen hands me his wet t-shirt, and I use it to wipe myself down as much as possible, while I count his abs and try not to stare at his hard nipples. When I'm done Sabin and Valen load up in an old Bronco, and the rest of us pile into Ryker's SUV. Ryker starts the car and "All My Life" by the Foo Fighters blasts through the speakers, scaring the shit out of everyone.

He scrambles to get the volume down and turns to me in the back seat. I scrunch my nose sheepishly.

"Sorry, I was kind of jamming when I pulled in here. You have really good music," I offer as consolation for the ruptured eardrums I just gave everyone.

He shakes his head, and a smile grows across his full lips. "I love music."

"He's an incredible guitar player," Bastien informs me. "And Knox can sing the panties off anyone."

Ryker and Knox chuckle.

"We'll have to go camping or do a bonfire night, then you guys can show Vinna what you can do," Bastien decides.

"I'll be sure to bring extra panties," I tease.

Bastien turns around in the passenger seat and gives me a big smile. "Does that mean you are going to stop avoiding us now?"

The easy happiness I was feeling blinks out, and I sigh. "No."

Bastien's smile dims, and I hate that he looks sad. I feel like I just kicked a puppy, but I can't get sucked back into this...thing that happens when I'm around them.

"I'm just here to learn about magic. I shouldn't be

focusing on anything beyond that. The paladin aren't teaching me shit, and reading only goes so far. When I'm with you guys, it's easy to forget that my life right now is a drama-filled suckfest.

"I don't want to add fighting with Sabin, and you guys fighting each other, to my suckfest. I'd love to say we can just keep it friendly, but if I'm being honest with myself, that's not going to work for me either. So avoiding you is the best plan I can come up with right now."

Bastien watches me for a minute and then silently turns to face the front of the car. I stare at the back of his head and his dark-chocolate wavy brown hair for way longer than is healthy. The silence in the car feels wrong. I want to take everything I just said and shove it back in my mouth, but it wouldn't change our reality. Everything about this sucks, but that's the story of my life these days.

24

I close the door of the Jeep and lock it with the fob. It looks more baby tank than I pictured, but I'm in love all the same. Neil showing up at the door was the best possible surprise, and it looks like my carjacking days are over. I dropped Neil back at his office, and now I'm taking full advantage of my freedom and getting to know this town on my terms.

I steer clear of the bars and instead step into the quiet bookstore. I grab a tote that's hanging at the end of a shelf and start adding books to it. A girl walks quickly around the corner and lets out a surprised yelp when she sees me, the books she was carrying going flying.

"Sorry, I didn't know anyone was in here," she tells me as she starts to pick up the books from the floor.

I bend down to help. "I didn't mean to scare you. I've been quietly stocking up."

I point to my bulging tote and smile. She smiles back and stands up. She's taller than me and slimmer—lean where I'm more muscular. She has shoulder length magenta hair that's cut bluntly and curled and tousled to perfection.

The color seriously compliments the pink undertones of

her fair complexion and her heart-shaped face. She smiles back, her eyes the color of milk chocolate, the smoky eye makeup she's rocking accentuating them in all the best ways. Her nose is delicate, and the septum ring she has makes everything about her look even edgier.

"Are you finding everything okay?" she asks me politely.

"Actually, I was wondering if you had any books about caster basics, like a *Casters for Dummies,* maybe," I ask sheepishly hoping my question doesn't offend her.

I let out a relieved breath when she giggles and tells me to follow her. She starts pulling books from shelves and leads me to a small table next to some comfy looking chairs.

There's no *Casters for Dummies,* but there are books explaining caster history, magic basics, and what to expect before your awakening.

"You have a little brother or sister going through the quickening?" she asks me.

"No, these are for me. I just recently moved here, and I'm trying to catch up on what I need to know," I admit, chagrined.

"Holy shit, you're Lachlan Aylin's niece, aren't you?" She takes a step back and studies me more intently. "I thought it was just a rumor," she tells me and points to the runes on my arms and hands. She inspects them more thoroughly, and I shift on my feet awkwardly.

"Yes to the niece question, and nope, not a rumor," I answer and run a hand over the runes on my arm.

"They're beautiful," she tells me, and I relax a little.

"I'm Vinna," I introduce myself, extending my hand.

She looks at my extended palm and then back up to my face, shock evident in her eyes.

"I should probably tell you I'm a shifter," she offers hesitantly.

"Cool."

I can't help but wonder if this has to do with my fight a couple nights ago. Do shifters hate me now or something? She looks at me quizzically and then shakes my still outstretched hand.

"I'm Mave," she finally offers.

We sink into the two comfy chairs and start asking each other questions. I tell her about how I ended up here, and she tells me about her pack and what life is like growing up in this town. I learn that casters aren't always on good terms with shifters which explains her hesitation when I first introduced myself.

"So what's it like living with the Fierro twins?" Mave leans back in the chair and fans herself with her hand. She raises her eyebrows suggestively, and I laugh and then fan myself too.

"Good to know I'm not the only one drooling over that whole coven," I admit.

"Ah, you have coven lust already? I was just talking about the twins, but I like where this is headed."

I laugh and then groan as I cover my face with my hands. *Coven lust*, yeah that about sums it up.

"Vin, you're the hottest ticket that's walked through the wards of this town. All that"—she motions to my face and body—"wrapped up in a cloak of mystery. Well, let's just say things are about to get really interesting around here," Mave declares and smiles, a glint of mischievousness in her eyes.

"Is that a good or a bad thing?" I ask, unsure.

"Probably both," she chuckles.

We talk for a bit longer as Mave tells me about all the caster boys that she thinks are worth paying attention to and catches me up on some local gossip. I have no idea about any of the people she's talking about, but it's fun to listen to her animated assessments.

I get lost in the easy back and forth of our *story exchange*, and I feel lighter than I have in days. Eventually, I check out and we exchange phone numbers, promising to do something soon. I walk out feeling excited about the new books and the new friend I made. As I make my way to the Jeep, I spot the sisters walking my way.

"Well, well, well, what do we have here?" I tease getting their attention.

"Vinna, love, what are you up to on this lovely afternoon?"

I point to the bags of books I just purchased. "I'm stocking up and poking around town."

"We're just headed to lunch. Join us," Lila tells me, snaking her dainty arm through mine.

"Are you sure? I don't want to interrupt girl time."

"Well, you are a girl, so you'd be adding to it, not interrupting it," Adelaide reassures me.

"Have you had Indian food before? That's where we're headed."

I shake my head and smile. "If you three like it, I'm sure it's amazing."

We're led to a table and handed menus. I don't get much of a chance to look at it though because people keep stopping by the table to say *hi* to the sisters.

"Everyone here seems to know you guys. Do you come here a lot?" I ask after the manager and several different waiters stop by to greet them and chat for a bit.

"We come here a lot," Birdie smiles fondly. "We've been eating here a couple of times a month for ages, but I also think the presence of a certain *mysterious niece* at our table is making us far more popular than we normally are." She winks at me.

"How does everyone know about me?" I ask, taking a bite of something that was just delivered to the table. "Wow, that's good. What is this?"

"They're called pakoras. Try it with this sauce," Lila tells me.

I proceed to stuff my face shamelessly, but the sisters are aware of my table manners or the lack thereof when it comes to good food, and they just smile at me encouragingly.

"Gossip travels fast around here. You're currently the talk of the town," Lila confesses.

I groan irritably.

"Don't worry. It will start to die down when everyone gets used to seeing you around," Birdie tells me.

"But speaking of gossip... what's going on with you and *the boys*?" Adelaide asks, trying and failing at sounding casual and barely interested.

I choke on the food in my mouth and start coughing loudly. I gulp water to clear everything away and take in the sisters' plucky grins.

"Nothing really, why?" I hedge.

"Just curious, I thought you guys were getting along, but lately you're more subdued and seem to be avoiding them. Did something happen?"

I look at each of their eager faces, which are patiently waiting for me to answer. I fidget in my seat for a minute, debating if it's weird to talk to them about what's going on. I'm out of my depth though, so maybe it's worth a shot. I take a deep breath and start to explain.

"We do get along, and I have fun with them. I click with them in a way I've never had before." I take a sip of the mango drink Adelaide told me I had to try. Shit, that's amazing. I point to the drink and give her a thumbs-up before continuing. "But it's also intense in a way that freaks me out. I'm attracted and drawn to them, and I don't know how to be around them without looking at them that way or wanting things I probably shouldn't."

All three of them nod their heads in understanding. I sigh and drown my sorrows in mango deliciousness, and it's quiet for a minute.

"Do they not want things to go further?" Lila asks me. "Because that is not the impression I get when I observe you all together or overhear their conversations," she says with a sweet smile and then gives me a wink. I can't help but chuckle.

"Um, I think most of them are good with letting things... progress, but Sabin made some points that have me questioning whether that's a good idea." I look at my hands. "Since then I've been taking a step back, trying to sort through what I think and feel about everything."

"What did he say?" Birdie asks, sounding a little more growly than she did before.

"I've only been a caster for a little while, and he thought things were moving too quickly."

"You've been a caster your whole life, you've just known that's what it was called for a short time. The fact that you've grown up the way that you have, dealing with everything you've had to deal with, puts you ahead of kids who grow up in this community, not behind them. I hope you know that, Vinna," Lila tells me fiercely.

"You're not lacking in anything that matters, and that makes you an incredible caster worthy of incredible things in your life," Birdie adds.

I give them a small smile. I never really thought about it that way. I've been focusing on all of the ways I'm behind or inadequate. I didn't really think about how I might be better off because of who I already am and what I've been through.

"He is right about some things though. I'd known some of them for like a day before things started getting...intense. That can't be normal, right? Is this a magic thing? Is it normal to feel this way about men you don't even know?"

The sisters chuckle and look at each other with knowing smiles.

"I want to say it's *not* a magic thing, but honestly we don't know much about the magic you have yet, so it'd be unwise to rule it out completely," Lila tells me. "But it sounds more like attraction to me, and when it comes to that, the best advice I can offer is to trust your instincts."

The other sisters voice their agreement.

Adelaide grabs my hand. "It will all work out, love, exactly how it's supposed to in the end. Trust yourself, trust others with your heart and vulnerability. You're an exceptional female, don't be afraid of happiness, fight for what you deserve."

25

"I need an *I heart korma* t-shirt," I tell the sisters as we walk into the house from the garage. "Besides everything you ladies make, it's my new favorite."

They dole out hugs as they head up to their apartment, and I walk into the kitchen. I hesitate for a second when I walk in and find the guys gathered around the island, dishing up ice cream. Their conversation comes to an abrupt halt, and I give an awkward, barely there smile before taking off for my room.

I unpack the bags of books and find a new home for each of them while I ruminate on the advice the sisters gave me at lunch. I want to be respectful of Sabin and how he feels, but the sisters are right. I'm not listening to my own instincts. I'm not listening to what I feel is right. Maybe it's selfish of me to decide that what I want trumps everything else, but when I listen to my instincts, I always end up exactly where I need to be. So why am I ignoring them now?

A knock on my door pulls my head up, and I see one of the twins poke his head in.

"Bruiser, can I come in?"

I nod my head at Bastien and give him a small smile. I

lean back against the built-in bookshelves, and Bastien plops his large frame on the sofa. The green in his hazel eyes is extra prominent today, and his gorgeous hair is down. It skims just past his collarbone, and his pecs flex enticingly as he sets his hands in his lap.

"New books?" he asks in an effort to skate around the awkwardness hanging around us.

"Yeah, just some basics so I can start figuring out how to use magic and not just read about it," I tell him and gesture with my thumb behind me.

"What's in the box?"

I look around and then behind me, searching for the box he's asking about. When I realize what it is, I pull the cedar rectangle down from the shelf and set it between my legs. I run my hand over the top of the smooth wood, tracing each of the four corners.

"These are my sister, Laiken's, ashes. I planned on spreading them somewhere, but so far I haven't found a place that felt right. So, yeah."

"What happened to her?" he asks, his voice laced with empathy.

"Beth happened to her." I scoff. "Beth was a user and a con artist. She got away with a lot, but she tried to blackmail this guy, and instead of him giving her what she wanted, he shot her, then he strangled Laiken and shot himself."

"Fucking hell. I'm so sorry; that's horrible."

"After Beth kicked me out of the house, she moved. I had no way to find her or Laiken, but once I had enough money from my fights, I hired a private investigator. I tried to get Laiken to come with me, but she wouldn't. I think Beth told her I had left her behind or something. She was so angry with me, but I should have fought harder for her."

"Bruiser, you were just a kid yourself. You can't blame yourself."

"It's impossible not to; all I have left are thoughts and memories—and this—until I find a place for her." I gesture at the cedar box and then place it back up on the shelf.

Bastien stands up and scoops me off the ground like I weigh nothing. He bounces back down on the sofa with me in his lap.

"I was three when my parents went missing. They were part of the paladin coven that disappeared with your dad. I've spent most of my life obsessed with trying to find them, or find out what happened to them. So I understand how easy it is to get lost in the what-ifs. Don't do that to yourself. Someone took my mom and dad, and someone took your sister, and the blame lies with those people. Don't take on fault that doesn't belong to you."

He runs his hand down my jaw and stares firmly in my eyes.

"Okay. I won't if you won't," I tell him, and a small guilt-infused weight lifts off my chest.

I marvel at Bastien's ability to be playful and silly, and yet still so emotionally in tune and mature when the situation warrants it. He sees so much more of me than I thought I was showing, and it makes me feel understood and validated. He can joke and tease with the best of them and then turn around and talk about real-life, tough shit in a way that makes me feel lighter and freer than I have in years.

He gives me a beautiful, heart-stopping smile, and I find myself wanting to run my fingers through his incredibly inviting soft waves. I squeeze my hands into fists and growl at myself. He's been here for five minutes, and already my self-control is being smashed into smithereens. I move to get out of his lap, and he lets me.

"Why'd you move? Did I make you uncomfortable?" he asks curiously.

"No, it just makes it harder to listen to whatever it is you came up here to say, instead of doing other things," I admit, uncensored.

Bastien's mind-numbing smile is back, and he pulls me back into his lap. Only this time, he positions me so that I'm straddling him instead of sitting sideways like I was before. *Well, crap.*

"I'm cool with other things," he tells me, and I feel the proof of his statement grow against my ass. I close my eyes and take a couple of deep breaths to try and refocus my brain.

"What's up?" I ask, trying to change the subject. I laugh when I realize the multitude of different ways he can answer that question. "I mean, what do you want?" I try again with another chuckle.

His smile turns salacious, and he grinds himself against me. "You don't know what I want, Bruiser? I need to make myself clearer?"

I stare at him and groan irritably. Why is this so easy and all so difficult at the same time?

"I mean what did you come up here to talk about?"

I give up my internal battle and finally run my fingers through his waves. Yep, just as gloriously soft as I thought they would be. Bastien hums in appreciation as my fingertips scrape across his scalp, and now it's his turn to close his eyes and attempt to control his breathing.

"I can't remember. It was something along the lines of: can we just pretend Sabin is a mute and never told you any of the shit he told you?" Bastien asks with a breathy laugh.

"I'm surprised Captain Cockblock let you come up here alone," I admit.

"Bruiser, let's get a couple things straight. Sabin's permission is not required. He doesn't *let* me do anything. He can feel how he wants to and behave how he wants to, but I'm not him. Also, none of us agree with his assessment of things. So please let it go and hang with us again. You know you miss us," he smirks.

I chuckle and then evilly grind against his massive hard-on, eliciting another groan from him. "Feels like you've been missing me, Bastien," I counter and high five myself internally for the sultry comeback.

"You're playing dirty," he accuses.

"I'm playing dirty? You started this," I laugh and tug lightly on the ends of his hair.

"I did, didn't I." He grins while I continue to watch, hypnotized, as his chocolate locks slip silkily through my fingers.

"Tell me you're going to stop avoiding us."

"I'll stop avoiding you," I parrot.

"I knew I could convince you. Are you sure you don't need more convincing?" Bastien wags his eyebrows suggestively.

"Sorry to bruise your ego, but *you* didn't convince me of anything. I got some good advice today, and it helped me see things in a different light," I confess.

"Bummer, here I thought I could add powers of persuasion to my magical resume."

Bastien sticks out his lower lip in a faux pout, and before I can second guess myself, I lean into him and take his pouty lip in between my own. I suck on it for a couple of seconds before I pull back to gauge his reaction.

I don't get very far before Bastien grabs the back of my neck and pulls my lips back to his. His kiss is fire and passion and everything I need right now. His tongue sneaks in to meet mine, taking things to a whole other level that sears the feel of his lips and tongue onto my soul.

The dam on my desire breaks, and I bury my hands in his hair, claiming him the same way he's claiming me. Need burns through every inch of me, and my magic begins to build in that same unusual way that it did with Valen and Ryker in the closet.

I moan my approval, and Bastien greedily swallows my pleasure. Our kiss slows and languidly, Bastien and I pull our mouths apart from each other. We're both breathing heavily, chests heaving with effort to fill our lungs and clear our minds.

Bastien brushes hair away from my face, and I pull my fingers through his waves one last time. I stroke the back of my fingers down his jaw, and he closes his eyes and leans into my hand.

"What kind of spell are you weaving over me, Vinna?" he asks with hooded eyes and want in his tone.

I laugh softly before stealing his lips again, this kiss slower and more appreciative. I try not to move against his hardness, but it's maddening to stay so still. I retreat, offering one last quick peck before climbing off him. Bastien groans in protest.

The space between my thighs feels empty, and a twinge in my gut tells me to do something about it. I ignore it and offer my hand to help Bastien get up.

"Let's go before I lose my virginity on this couch," I tease.

Bastien stills immediately and gapes at me. "Wait, what?"

"What?" I ask, unsure why he's shocked.

"Uh, I just thought otherwise, you're so...not virginal."

I laugh. "What does that even mean?"

Bastien runs his hands through his hair. "I don't know. You're not shy or awkward. You seem comfortable with things."

I snort. "Yeah, it's called romance novels and masturbation, and not always in that order."

Bastien lets out a surprised chuckle, and I can't tell if he's embarrassed to be talking about this or interested.

"I don't think you have to have sex to be sexual. I know what it entails. It's also something that's incredibly intimate to me, and until now I just haven't met anyone I could be that way with."

"I'm not going to lie, Bruiser; my inner caveman really likes that."

I laugh. "Don't get any ideas about clubbing me and hauling me off to be at your mercy. I will kick your ass."

Bastien chortles. "Don't knock it till you try it; you might like it kind of rough."

I laugh even harder and then clench my thighs together at the exciting thought of rough sex.

He rubs his palms together nefariously. "Are you ready for the corruption of your innocence to commence, Bruiser?"

"Please, do you know who you're talking to, what innocence?"

We both laugh.

"This is going to be fun," he teases, in a singsong voice and gives me a quick peck.

I push his hulking form out of my room, all the while internally shouting, *fuck yeah it will be.*

26

The ringtone on my phone loudly serenades me, and I'm forced to abandon my dream. I blindly grab for the noisy device, refusing to open my eyes. After a couple of misplaced slaps against the cool wood of the side table, I finally find the phone underneath my grip and bring it to my ear.

"Hello?" I greet, my voice is deep and groggy with sleep. No one responds, and I listen to the silence a few seconds more before I finally open my eyes to see if the call disconnected. It's still active, so I try again.

"Hello, anyone there?"

Silence.

An odd feeling trickles down my spine. "Talon, is that you?" I ask, and the call abruptly disconnects.

My head falls back onto the pillow, and a few breaths later the phone rings again. I don't check the caller ID just answer it quickly.

"Talon, are you okay?"

"Who's Talon?" a smooth, melodic female voice asks me. I look at the caller ID and see it's Mave.

"Just an old friend I'm trying to get ahold of," I croak, still not all the way awake.

"Gotcha, what are you up to today besides sleeping?" Mave teases.

"Hanging with you obviously," I supply.

"Excellent. You need a swimsuit, a towel, and a desire to walk on the wild side."

"Check, check, and check. Where should I meet you?"

"I'll text you directions, and you can come pick me up."

"Sweet, I'll let you know when I'm on my way."

Mave hangs up. No *goodbye* or *see you later*, and it makes me laugh. She's definitely my people, straight to the point with no side of bullshit. I roll out of bed and get cleaned up. I open my swimsuit drawer and pick out a bikini. I throw on a loose tank top and some denim cutoff shorts. I use my magic to counteract my bed hair, and it's shiny and voluminous in seconds. Man, I love magic.

The drive to the address Mave sent me is beautiful—not that there's much ugliness in Solace in general. The trees are much more condensed where she lives, and I picture wolves and other shifters being right at home amidst this wilderness.

Mave and three other people are standing at the end of a dirt road that apparently leads up to where her pack lives. I pull over, and everyone climbs in.

"Vin, this is Kaika, Tru and my little brother Macon."

I say hello to all of them and throw in a friendly wave. They all grunt various versions of hello, and one semi-grumpy *hey*.

Kaika and Tru look like they'd fit right in with Jacob from *Twilight's* wolf pack. They both have black hair, black eyes, and tan skin. Kaika's hair is long and straight, and Tru's is buzzed. Macon looks like a smaller version of Mave. He has the same lanky build and heart-shaped face. He's missing the septum piercing, and instead of having magenta pink hair like his sister, his is a medium length, blue-black.

"Nice wheels," Mave tells me, rubbing a hand over the interior of the door.

"Yeah, did daddy buy it for his little princess?" Kaika mocks from the back.

I find his eyes in the rearview mirror. "No, I bought it from all the money I made being a badass," I say, overly sweet and cryptic while fluttering my lashes at the presumptuous prick.

"Kaika, shut up." Mave turns around and punches him in the thigh. "I told you she's cool. Try to be at least ten percent less miserable so you don't scare her off."

She turns back around, and we smile at each other. I pull off on a dirt road that takes us to a bigger dirt clearing that Mave tells me to park in. We all unload, and I follow them through the trees to a lake that's surrounded by a sandy shore. Solace is seriously the land of endless lakes.

Mave points out some layers of cliffs to our left. "That's what we're doing today. You ready for a cliff jumping good time?"

I laugh as I take in the rocky wall face. Macon doesn't wait for anyone's invitation. He strips off his shirt and sprints away, leaving a trail of hoots behind him. Mave cracks up.

"He's the adrenaline junkie in the family. As soon as he caught wind that I was coming here, he was begging me to come. We probably won't even see him again until it's time to leave."

I chuckle and watch him disappear around a huge boulder. Tru lays out a blanket, and we settle our stuff on it. We all strip down to our swimsuits, and I excitedly follow Mave to the second level of cliffs. The trail up to the different levels of rock is smooth, which shows just how often people trek up here to do this. There's a light breeze that's keeping the heat at bay, and the water below us is sparkling and inviting.

"Tru, you jump first to show Vinna the best way to do it," Mave instructs.

Tru nods his head and without any hesitation leaps silently from the safety of the cliff's edge and plummets toward the water. My heart picks up its pace, and I quickly move to the rocky edge so I can see how he enters the water. Tru breaks the rippled surface feet first and starts paddling to shore.

"Do you want to watch again, make sure you've got it?" Mave asks me.

"Nope, I think I'm good," I say enthusiastically. "Any rocks or other things down there I should be worried about?" I ask as I assess the cliff's edge around me and the water below.

"No rocks, and the lake monster only hunts at night, so we're good."

I stare at her, trying to figure out if she's serious or not. My initial instinct is to laugh and blow off her obvious joke, but now that I know there's this whole paranormal world out there, I'm not so sure she's not completely serious.

Mave stares at me straight-faced before a smart-ass glint sneaks into her features.

"Vin, you're making this too easy."

Mave cracks up, and I flip her the bird before I join her. I give one final chuckle and step back a couple of paces. I put my fist out, and Mave bumps her knuckles against mine. I take a running leap off the cliff. *Holy shit.*

The weightless feel of falling is completely liberating. The wind aggressively caresses up my body, taking my excited shouts with it, before I'm enveloped by the cold water of the lake. It's easy to see why Macon loves this so much. My head breaks the surface of the water, and Mave hoots and hollers her approval of my first jump. I have a huge smile on my face. *Oh, hell yeah, I'm doing that again.*

We spend the next few hours climbing up to various heights in the cliff face and then hurling ourselves over. The highest I managed was a little over forty feet, but it stung going into the water, and I decided that was as high as I wanted to go. Mave stayed with me, but Kaika, Tru and Macon were all jumping from insane heights.

"Your friends are mental," I tell Mave, as we watch a cannonball contest commencing from what has to be seventy-feet up from the water.

"Shifters have strong bones and a seriously high pain tolerance," she offers in explanation of their crazy-ass shenanigans. "Come on, let's go eat; I'm starving."

My mind jumps back to the arena and the sound of Torrez's jaw breaking. I shake it off and follow Mave back down to the blanket. She hands me a sandwich from a stack inside the small cooler they brought, and I pull out the bag of drinks I stole from the kitchen. I hand over a water and a soda, and we dig in.

I savagely devour the sandwich in no time, and Mave tosses me another one. I inhale it and then lie back and soak up the sunshine.

"What's your family like? Is Macon your only sibling?"

Mave snorts into her soda. "No, there are eleven kids in my family. Macon's second to last."

"Holy shit, that's a lot of brothers and sisters," I declare as if Mave wasn't aware of this fact until I dumbly pointed it out.

"Mostly brothers. Only one little sister," she corrects.

"Where do you fall in the lineup?"

"Right smack dab in the middle," Mave chuckles. "I like it though. Maybe it's the wolf in me or my own twisted nature, but I like the chaos and comradery that comes with growing up in a big wild family."

"I could see that," I admit. "So tell me about shifters."

"Hmmm, where to begin...there's a ton of different kinds of shifters. Solace pretty much only has wolves and cougars, but shifters live all over. We tend to be predatory animals: foxes, bears, wolves, big cats, eagles, etc. We can heal pretty much anything except for a missing head. What else do you want to know?"

"I don't know. What's it like? Do you like being a shifter?" I ask.

"Yeah, I like it, I also don't know any different. I've always been a wolf. The pack can sometimes be hard. You have to listen to wolves above you in the hierarchy, but that's life anywhere you go. I like the wildness and power that I have as a wolf. I like being part of a pack; they belong to me, and I belong to them."

I nod my head in understanding and try to picture Mave in her wolf form. I want to ask her what she looks like as a wolf or what it feels like to shift, but I don't know if that's considered rude. I don't want her to feel like a spectacle. I give her a big smile and get up and wade into the lake, and Mave follows me in.

"How do you like working at the bookstore?" I ask, changing the subject.

"Oh, I don't really work there. Some members of the pack own it, and we all help each other out when needed. My day job is at the local tattoo shop."

"You're a tattoo artist?" I ask, obviously surprised and noting the complete lack of any tattoos anywhere on her body.

"No, a piercer," Mave grins and flicks her septum ring. "You should come by sometime. I'll give you the friends and family discount," she tells me, with an enticing singsong voice. "You could definitely pull off a nose ring with that cute little nose you've been blessed with."

I chuckle at her enthusiasm.

"No face piercings for me. They can be used against you too easily."

Thoughts of a nose ring or belly button ring getting pulled out in a fight, makes me shudder. I don't even have my ears pierced for this reason. Mave looks at me curiously.

"Hmm, something more discreet then," she smirks. "A couple nipple rings, maybe?"

I laugh. "I don't think I'm wild enough to pull that off."

"Oh, I doubt that," Mave chuckles. "You were raised as a non, with monogamy and all that, but how many days were you here before your *coven lust* kicked in?" She winks at me, and I laugh even harder. "There's no way you'd abandon the non-mentality you grew up with for the polyandrous ways of the casters unless you had some kink inside of you." Mave's smart-ass grin grows wider, and then she bursts into laughter and splashes me.

"Come on, Vin, your secret's safe with me."

She squeals when I pelt her with water.

"Admit it. You know you own a very used copy of *Fifty Shades of Grey*!"

I start laughing so hard I can't breathe. "I own the whole series," I admit through bursts of laughter as splashes rain down on me. Mave loses it with my admission, and we're both holding our sides as we laugh our asses off.

"Let your freak flag fly, you kinky witch."

Voices on the beach draw our attention. I look over, expecting to find Mave's friends, but it's a different group laying out blankets right next to ours. Mave stiffens beside me.

"Shit," she mumbles quietly.

"What's wrong?" I ask, and my adrenaline rises in response to her sudden distress.

She looks away from the newcomers and back to me. "Do you care if we leave?"

I study her for a beat. It's obvious she feels bad for asking. "No, that's cool, are you okay?"

"Yeah, I'll explain in the car."

Mave hesitantly swims toward the shore, and I follow. Her demeanor visibly changes, she's hardening and fortifying, but I don't know why. Every ounce of laughter and happiness that was just in her eyes has been shuttered away, replaced by a cold ferocity.

My senses are on alert as we wade out of the water toward our things. I feel eyes on me, but I don't look around for the source. Neither of us bothers to get dressed, as we start to pack everything up. I'm shoving my clothes in my bag when Mave's head snaps up. I follow her gaze and spot Kaika, Macon, and Tru rounding a corner and walking toward us.

"Shit, shit, shit!" Mave harshly whispers.

I look from her to her friends and then finally to the group of newcomers. A couple of guys from the new group hone in on the male shifters. Kaika and Tru slow, almost imperceptibly, as they register the new arrivals.

"Tru," a male voice shouts from the new group.

"Here, Tru, come here boy."

A burst of laughter follows the obvious insult. I look back at the newcomers, completely disgusted with the taunt. Mave mentioned that shifters aren't always on good terms with casters. With the tension now radiating from Mave and her packmates, it's clear I'm about to get a front row seat as to why.

The group of new arrivals is big. There are eight guys and two girls, but only four guys in the group seem to be outwardly amused by the taunting of the shifters. The other guys are merely watching with various looks of boredom or disinterest on their faces.

I pause at the set of gray-blue eyes that are trained on me. The eyes belong to a tall blond guy. His hair is short, and an unruly curl gives it a hot bed head look. The contrast of his dark eyebrows and tan skin against the lightness of his eyes and hair gives him a striking and drool-worthy visage. His stormy-blue gaze tracks me with shrewd intensity, and I match his stare for a minute before looking back toward the shifters.

Macon, Kaika, and Tru almost reach us when a stocky guy grips Tru's arm and yanks him toward the offensive group. I expect Kaika or Mave to react to the manhandling, but Kaika is staring at the ground and Mave is watching, but she's not doing anything about it. Kaika and Macon stop in front of us, and Mave starts handing them the things we brought.

Tru is forcefully guided over to the group of troublemakers. I only catch phrases here and there, but I hear something about a *game* and to *tell them when*. I'm trying to figure out what the hell is going on when, out of nowhere, a guy punches Tru in the stomach. He crumples over from the blow.

The assholes laugh, and the kid that threw the punch looks toward the bored faces of the other six people he came with like he's seeking their approval. I step away from Mave and calmly walk into the ring of assholes. I step in front of Tru to face off with the group of bullies.

"Want to explain to me what you're doing?" I ask evenly.

"It's a game, right, Tru? As soon as he says *when*, we stop," the asshole to my left explains with a laugh.

I've only known Tru for a handful of hours, but I've noticed that he hasn't spoken a word the whole time. Maybe he's the strong, silent type, or maybe it's something else, but it's clear these assholes know that no matter what they do to him, he's not going to *tell* them to stop.

I turn to look at Tru, narrowing my eyes at the stocky asshat who still has his arm around Tru's shoulders. He wisely drops it. I hand my keys to Tru, hoping he'll take the hint and get Mave and the others in the Jeep. Tru's eyes are filled with fire, but his body language is surprisingly submissive.

It bothers the shit out of me to see that he's tempering the fight in him with inaction. I turn around and start backing up into Tru's body, forcing him to step out from the group in order to make room for me.

"Sounds fun. I want to play, but I go first," I say sweetly.

He snickers uncomfortably and looks around at his friends. When no one steps in to tell him this is a bad idea, he agrees with a shrug and a smirk. I step up to him and give him the most demure smile I can muster.

I call on the runes on my arm, wanting a little extra kick in my punch, and I hit the guy hard on the side. I feel the distinct crunch of broken ribs, and he crumbles in on himself, immediately screaming in pain. I step back to give him room to writhe and look at the other three assholes in challenge.

The stocky one looks furious. "What the fuck did you do?" he rages at me, trying to get in my face. I grab him by the neck, lift him off the ground, and then slam his body down flat into the sand. I use enough force to knock the wind out of him but not enough to break anything. I lean over the asshole while he gasps for air, and I wait until his eyes focus on me.

"Tell me *when*," I mock.

I stand up and silently dare anyone else to play. When no one else approaches me, I look each and every one of them in the eyes. Not just the bullies, but the rest of the group who just stood by and watched. I shake my head in disgust at them. I look at the two guys on the ground then back up at their group.

"This bullshit stops now. Don't touch any of the shifters again."

I look over to find the guy with the overcast blue eyes and stare at him until he gives me the slightest of nods. I take that as agreement and walk away, snatching my bag from where I dropped it and head toward where the Jeep is parked.

Mave and her friends are grouped by the beach entrance instead of in the car where they should be. I approach them, and Tru hands me back my keys. We all climb into the Jeep, and I drive toward where I picked them up. I give them and myself about ten minutes to process things before I break the silence.

"Anyone care to fill me in?" I pose to no one in particular.

It's silent for a minute longer before Mave speaks.

"We've had trouble with that group before," she offers vaguely.

I patiently wait for her to elaborate.

"They know our pack is easy prey because we won't fight back."

I look at her with confusion.

"Our alpha works with the casters' Elders Council. Two of the guys in that group are the sons of elders. If we fight back, we could jeopardize our alpha's working relationship with the council, which would be really bad for the pack. We've been ordered not to engage any of them for any reason."

I nod my head absently. "Is that whole group a coven?" I ask, trying to piece things together.

"No, only four of them are a registered coven. The extra guys seem to think they're going to be brought into the fold, and the girls are probably auditioning for a place too," Mave informs me. "The actual coven never lifts a finger toward us, but they also don't stop their cronies from doing anything either," she adds. "Now your turn."

"My turn to what?"

"Explain what in the name of *terminator* happened back there?"

I chuckle at the wide-eyed, excited look on her face. "I used to fight for a living. It's what I did before I found out I was a caster and my uncle found me and brought me here."

"Thank you, Vin. It means more than I can say that you stood up for us. Tru doesn't talk unless it's in the pack link, but he says thank you, too." Mave is quiet for a minute, and then she suddenly starts giggling. "Holy shit. I had to stop myself from laughing when you picked Harris up by the neck. It was beautiful," Mave tells me, and she closes her eyes like she's happily reminiscing.

A grumbling laugh starts in the back seat, and we both look back to discover it's grumpy Kaika laughing his ass off. Mave and I look at each other, completely stunned, before breaking down and joining him in fits of hysterical laughter.

27

I make it up to my room without running into anyone, which surprises me. I shower and change into some cotton shorts and a loose, slouchy top that likes to slide off my shoulder. My right hand is sore, and my knuckles are bruised from the punch I threw. I dry my hair with magic and head down in search of a healer.

I spot Lila in the kitchen, and she tells me Evrin's out, but Ryker and *the boys* are playing pool downstairs. She hands me an ice cream cone I thought she was making for herself, and I give her a quick hug before I clomp down the stairs.

I crack open the door to the billiards room, just as someone breaks and the grouping of balls scatter all over the felt tabletop. Five sets of eyes shoot over to me, and I smile at them self-consciously. Knox leans over to take a shot, and I take the opportunity to stare at his ass and the muscles in his back. I shake away my lusty thoughts and take a lick of my ice cream cone as I make my way over to where the other guys are sitting on a set of sofas.

Valen grabs me and pulls me into his lap, shoving his face into my hair and the crook of my neck. I laugh as he starts inhaling deep breaths and gives me a playful bite that sends a shiver down my spine. I love how assertive the twins are. They both exude this confidence and comfort with who they are, and they don't hesitate to take what they want.

Bastien takes my feet in his lap and grabs my hand that's holding the ice cream cone so that he can steal a taste. *These sneaky twins are always jacking my food*, I grumble to myself and yank my cone away from him. He laughs and winks at me.

"I thought you said you weren't going to avoid us anymore," Bastien asks, his playful smile turning a little sad.

"I'm not," I reassure him, feeling confused by his question and reaction. I run the back of my hand along his jaw, and he leans into the caress.

"Where have you been all day then?"

Ahhh, that's what's going on.

"I went and hung out with Mave. I met her the other day, and she invited me out."

After explaining who Mave is and how we met, in exacting detail, my answer seems to appease him. Bastien twines his fingers with mine, rubbing his other hand over my shins, his smile happy and carefree again.

"Where'd you and Mave go?" Sabin inquires, watching Bastien and Valen keenly.

Sabin stands in the corner, holding a cue stick, waiting for Knox to finish his shot. He gives me a gentle smile, and his dimples make an appearance. I give him a small smile back and then wince in pain when Bastien unknowingly squeezes my bruised knuckles.

Sabin catches my pained look and rushes over. I hiss and try to pull my hand free which makes everyone else take notice. Bastien brings my hand closer to his face and narrows his gaze at me when he takes in the fucked up state of my knuckles.

"Bruiser, what's with the bruises?"

I laugh at the Dr. Seuss sounding question. "It's not a big deal. I came down here to see if Ryker could work his magic, pun intended, before you two started distracting me." I chuckle again at my own joke, but apparently I'm the only one who sees the humor.

"How'd that happen?" Knox asks me, a tick in his jaw.

"We were hanging at this lake, and this other group showed up and started harassing Mave's friends. I just pointed out some reasons why they shouldn't do that," I finish, pointing to my bruised knuckles.

Sabin runs a hand over his face. "Vinna, shifters are more than capable of defending themselves. You should know this after seeing what they can do at the fights. Don't get involved in their feuds."

I stare at Sabin, irritated, and wish I could take the smile I gave him earlier, back. "Thank you for that useless opinion, but they can't retaliate against this coven. Mave's alpha doesn't want them to do anything that could mess with his relationship with the Elders Council, so they have to just take what's done to them. But seriously, even if that weren't the case, I'm perfectly capable of judging for myself what I should and shouldn't be involved in."

I pull myself free from Valen and Bastien's laps and sit on the arm of the sofa on the opposite side of them. Bastien and Valen shoot a warning look at Sabin. A twinge of regret snakes through me, and I realize that I can't punish the others every time Sabin pisses me off. I can't withdraw from them just because I want to withdraw from him.

"Wait, it was a coven that was starting shit, not other shifters?" Sabin asks confused.

"It's kind of complicated," I tell him. "The dudes that are actually in the coven didn't really do anything other than watch, but the group of casters that hang out with them started everything. I only got involved when they hit one of the shifters."

"But what does that have to do with the Elders Council?" Sabin asks me.

"I guess two of the guys in the coven have dads that are elders."

Understanding dawns on all of the guy's faces.

"What did Enoch do when you fucked up the two guys?" Bastien asks.

"Who's Enoch?"

"Tall, blond hair, blue eyes," Sabin describes to me.

"Yeah, that guy was interesting. He just watched me. He didn't say a word. He didn't try to stop anything. He just nodded at me when I told him they wouldn't touch the shifters anymore, like some pretty boy Godfather."

Knox cracks up and walks over to press a kiss to the top of my head. He swipes my ice cream cone, but I'm too focused on the other guys and the look they're giving each other, to object. I'm about to ask them what's going on when Ryker pushes my knees apart and steps in between my legs.

He takes my bruised hand in his, and the heat of his magic banishes the pain away. He brings my knuckles to his lips and kisses them softly. Flutters fly low in my belly.

"You know the way you do that, it's not exactly a deterrent for getting injured," I explain, as I squeeze my thighs against the sides of Ryker's legs.

"Anything else need my attention?" he asks dropping his gaze to my lips.

I put my hands on the backs of his denim-clad thighs and tilt my head back in invitation. A throat clears loudly in the room, unnecessarily reminding us that we're not alone.

"Captain Cockblock to the rescue," I chant.

I scoot back on the arm of the sofa, away from Ryker. I give a mock salute to Sabin that morphs into the bird, and the other guys chuckle. Not to be deterred, Ryker drops his weight onto the sofa and snakes an arm around my waist. He sends a challenging look to Sabin and pulls me down between his legs. I lean into him and press my back against his chest. Sabin watches for a second more and then moves to the table for his shot.

I can feel the hardness in Ryker's jeans against my lower back, and I can't lie, I like this reaction to me. I let out a deep breath and relax into him. One of his strong hands rests on my thigh, and he absently starts to run his fingertips over my skin. Goosebumps spring up all over my body. Ryker notices and breathily chuckles in my ear.

"So tell me about your magic," I prompt the room in an effort to distract myself from how good Ryker feels against me.

"Do you have an idea of what kind of magic you think you have?" Ryker asks with excitement in his voice.

"I have no idea. The books describe how different magic is supposed to feel to a caster, but it's confusing the fuck out of me. I must not understand it properly, because I feel a jumble of what the books describe and not just one specific thing."

They all nod their heads in understanding, which makes me feel a little better. The books make it sound so easy to figure out what your magic is, and I've been feeling like an idiot.

"For most of us, calling our magic and directing it is a visual thing. We picture what we want to accomplish, and we weave that intent with the magic itself and then send it out to do what we want. All the branches have limitations and possibilities, and you learn what they are over time," Valen explains.

"Spell magic, however, works very differently than the other branches," Knox tells me. "I have to know about the potential and the properties for anything in the world that could be used as an ingredient. I have to know how to combine those things to get what I want, and I shape the intent of the spell through words and processes, not visualization. Kind of like baking, you have to add things in a specific order to get the end result that you want. With Spell magic, the words you speak into a spell matter, too."

"That sounds real fucking complicated," I tell Knox, and he laughs.

"Yeah, I was a little freaked out when I found out I had Spell magic, but what can you do?"

He shrugs, and I smile. I don't know if I'll be as laid back as he is if I have Spell magic.

"So Ryker heals, and Knox spells, what do you guys have?"

"I have Elemental magic," Sabin tells me.

Valen raises his hand slightly. "I have offensive magic."

"And I have defensive magic," Bastien finishes with a wink.

I rest my head back against Ryker's shoulder and think about what Valen said about visualization and weaving that with magic in order to direct it. That's kind of what I do with my runes, I suppose. I think about which weapon I want and the runes that create that weapon. Then I feed magic into those images, and the weapon I want pops into my hand. I smile feeling like I finally understand that part of things.

Lila calls down to us for dinner, and everyone but Ryker and me rush out at the promise of food. I'm slow to get moving, due to the hypnotic state I'm in from Ryker playing with my hair while I'm lost in my thoughts. I head to the door, but when I pass the pool table, Ryker tugs on my hips, stopping me, and then he turns me around.

He grabs on to my waist and lifts me to sit on the edge of

the pool table. I squeak in surprise, and he chuckles. His eyes are filled with laughter, and his smile is devastatingly gorgeous. Ryker cups my face gently in both of his hands and leans into me. His lips are centimeters away, and I close my eyes and feel his breath against my lips.

"Vinna, I'm dying to kiss you."

He runs the tip of his nose in a circle around the tip of mine but still doesn't close the distance.

"Then why aren't you?" I ask wantonly.

In the next breath, he gives me exactly what I want, and I finally feel his mouth against mine. I sneak my hands under the hem of his shirt and run them up his sides. He guides my head back with his hands and deepens the kiss.

His tongue guides mine expertly, fusing us together and coaxing my soul out to dance with his. I swallow his moan when I bring my hands to his chest and run my fingers over his hard nipples. Ryker sucks on my bottom lip flicking it with his tongue, and it sends bolts of yearning straight between my thighs.

He takes hold of my top lip and then returns to my bottom lip, the tips of our tongues teasing and testing, before he breaks away. Ryker tilts my face to the side to give himself better access to my neck. He starts a trail of kisses and gentle nips from the lobe of my ear to the runes on my shoulder.

He lightly runs his tongue over my runes, and I moan at the sensation it creates. I'm so wet it's probably visible through my dark shorts, but his tongue on my runes has my magic reacting in that strange way that happens whenever I get intimate with any of them.

Ryker runs the tip of his nose up the side of my neck.

"I just wanted a kiss, but now I don't want to stop."

He nips my earlobe and then sucks where it connects to my neck. I moan again, and he moves his hands under the hem of my shirt caressing up my back. He brings his face in front of mine, and I lean in for another kiss.

"No one's asking you to stop," I surprise myself by saying.

I feel his smile against my mouth, and it coaxes the corners of mine up too. He steps back from me, doing the exact opposite of what his words and eyes are telling me he wants to do. His strong hands and arms leave my skin, and I groan at the loss.

"Don't tempt me more than you already are, Vinna," he chuckles.

"Why not?" I whine.

Ryker laughs and threads his fingers with mine. He pulls me from the edge of the pool table, and I look back, surprised that I haven't left a puddle behind. I climb achingly up the stairs and find the other guys waiting for us.

No one, including Sabin, says anything. Bastien gives me a quick wink, and that's the only acknowledgment I get from any of them about what Ryker and I were obviously doing downstairs. Their lack of reaction feels natural and complicated all at the same time.

28

We all dig into another incredible meal from one of the sisters, and when I'm done, I check if the coast is clear and dash into the kitchen. I manage to booty bump Lila out of my way and make it to the sink.

I can only manage to turn the water on before Lila starts to tickle me. I screech and try to scramble away, and Lila easily plucks my dishes from my laugh-weakened hands. She's already scrubbing them before I can get a hold of myself to retaliate.

"This isn't over Lila. Your washing days are numbered," I declare with exaggerated authority.

She giggles and blows soap suds in my direction. I glare at her, trying not to smile, and I turn around to find the guys smiling and laughing at me.

"What was that about?" Bastien asks me through his laughter.

"They won't let me wash my own dishes," I tell him incredulously. "That's me battling for my right." I raise my voice, making sure Lila can hear me over the running water. She giggles.

"That was hilarious," Knox declares breaking into a fit of laughter.

"I never thought I'd see Vinna bested, but alas, the day has arrived," Sabin winks at me, passing me and handing Lila his plate. He gives her a quick peck on the cheek and thanks her for dinner.

"Ah, so food is the key to your affection," I tease him, and he shakes his head at me, chuckling.

All the guys line up and hand their plates to Lila, like good little boys. She even shoots me a look that says, *see, that wasn't so hard, now was it?*

To which I reply, "You're all sheep. Will none of you join my revolution?" I'm trying to channel my inner *Braveheart,* but I sound more drunk Jamaican than Scottish. The guys roar with laughter, and I concede my loss. Valen throws me over his shoulder and starts to take me back downstairs.

I lean up on his back and yell, "You haven't seen the last of me, Lila," and proceed to cackle an evil laugh that would make the wickedest of TV villains proud. A slap to my butt turns my evil cackle into a startled squeak, and that sets the guys off even more. They're bent over and crying with laughter. Even Sabin's cracking up, and that's saying a lot.

I hang over Valen's shoulder, happy to pretend I'm the sack of potatoes he's carrying me like. He makes his way to the theater room then pulls me from his shoulder and sets me back on my feet.

I take a minute to let all the blood rush from my head back into the rest of my body and then race Valen to *my spot.* He muscles ahead—damn shorter legs—so I leap at him spider monkey style trying to keep him from winning.

We both fall back into the spot at the same time, and Valen isn't the slightest bit fazed by my efforts to push him out of the corner. He simply repositions me against him, the way I was when we woke up from our first movie night.

This time I'm not as confused or hesitant, and I make myself comfortable against him, shoving my hand up his shirt and resting it against his warm chest. He doesn't seem to mind and grabs my knee, pulling it up and over his hips. He leaves his hand tucked in the crook of my knee, and the other rubs small circles over my lower back.

The other guys chuckle at our antics and settle in. Sabin puts on a movie, and I can't help but sneak glances around the room at the others. I wonder what they think about all of this. I kissed Bastien and Ryker less than twenty-four hours apart. Now I'm sprawled across Valen like it's no big deal, thinking about how I'd like to make out with *him*.

I know this is how things are supposed to work for casters, but how is none of this weird for them? Better yet, why is this not weirder for me? Maybe Mave was right, and I am a closet freak. The fact that my libido currently has her engines shamelessly set to *full steam ahead* does support that theory.

So far I'm only kissing these guys, but what happens when it goes beyond that—which if I'm being honest could be any moment now, with the way these boys kiss and how incredibly attracted I am to them. If I decide to have sex with one, will it piss off the others?

What if I have sex with one before I even kissed all the others? Do they talk to each other about this stuff? *Fuck.* Does it bother Ryker that I made out with him earlier, but now I'm cuddled up with Valen and not him?

I glance over at Ryker, but he's focused on the screen. My quick peek causes me to rub my cheek against Valen's chest lightly, and he kisses the top of my head. I'm not focused on whatever movie is playing, but it must be funny because Valen's vibrating with laughter.

An endless amount of questions rapidly fire through my gray matter, but the vibrations of Valen's laughter and his hands sliding through my hair are enough to quiet my frenzied thoughts, and before I know it, I'm soothed to sleep.

* * *

Soft lips on my forehead rouse me from my sleep. The soft, steady touch of fingertips across the runes on the back of my thigh turns me on, and my magic starts to wake up alongside me. *There must be something with these guys touching my runes*, I ponder sleepily.

That'd be the only thing that would explain the magical current and heat I suddenly feel building in my chest. It happens every time I'm intimate with these guys, and the only overlap is them touching or kissing my runes.

An intense crackle of magic moves over my skin, and I sit up quickly and scramble off of Valen.

"Vinna, it's just me," Valen tries to comfort, but another crackle of magic lights up my skin, and I look at him with panic in my eyes. He reaches for me concerned, and I scramble even further away.

"Vinna, it's okay, you're safe," he reassures me.

"I know it's you, that's not the problem. I just don't know what the fuck is going on with my magic."

A huge pink crackle of magic moves up my arms, and I freak out. I barely hear Valen's whisper of "*holy shit*" before I'm sprinting out of the theater room and up to my room as fast as my legs will carry me. The more distance I put between us, the more the pressure in my chest decreases.

I make it up to my room and throw the door open. I take deep breaths to try and calm my magic down. I hear Valen's footsteps just slightly over the pulse in my ears. I turn to shut my door so that I can lock him out, but I'm too late. The door latch clicks shut behind him, and he walks tentatively toward me.

"Valen, please," I plead. "I don't know what's going on." I put my arms up, begging him with my words and body language not to come any closer.

"Vinna, it's okay, I'm trying to help you. You just need to ground your magic."

He steps closer despite my protests, and another crackle of magic blinks up my body, lighting up the darkness in my room.

"You're like a living plasma ball," Valen comments absently, as he watches magic flicker and flash across my skin like lightning.

Valen's comment pulls me from my panic, and I almost chuckle. I do look like a plasma ball.

"This won't hurt me, Vinna, it's okay," he assures me.

He runs his fingers through my hair and grips my nape. When his hand lands on the two lines of runes on the back of my neck, a rush of magic moves from me to him. I gasp at the feeling, and the flashes of pink and orange magic that are streaking across my skin morph into a deep purple.

Whoa, my magic's never been purple before. I stare transfixed as the violet streaks flicker up Valen's arms and then sink into his skin. He closes his eyes and releases a deep moan.

"It's hurting you," I accuse and try to step out of his grasp.

Valen opens his eyes and pulls me even closer. "It doesn't hurt; it feels fucking amazing."

I barely have time to think *what the hell* before Valen runs his fingers down the runes on the back of my neck. His touch sends a jolt of sensation and magic through me, and it snaps powerfully to my center. I moan and suddenly feel like I'm on the verge of an orgasm.

"See, it doesn't hurt."

"Are you grounding it? Will this stop soon?" I ask, feeling a lot less panicked and a lot more turned on.

"I can't ground it. It's not an overload of magic. It's something else...your magic is doing something to mine," Valen confesses, and another erotic moan escapes his lips.

"That doesn't sound good!" I squeak at him, but he laughs quietly.

"Ignore whatever it sounds like because it *feels* fucking incredible."

His gaze traps mine, and he leans down. He waits a hair's breadth away from me, silently asking me if what he's doing is okay. I close the distance, and he hungrily kisses me. His lips on mine send another jolt of magic from me to him, and we both moan at the ecstasy it evokes.

It's like I can feel him everywhere, his tongue against mine, his mouth, his body. I can't feel where he begins and I end. His kisses possess me, demanding ownership of my mouth and body, and I gladly give it over to him. His lips break away from mine for less than a second as I tug his shirt over his head. As soon as he's clear of it, his lips crash back down to mine where they belong.

Valen nips at my bottom lip, and I moan into his mouth. I run my hands over the muscles of his arms and chest, everything defined and stone-like under his soft golden skin. *He feels incredible...he feels...like he's mine.*

I pause at the intense possession that's coursing through me, but Valen's hands slowly pull up the hem of my shirt, and suddenly that's all I can focus on. I reach down to help him pull it off. My hair cascades down my naked back, and Valen closes his eyes when he feels my bare breasts against his chest.

He kisses me again, and we move entangled to my bed. I scoot back to the center of the bed, and streaks of moonlight shine through the windows to caress my skin. Valen takes in a deep breath and pauses to take me in.

"By the moon, you're gorgeous."

Valen's eyes are filled with worship and hunger. He climbs over me, and I spread my legs in invitation. He settles his hips against mine and kisses me slowly and passionately. I can still taste his frenzied want, but this focused intensity is everything right now. He runs a hand up my side, and his thumb gently caresses the side of my breast.

His lips pull away from mine and move down my neck. His tongue finds the runes on my shoulder, and a new surge of magic jumps from me to him. I'm gasping and grinding my hips against him wanting more.

He sucks my aching nipple into his mouth and flicks his tongue against its hardness. I whimper and arch my back involuntarily, as my body responds shamelessly, demanding more. Valen's mouth draws out the most incredible sensations, and he moves from one nipple to the other.

My fingers are tangled in his long, dark chocolate brown curls, and I tug lightly as I grind my clit against his hard-on. Valen releases my nipple with a final flick of his tongue and brings that incredible mouth back to mine. I mewl with need, but I pull his face away from mine.

"Valen, you have no idea how much I hate saying this, but we can't have sex tonight."

I prepare to explain that all of us need to talk and discuss a lot of things before any of us take that step, but he makes the need to justify myself unnecessary.

"No sex, got it. Can I do other things?"

His quick acquiescence makes me smile. "What other things did you have in mind?"

He absently runs the back of his fingers over a firm nipple, and I arch my back into his hands. His sexy smile steals my breath and almost steals my *no sex* resolve.

"Can I taste you?"

I picture his head between my thighs, his lips wrapped around my clit, and the image itself almost makes me come.

"If we did that, then I don't think I'd want to stop," I admit.

"Hands only? How do you feel about that?"

I reach down and unfasten the top button of his jeans.

"I feel good about hands," I tell him, and I glide the zipper down.

Valen slides down my body to kick off his jeans. He snakes his thumbs into the waistband of my shorts and pulls them down. I lean up on my elbows and unabashedly drool over how incredibly stunning he is in his boxer briefs, his cock bursting to escape the confines of the fitted cotton.

He sexily climbs back over me, and I eat up every inch of him with my eyes. Instead of settling back between my thighs, he lies on his side next to me. He claims my lips in another mind-altering kiss and pinches my nipples between his fingers. I cry out in pleasure, and purple magic sparks all over both of us.

Valen moves his hand maddeningly slowly from my breasts, down my stomach, and over the outside of my underwear.

"You're soaked," he groans against my lips.

He watches me brazenly as he slides his fingers inside my underwear and rubs a quick circle around my clit. I close my eyes and arch into him, reveling in the sensation. He moves his fingers down and separates my folds where he rubs and plays with the wetness there.

He dips his fingers slightly inside of me giving me just a taste of what it would feel like to be filled by more. He watches me start to come undone, and I reach into the band of his boxer briefs and take hold of him. It's my turn to watch his reaction as I touch and explore.

My fingers almost come together around him, but they don't connect as I stroke up his shaft in search of his tip. Precum drips against my palm, and I feel the accumulation of it in the wet fabric of his underwear. I fucking love knowing that he's dripping because of me.

Valen pulls my wetness over my clit and starts to massage it all around. I mewl and rock my hips against his finger, as I tighten my hold on him and stroke down his shaft. We both watch the pleasure the other feels, as strikes of magic flit all over our almost naked bodies. The pressure of my magic builds alongside the pressure of the impending orgasm Valen is coaxing from my body.

He dips his fingers back inside of me, going deeper this time, and begins to gently stroke in and out of me. His thumb rubs against my clit simultaneously, moving faster and faster, and an orgasm tears through me. A pulse of purple magic ripples out of me and slams into Valen and then out of the room.

The flow of magic out of me extends my orgasm and makes it more intense than anything I've ever felt. As my magic flows through Valen, he grinds into my grip and swells in my hand.

He pulls away from our kiss, crashing his face into my hair as he thrusts into my hand and shouts out his release. The French doors in my room vibrate slightly from the pressure of my surging magic, and we both pant and groan as we ride out our orgasms.

Valen's fingers are still inside me as my body starts to come down from the rapture of everything that just happened. He withdraws them slowly and the aftershocks of his touch twitch and quake through me. We both lie back, floating in bliss and trading compliments until Valen leans over and steals a quick kiss.

"I'm going to get cleaned up and be right back."

I peck him again and watch him scoop up his clothes and tiptoe out of my room, closing the door behind him. *Man, orgasms are way better when someone else is giving them to you.* I lie for a little longer, smiling and feeling blissed out before I finally move to the bathroom. I clean up, change my underwear, and slip on a tank top.

I flick off the light and walk into the moonlight soaked bedroom, where I find Valen already snuggled under my covers. I get into bed and crawl over him purposefully clumsy. We both laugh, and I snuggle into my pillow. Valen pulls my back against his chest and kisses my shoulder and then my neck. We both simultaneously let out a satisfied sigh and then crack up at the synchronicity of it. Valen squeezes me tightly against him, and I succumb quickly and happily to the call of my dreams.

29

Searing pain pulls me from peaceful oblivion. It steals my breath, and I clench my jaw against the strangled scream that rises in my throat. I don't panic, this brutal pain and I have met before, and I know it will stop, as quickly and mysteriously as it started.

The burning pain is focused on my hands, chest, and head just behind my ear. Thank fuck it's not all over my body like it was on my sixteenth birthday. I pant shallowly and let out a relieved whimper when I feel the white-hot waves begin to recede.

The pain disappears completely, and I know it's left behind more than just its memory. I take deep breaths and feel my clenched muscles start to unlock. I sit up in bed. The sheets pool at my waist, and my tank top clings to my clammy skin.

I scan my hands for what I know will be there. On both of my ring fingers—where there was previously only an eight-pointed star rune—I now have five new runes. They stretch down to the base of my finger, taking up the whole width.

I pull the neck of my tank top down and find a smaller

set of runes on my sternum nestled between my breasts. I stare at it for a second before I push my breasts together and all but the star rune disappears inside the line of my cleavage.

I throw my covers off and drag my tired feet to the bathroom in search of a mirror so I can look behind my ear where I know new runes have etched themselves. I flick the light on and squeal in shock when I find Valen on the floor, leaning against the wall, grimacing in pain.

"Holy shit, are you okay? Why are you on the floor?"

Valen puts his hand over his eyes to shield them from the light I just turned on.

"What the fuck!" I shriek as panic grips me, and I scramble away from him in a backward crab walk.

On Valen's ring finger is a set of black runes. They start with an eight-pointed star on the skin below his fingernail and mark his whole finger to its base. I run my gaze over his other hand, resting palm down on the floor, and see the same runes on his other ring finger.

I cover my mouth with both hands trying to hold in the shocked gasp attempting to escape. *What the hell, how does he have runes?* Valen reaches for me, confused by my reaction. *Has he not seen them? Fuck, is he going to be mad?*

As he stretches his arms to me, I catch the line of runes on his sternum centered between his defined pecs. I scramble back further away from him and clip my shoulder painfully on the door frame.

"I'm so sorry!" I cry out.

"Vinna, no, shit! What are you talking about?"

Valen leans toward me, and I'm on my feet and running away from him before he can get up off the ground. A few steps out of the bathroom doorway, I slam into an unyielding wall of muscle. I bounce off of Sabin, and he grabs my shoulders to keep me from tumbling to the ground.

Sabin takes in my terrified expression and immediately moves me behind him as he assesses our surroundings, looking for the cause of my fear. Valen comes running from the bathroom toward us, and Sabin tenses.

"What the fuck is going on?" he growls at Valen.

"That's what I'm trying to find out!" Valen snaps back and reaches for me again.

My bedroom door whooshes open, and three more tousled, pajama-clad bodies stomp into the room. Did they all move into Lachlan's house and I didn't notice? What are they doing here this late at night? Sabin blocks Valen from moving past him to get to me. He turns to say something to Valen, and I see black runes marring the skin behind the back of his ear.

Sabin has matching symbols on his fingers, and they're the same symbols on me, on Valen. I look to the other guys...they all have them. I run a shaky finger over the skin behind my ear, no doubt where I'll find my own matching set of ebony runes.

What the fuck is going on?

I stare at them horrified. Ryker moves toward me, but I quickly back away, shaking my head at him. *What the fuck is happening?* I don't know how, but I know somehow this is my fault. *Did I do this to them? Did my magic do this to them? But why? Fucking hell, what is wrong with me?*

"Nothing's wrong with you. This isn't your fault."

I open my mouth to argue with Ryker but stop confused. *I didn't say that out loud.*

My eyes widen in shock, and their looks mirror mine.

Can you hear me? I ask in my head, and my knees wobble when they all chorus "yes."

"Can you hear us?" Bastien asks me, and the room grows quiet while I search for their voices inside my head.

"I only hear me."

In shock, I run my finger over the runes on the side of my head again. Maybe it only works from me to you? Can you hear everything I'm thinking? Oh god, this could be really bad for me. Are they going to know everything I think about them? After a couple of seconds of them staring at me blankly, I make the connection.

"Bastien run your finger over the runes behind your ear."

He does and then looks at me, obviously waiting for an explanation. I don't say anything else, I just wait.

"*Okay... I guess she's not going to tell me the point of doing that. Look at her face, stay focused on her face. It's cool that she's in her underwear, no big deal. Fuck, that body though, I want those incredible legs wrapped around me... Nope, NO, don't be that guy! Just keep looking at her face until she tells you what the hell is going on. That drop-dead sexy, gorgeous face. Why is Val smiling at me like that?*"

A blush creeps up Bastien's neck when he realizes we can hear what he's thinking. His smile is sheepish for all of two seconds, until suddenly an image of me straddling his lap while we kiss and I grind against him, pops into my head.

"Bastien, stop!" I frantically shout at him, and he touches his runes, turning the mental link off.

He gives me a wink and an unapologetic saucy smile. Sounds of amusement and Sabin's huff of exasperation bounce off the walls of my room. I exhale a shuttered breath, my gaze flicking from one shirtless body to the next. How the fuck has my magic connected us, and why?

I quickly scan every exposed inch of their bodies, as I search for any other visible runes, but I can only see the same runes that showed up on me tonight. I wade through the onslaught of possibilities as to how this happened, when something clicks, and my shocked and horrified gaze finds Valen.

"Oh fuck, it was that pulse of magic."

He looks at me confused.

"When I...when we..."

I motion from him to me. My eyes flit like a hummingbird around the group, embarrassment keeping them from landing anywhere.

"That purple magic that we felt, I think it did this," I say as I gesture to the bed.

I look back to Valen, and understanding dawns on his face. Four heads immediately snap from the bed to Valen.

"Wait, did you two..." Knox's voice trails off.

"None of your business," snaps out of Valen's mouth, at the same time I shout, "NO!" and heads swivel back and forth between us in confusion.

"We fooled around, that's all. We stopped before..."

I was about to say *before things went too far,* but judging by the runes now marked on their bodies, I'd say things clearly went plenty *far*.

"Either way it's not really any of your business," Valen claims again, stepping toward me.

Sabin steps into his path. "None of our business? How is this"—Sabin points to the runes on his chest—"none of our fucking business? I asked you guys to slow down, to use more than your dicks to think about what you were doing. Now look at what's fucking happened!"

"I wasn't thinking with my dick, and if you'd stop being scared shitless of getting hurt, maybe you'd finally admit that there's more to *all* of this than just that!" Valen seethes at Sabin.

"Fucking relax, Sabin, it's obvious that they had no idea

this would happen; look how panicked Vinna is," Knox defends.

Five sets of eyes find their way to me, but I'm staring at Sabin.

"I'm sorry," I choke out as guilt strangles me.

Sabin doesn't want a relationship with me. He's made it clear he doesn't want any of them to have a relationship with me, and now I've somehow marked them. Worse, I've marked *him*. I've forced some kind of a connection he doesn't want. Despair bubbles up inside of me.

"I have no idea what I did, but I swear I'll figure out a way to fix it."

I drop my face into my hands, unable to look at him anymore. I feel awful. I had no idea that this forced connection was even in the realm of possibility, or I would have never done anything that would have forced it on them like this. Sabin warned me that I didn't know what my magic could do, but I thought what I wanted was more important than his concerns.

Fingers wrap around my wrists and gently try to pull my hands from my face. I keep them firmly in place unable to look any of them in the eye anymore. A hand brushes through my hair and someone leans down to my ear.

"Look at us, Vinna," Ryker whispers. "Don't hide from us, don't withdraw again."

His lips gently kiss the new runes on my fingers, and an involuntary shiver of pleasure radiates through me. Ryker pulls me to him, and I give in and drop my hands from my face. His chest is pressed against mine, and I find myself beginning to automatically and effortlessly match his breathing.

"We don't blame you, so don't blame yourself. No one is mad," Ryker tells me, and I automatically glance to Sabin.

"He's right, I'm just shocked," Sabin grumbles.

"I don't know what the big deal is; I think this is fucking awesome," Knox offers.

I look over at Knox, taken aback by his excitement. I really shouldn't be surprised by his sentiments. He's the king of rolling with the punches, and when it comes to me, Knox always sees the silver lining.

"What? We can hear each other's thoughts when we want to. That ups our badass factor by a fucking shit ton. We're paladin. How much better are we going to be as a coven with this ability?"

A couple grunts of agreement sound off from the other guys.

"I fucking love the upgrade, Vinna, so don't stress," Knox exclaims and shoots me a supportive smile and a quick wink.

I look around to the other guys, gauging their reactions to Knox's comments, and oddly their nods and smiles seem to agree with what he's saying. I take a fortifying breath and step out of Ryker's arms. Exhausted, I plop into a chair and wait as the guys all do the same. A sigh of relief and acceptance flows from everyone as they sit down.

Alright, now that my emotional breakdown is on pause, it's time to sort out what the hell we do now. It's reassuring to know that they don't seem to think this is a bad thing. They're definitely taking it better than I did when my runes showed up. I was completely panicked and terrified in the beginning. It took some time, but now I love them. Everything that they do, everything that I am because of them, I can't imagine a *me* without the runes.

"Want to use your runes and let us in on what you're thinking, Bruiser?"

I look at Bastien and give him a small smile.

"I was just trying to sort through how I feel about this. On the one hand, I feel terrible, like I've forced this on you whether you want it or not." I look from Bastien to the rest of them. "On the other hand, I love my runes. It feels right in a way that I can't explain, that you have them too." I look down at my hands and trace the runes on my fingers with my eyes. "But that makes me feel really selfish and shitty, which brings everything full circle back to feeling terrible."

"You weren't alone in this; something about our being together triggered this. That means I am just as much to blame in all of this as you seem to think you are." Valen leans toward me. "I can tell you that I don't feel violated or upset in any way, and I wouldn't change *anything* about how I got the runes."

Valen grins brazenly at me. Our entwined tongues and the feel of his skin against mine, quickly flashes through my mind, heat seeps into my gaze at the recollection. Knox clears his throat, and I blink away the desire I'm feeling to look at him.

"I think, for scientific purposes of course, that it's important to recreate whatever it was you were doing when the magic was triggered. It would help us to better understand how—and maybe why—this happened, and hey, if we end up with more cool abilities, I'd put that in the plus column. With that said, I would like to personally volunteer."

Knox stares at all of us straight-faced and then raises his hand like he's waiting to be called on. Bastien is the first to release his guffaw of laughter, and he's quickly joined by the other guys.

"What? It's for science," Knox defends, trying to fight off the laughter that's breaking through his faux-innocent façade.

His eager and heated eyes lock onto mine, but a smirk finally breaks through, and we both join the others in slap-happy laughter.

Out of nowhere, Bastien shouts, "I volunteer as tribute!"

in a dramatic rendition that would make Katniss Everdeen proud, and we all fall back into hysterics.

I lean back into my comfy chair as I come down from the laugh high. I catch Sabin and Ryker both sneak a few glances at my new position which is giving them a peek between my legs. I probably shouldn't mess around, given everything that's happening right now, but I can't pass up the opportunity to fuck with Sabin.

I spread my legs a little wider, teasingly, and Ryker immediately looks up at me, knowing he's been caught. He smiles and gives me a cheeky wink, and I chuckle. My laugh seems to snap Sabin out of his focused attention on my underwear-clad crotch.

"Captain Cockblock, I didn't know you had it in you," I tease, enjoying the deep shade of red that consumes his cheeks at getting caught perving out.

Sabin shakes his head abashed, but when our eyes connect again, the longing I find there has me choking on my amusement. A dimpled smile sneaks across Sabin's face at my shocked reaction to his desire. *Whoa, where the hell did that come from?*

30

"Alright, now that everyone's calmed down," Bastien says, winking at me, "let's talk about what all of this means."

Seriousness and focus shutter down over each of us as we wait for Bastien to continue.

"Obviously we need to talk about the runes, but I also think we need to talk about what's happening between all of us."

Each of them looks to me and waits for some sign of approval or disagreement. I just shrug.

"I guess the first thing to ask is if everyone is okay? I'm sure you all felt what I did, and waking up in a fuck-ton of pain is not going on my favorite things list," Bastien admits.

"No shit," Knox agrees. "That's what it felt like to get all of your runes?"

"No, the first time was *way* worse. The pain was all over my body, and I legitimately thought I was going to die. This time was easier," I shrug nonchalantly. "I also knew what was happening this time, since it had happened before, so it didn't freak me out as much," I explain, and I catch a couple of them wincing.

"And you were all alone. You didn't even know you were a caster," Ryker reminds everyone, a reverent tone in his voice.

I look down and run my finger down the runes on my sternum. I can picture myself at sixteen, sitting on my bathroom floor, trying to sort through what the hell was happening to me. I can feel it like it was yesterday, how lonely and confused I felt.

Valen reaches out and takes my hand. He laces our fingers together and gives me a comforting smile. The feel of my hand in his pushes the memory and the shadow of loneliness away, and I smile warmly at him.

"I think we just found out what these runes do," Sabin announces, gesturing to the marks between his pecs.

I look at him curiously.

"I can feel you, Vinna. I think we all just felt what you were feeling." Sabin looks around for confirmation, and the other boys agree.

Shit. I run a finger over the runes on my chest again.

"Sorry, I wasn't thinking, I should know better than to activate them."

Valen squeezes my hand. "You're not alone anymore; you have us."

"Do I have you though? I haven't had my reading. We have no idea what that might change, and just look what I've done to you all already. How can any of you be on board for this?" I ask, pointing at his runes.

"I already told you, I'm in. That feeling of rightness that you mentioned, I have that too, and I trust it," Valen reassures me.

"I know this is new, but I think it's safe to say that none of us have ever felt the way that we feel about you. That's a little scary, but it's also incredibly exciting, and just like Valen said, it feels right for all of us," Ryker adds.

I look at Sabin and wait for him to disagree or tell us how crazy we all are, but he doesn't say anything. He just stares at me like he's trying to solve a puzzle. I have no idea if I'm the puzzle or if he is, but the fact that he isn't telling all of us to slow down or fuck off surprises the hell out of me.

"Okay, so how does this work then?" I ask no one in particular.

"What do you mean?" Ryker queries.

"I mean, we're what...dating...a couple? No, that wouldn't be right, we'd be a sextuple." I look at each of them, trying to fight some of the nerves I'm feeling. "There are five of you and one of me, which is a great start to a romance novel or a wet dream, but in reality, it's all so much more complicated than that." I fidget in my chair. "Relationships between two people can be hard, so how the hell does it work with six of us?"

I run both of my hands through my hair in exasperation.

"How do I make sure that each of you is getting what you need? Do you get jealous if I'm paying attention to one of you, like cuddling with one of you during a movie or things like that? How does being physical and sex work? I mean, I know how it works, but in a sextuple, how does it work?"

I look at all of them as I feel a rising panic.

"I'm not going to lie, the thought of having sex with all of you at the same time scares the shit out of me, so is that up for discussion, or is it mandatory?"

A roar of laughter stalls my nervous rambling, and I watch all of them—including Sabin—bend over and laugh hysterically. I tuck my legs up under me and wait for them to recover from what apparently is the funniest thing they've ever heard.

"Is it mandatory?" Bastien repeats, barely able to get the word out, he's laughing so hard.

They laugh for a solid couple of minutes before they manage to calm down.

"I would say yes to the sextuple question," Knox declares, wiping laugh tears from his eyes, "Which means we're all with you, and you are with us, and no one strays from that," he finishes, more seriously.

"This works like any other relationship, Vinna. We've all grown up understanding that we'd share a mate. We know that it will require effort and openness from all of us. Some things will be challenging, and there will be opportunities to learn and grow as we get to know each other better," Ryker offers.

"Different covens handle things differently. There's not a one size fits all solution or way to go about this. We could try for some sort of a schedule, which sometimes helps to ensure everyone has equal time and access to each other," Sabin tells me, and I stare at him and try to picture how that would work.

"In the coven I grew up in, they rotate days. If it's your day to be with your mate, you can plan a date or special time together, you sleep in the same bed that night, things like that. The coven still works together during the day, so they all spend time together, but your assigned day is your dedicated time with your mate," he further explains.

"My parents' coven is similar, but not as structured," Knox adds. "In the beginning, they all sort of just went with the flow of things, but a pattern of sorts still developed. They each take turns spending alone time together. But it seems they all communicate a lot about who needs what and work around that. Like if their compeer is having a rough time and needs their mate, they will make adjustments and switch things up."

"Compeer?" I ask.

"That's what we call each other. You'd be our mate, and we'd be each other's compeers," Knox clarifies.

"There might be times when we get jealous or maybe frustrated, but if we're all open and honest about what we need—when we need it—then it won't be an issue. It doesn't bother me if you are snuggled up with my compeer in a movie, but if it's never my turn to get in on those snuggles, then it would start to bother me," Bastien answers. "If that were to happen, then it's my responsibility to bring it up to everyone as soon as I feel bothered, so that we can figure out a solution."

I sit quietly for a minute and think about what each of them explained. "But how does it work in the beginning? You know, that honeymoon stage when it's all hot and spontaneous and all of that? How does that work with five different guys needing equal affection, passion, and time? You just have to wait until your day?"

Valen chuckles. "We'll have to figure that out. We've all grown up around this, but none of us have actually been in a relationship like this before. We're probably not going to get things perfect right from the start. Like Bastien said, we have to be straight up and quick to explain what we need and want from each other, and eventually we'll figure out what works best for us."

I notice that no one has really addressed the group sex question—well, other than to laugh at it. I'm about to ask again when all of our runes start to glow a deep orange. The guys all look at their hands and chests and then at each other, surprise and questions are written all over their faces. My magic starts to burn inside me, demanding my immediate attention and action. I'm off the chair in a flash as I follow the warning of my instincts.

"They're trying to get in," I whisper.

31

Sabin grabs my waist as I try to shoot past him.

"We'll go get the paladin, they'll know what to do," he tells me, at the same time someone else asks, "Who's trying to get in?"

He lets out a frustrated growl when I expertly yank my wrist from his hold. Ryker and Knox move in front of my bedroom door, blocking the only exit they see in the room. *They're not going to be happy when they realize that's not the door I'm headed for.*

I leap over my bed and fling open the French doors that lead to my balcony. I jump up onto the stone railing without hesitation and activate the runes on my legs and feet. Then I leap out into the cool darkness of the night. I call on both of my short swords from the runes on my ribs and grip them tightly as the wind whips past me in my freefall to meet the ground.

I land effortlessly, slightly crouched on the manicured lawn of the front yard. Swearing and shouts sound off on the balcony above me, but I focus in on the things I sense outside of the barrier. I realize then that the magic I fed into the barrier the first time I crossed it with Lachlan and his coven, not only strengthened it but connected me to it.

I'm not the magical version of duct tape, I grumble to my magic. But apparently, it doesn't agree. I can feel each move against the protective barrier as if it were against my body directly.

Something is slamming against the shield, trying to make cracks and access points. Other things seemed to be almost feeding off the magic of the barrier. The attacks feel malignant and cold against me. I can sense that the barrier is surrounded by an all-consuming darkness, the malevolence of which sends warning shivers throughout my whole body.

Magic swells up inside me in response, and a fierce possessiveness overcomes me as I think about anything breaking through and hurting what's mine. A feral growl rumbles in my chest, and I bellow a challenging roar at anything that would fuck with me. *Whoa, where the hell did that come from?*

Letting the magic guide me the way it always does, I let it continue to surge in me until I can barely take it. Just when I feel like I'm going to explode, I crouch and slam my blades into the grass-covered ground. I hold onto the hilts of my magic-forged weapons and feed power through the blades and out into the barrier.

The protective dome that shields us from the threats, throbs with pink and orange light and becomes more than a simple force of protection. It morphs into a weapon. The barrier strikes out at anything and everything attempting to breach it, and I'm rewarded with blood-curdling screams and roars of pain.

I continue to feed magic into the barrier, but suddenly the threat seems to blink out. Grass-muffled footsteps rapidly approach me, and I whirl around, a blade at the ready. Silva stops abruptly, inches separating his throat from the end of my short sword. He visibly swallows, and I quickly drop my hand and calm my magic. He takes a step back, and the rest of Lachlan's coven reach us.

I look past them, searching for the guys, but I don't see them anywhere.

"They're inside. We told them to guard the house, as a second layer of defense," Lachlan tells me in answer to my unvoiced question.

"What the *Xena: Warrior Princess* kind of shit is going on out here?" Evrin asks me, scanning my stance and the short swords in each hand.

I let the weapons go, the runes on my ribs reabsorbing their magic, and then I stand up straight. I almost wobble as my suddenly tired muscles seem to be struggling to cooperate, but I mask it.

"Someone or something was attacking the barrier. They seem to be gone now, or at least I don't feel them anymore," I explain.

I turn around to scan the darkness again, as I try to look and feel for a threat or any trace of whoever was just here. Silva gapes at me but snaps out of it as Lachlan organizes patrols. He sends them off to assess and collect clues, but he stops me when I try to join them.

"You're in your underwear. Go get dressed while we figure out what the hell is going on."

I dismiss his aggravated tone and take one more look around before I nod and make my way to the front door. I gently close it behind me, feeling drained from all the magic I just used, but I don't manage one more step before the guys are on me. They're all shouting at once, and I pick up on several—what the fucks—some—you scared the everloving shit out of me—and a whole lot of—don't ever do that again.

Ryker pulls me to him and starts running his hands all over my body in search of injuries. It dawns on me that I should do something to assuage their concern, but instead, I'm super focused on Ryker and his roaming hands. *Down, tiger.*

"You just sparked up and jumped off the balcony, like you were Selene in *Underworld*. I was terrified and turned on at the same time!"

Knox's confession breaks through my yearning for Ryker and his magic hands, and I look up at him. He looks cautious and lustful, and it makes me chuckle.

"Oh, and now you're going to laugh at me, Sparky... that's it."

Knox bends down and throws me over his shoulder. I squeak in surprise and start laughing even harder. He swats my butt playfully and then rubs the sting away, as he mumbles quietly about how *I need to be taught a lesson not to literally leap into danger*.

Knox carries me up to my room while I fill the others in on what happened. I don't fight being carried around like an invalid because I'm seriously so tired right now. I laboriously pull on some leggings and zip up a hoodie over my tank top. I try to finger comb some tangles out of my hair, but I give up and use my magic to tackle the windswept nest.

We all trickle back downstairs and wait in the living room for the paladin. I try to stifle a yawn, but it escapes and releases my inner Chewbacca. I expect to be teased about it, but instead, it seems to have set off yawns in all of the guys. I smile and slowly blink, my eyes feeling gritty and heavy. I lean into Bastien, and Knox pulls my feet into his lap. Any traces of adrenaline in my body are now long gone, and I'm defenseless against the exhaustion.

* * *

I groan as I close an old book that's about six inches thick.

"There's nothing in this one," I announce to the room.

The guys are sitting all around me in Lachlan's office, each of them scouring through their own tomes. Lachlan looks up from his laptop at his desk and takes note of the title of the book.

"I'll mark it off the list."

It's been a couple of days since I magically marked the guys and we had an attack on the barrier that surrounds the paladin's home. They've deduced that it was a group of ten to fifteen *somethings* that attempted to break in, but no one seems to be able to agree on what those *somethings* might have been.

My vote is for the lamia, but the tracks found around the barrier don't help pinpoint the paranormal species that created them. It could very well be lamia, or it could be casters, or shifters, or the stars only know what else. There has been a lot of speculation back and forth about who or what it could have been, but the uncertainty now floating around the house is unsettling.

I fully passed out and completely snoozed through what must have been an awkward conversation with Lachlan and the coven about the new runes I managed to gift to the guys. Pretty much seconds after I woke up in a puddle of drool on Bastien's shoulder, Lachlan forced us to scour the caster digital archives and his library in search of answers that would explain just what in the hell I did to them.

I'd much rather be trying to solve the mystery of who the fuck tried to get to us the other night. Especially since this boring book search has yielded a shit ton of nothing as far as answers go, but --according to Lachlan—my help is not needed.

"I'm done for the day," I announce, and I heave the heavy-ass book I just finished onto a shelf and dust my thighs off.

I weave my way out of the office, irritated. We haven't found one matching rune in all of Lachlan's sources. There are zero mentions of any casters having runes on their bodies, and a whole lot of nada when it comes to information about the connection the guys and I now have.

My magic just keeps upping the ante on my freak factor, and I feel like all of the paladin are watching me, waiting for the next crazy thing my magic is going to do. The itch of eyes on me is constant, and it's making me grouchy.

I touch the runes on my ear to amplify my hearing as I make my way to the kitchen. Aydin has started a *game* where he tries to surprise attack me. I don't know what purpose it serves, but it's been the most entertainment I've had in the past couple of days.

It's becoming a habit to listen out for him so I'm not surprised when he's waiting for me around some corner or various other blind spots in the house. I swipe a drink from the fridge, and Birdie subtly points to the pantry.

I don't tell her I can already hear his breathing and the steady staccato of his beating heart; I just give a thankful smile.

"Aydin, I know you're in the pantry," I announce before taking a swig of cold soda.

"How do you do that?" he pouts and slinks out of the pantry door.

"Birdie ratted you out."

I tip my soda bottle to her in cheers. She laughs and tries to look innocent as Aydin prowls toward her.

"Birdie, I've known you longer; you should be helping me."

"I am helping you, dear, helping you not get your butt kicked," she pats his cheek and laughs.

"You want to spar?" I ask through my giggles and shoot a wink to Birdie.

"I can't. It looks like we've got a new case coming in. Some unusual lamia activity that needs to be looked into."

"Is that connected to what happened here the other night?" I ask.

"Doubt it."

He's already walking away before I can ask him more about it, but a tingle of suspicion crawls up my spine.

Bastien brushes up against my back, and it chases away the eerie feeling. I lean into him automatically, and his arms wrap around me from behind. He steals my soda and loudly slurps down a big gulp before handing it back to me. *The dirty rotten thief.* The other guys all slowly trickle into the kitchen, apparently also giving up on another torturous day of looking through old dusty, useless books.

Birdie slides a plate of homemade chocolate chip cookies across the counter, and we all go into an instant feeding frenzy. Each of us savagely fights for a cookie, like somehow there won't be enough for all of us and there's no hope that cookies will ever be baked again. It's beyond ridiculous and hilarious.

Bastien pulls a cookie-filled hand toward his mouth, but I redirect it and manage to steal a huge bite. It's then I learn that it's okay when he and his brother steal my treats, but they can't take what they dish out. The look on his face as he stares at the missing bite in his cookie screams betrayal.

I see the torturous glint in his eye, and I break out of his grasp and run.

"How could you do this to me, Bruiser?"

"Oh, so you can take but not give?" I accuse.

"I can give, Bruiser, stop running and see what I've got in store for you."

His tone turns salacious, and I laugh as we circle the island opposite each other. Sabin walks into the middle of this ridiculous—but entertaining—cat and mouse game, and I slam into him in my attempt to avoid Bastien's attempt to tackle me. Sabin grabs my waist to steady me and then looks at all of us in an effort to figure out what's going on. I hold up my hands innocently.

"He started it, Captain," I declare, and then salute him.

Sabin rolls his eyes.

"I'm not here as acting hall monitor." He rubs his hand over the nape of his neck. "I actually wanted to ask if you'd hang with me for a bit?" he offers cryptically.

I look around, waiting for whoever he's asking to respond, but everyone is staring at me. I look up at Sabin and realize he's asking me to hang with him. Bewilderment stalls my response, and Sabin fidgets nervously at my silence.

"Um, sure," I finally manage to squeak out.

He relaxes and gives me a devastatingly handsome smile that makes his dimples come out to play. I'm instantly reminded of the *heartbreaker* I initially pegged him as and not the rigid Captain Cockblock that I've later come to know.

"Put on some jeans and shoes," Sabin instructs me, and then he grabs a cookie and walks out.

I look over to the guys, wondering if they're just as shocked as I am by this turn of events, but they all just shrug. Quick as lightning, I snatch the last cookie on the plate and sprint for my room. I slip on some skinny jeans, lace up my black combat boots, and keep on the dark green slouchy shirt I was already wearing.

I dash out of my room, and I'm surprised to find Sabin leaning against the wall just outside of my door. He's in a pair of well-fitted jeans and an ash-colored t-shirt, and I can't help but take in how incredibly gorgeous he is. If only he wasn't such a dick. His brown hair looks like he's been running his fingers through it, and it makes him look a little more rugged and a lot less controlled.

His tattoo stands out in contrast to his light gray shirt. Below his elbow, the tattoo is a reflection on water of trees and the night sky. Above his elbow is a detailed tree line that reaches up into a sky full of stars, with a full moon sitting on the top of his arm into his shoulder. It's stunning, and I want to sit and trace all the beautiful detail that I know I'd find if I could just get close enough.

"Where are we going?" I ask as I try to rein in my pathetic mental worship of an asshole who confuses the shit out of me.

"You'll see."

32

Sabin leads me down the stairs and out to the garage. He straddles an ATV and motions for me to get on. I keep my distance from him so he can keep it *classy and respectful,* exactly what he accused Valen of *not* being the last time I was on an ATV. We drive out of the garage and hang right, driving in a direction I haven't explored yet.

"Is it safe to leave our barrier, with what just happened?" I yell to him when I realize how far out we are going.

"Yeah, we'll be entering another protected barrier right away, so no worries."

The telltale tingling sensation of magic sweeps over me when we leave our barrier and enter the new one. I breathe a sigh of relief when my magic doesn't spaz out and do anything crazy.

We ride for a while before the trees start to clear to make way for green manicured lawns. We drive in the direction of a huge building, and I suddenly remember that there are stables on the property next to the paladin.

I can't contain the excited squeal that tumbles out of me when I realize where we're going. Sabin laughs. We stop next to the building, and he turns off the ATV.

"I take it you know where we are?" he asks with a dimple-filled smile.

I nod my head excitedly.

"Should I interpret your girly squeal as an indication that you ride?"

"I've never ridden anything, but I've always wanted to."

I wait for Sabin to call out the innuendo, but he just smiles.

"Good to know."

The stables are pristine. The stalls are enormous with intricately carved wood and iron doors, and it's incredibly clean. It's clear these horses are living in the lap of luxury. I don't know how many stalls we walk by before Sabin stops. He grabs a rope and opens a door. He motions for me to step in behind him, and I follow obediently.

"Hey there, buddy," Sabin coos. "You down for some exercise and a little showing off?"

He clips a rope to the halter of a humongous gray horse and then casually hands the rope to me. He walks out of the stall, leaving me all alone, and I'm stunned that I'm now standing here without any additional instructions. I hope this horse is happy to stand around because, if it wants to go anywhere, I doubt my puny little self and this rope are going to stop it.

"Hey there, gorgeous," I say, getting fresh and planting a kiss on its nose. "Aren't you quite the handsome devil?"

I duck a peek to confirm that handsome is an appropriate descriptor, and he lets out a snort of agreement. I chuckle and start to run my fingers up and down both sides of his neck. He brings his head down level with my chest and leans into me.

"Oh, you like that do you, some good scratches."

The clop of hooves fills the air, and Sabin reappears outside the door, leading another horse.

"It's good to know your spell affects males of all species and not just casters," Sabin teases me, gesturing to the horse cuddles I'm currently receiving.

I wag my brows. "Careful, Captain, or you might be next."

Sabin mumbles something under his breath, but I don't catch it.

"Follow me."

He jerks his chin toward the entrance and starts leading his horse away. With Sabin's help, I coax my huge horse out of his stall, grateful that he's a good listener, because we both know he could take me out if he wanted to.

My horse's huge frame is wrapped in a stunning dark gray color, with light gray dappling on his front legs and butt. His mane and tail are a beautiful contrasting white-gray. He looks so unique and regal.

"What's his name?" I ask, awe clear in my voice.

"That's Darcy," Sabin calls over his shoulder as we round the front of the stables. "And this is Bennet."

His voice has the same fondness that I heard when he was talking to Darcy earlier, and I catch a curious blush that creeps into his cheeks. He shows me how to brush the horses and then disappears to get their *tack*. I brush Darcy and then Bennet as Sabin makes several trips back and forth to get everything we need to ride.

Bennet is just slightly smaller than Darcy but not by much. Where Darcy is dark, Bennet is light making them opposites in a way. She's light gray everywhere with dark spots all over, except her face. Her hair is black, and she has black stocking-like marks on all of her legs.

I trace the patterns in Bennet's fur with my eyes as I stroke long lengths down her sides and back. I freeze when it dawns on me why the names sound so familiar. *Mr. Darcy* and *Ms. Bennet*. I laugh, their owner must be a *Pride and Prejudice* fan.

"No one cares that we're taking these horses?" I ask as Sabin starts to organize everything he's brought out to put on the horses.

"They're mine. I board them here."

I jerk my head in Sabin's direction, completely shocked at his revelation. Sabin is the *Pride and Prejudice* fan?

He gets Darcy kitted up and talks me through everything that he's doing and why. He helps me climb up on Darcy's back, and I get a quick crash course on how to handle him. I run my fingers through Darcy's mane and watch as Sabin hooks a rope to Darcy's halter. He walks us into a paddock and gives the rope in his hand some slack.

"Alright, Vinna, I'm going to have you and Darcy ride for a bit in here so you both can get used to each other. I'll help you get a feel for some different speeds on him, but if it's too much too fast, just pull on the reins, and he'll stop. Okay?"

I nod my head, and Sabin teaches me how to click my tongue just right to make Darcy move. His gait is smooth and slow, and it's surprisingly easy to get comfortable up on the back of this giant gray Andalusian.

"Tell me about how you came to be the proud owner of these two beautiful horses?"

Sabin shrugs. "Some people save up for a car or something like that, but I saved up for these guys. I bought Darcy first when I was twenty, and then Bennet a year later. I've always loved animals in general but especially horses, and I always knew I wanted a pair."

"Did you name them or is that pure coincidence?"

A blush creeps up his neck, and it tells me everything I need to know.

"You're a romantic!" I exclaim, my voice laced with shock and accusation.

"Don't say it like it's something dirty," he scoffs. "Is it so hard to believe?"

I stare at him thoughtfully and mull over that question. I have my opinions about Sabin and how he acts, but I haven't the slightest clue about the *why* behind what he does. I have no idea what makes him who he is. I think about that and realize that it changes the lens that I see Sabin through in a surprising way.

"I don't *really* know you. So, no, it isn't hard to believe," I admit. "Solve the mystery then and tell me about yourself, Sabin Gamull."

I pat myself on the back for remembering his last name, then lean over and actually pat Darcy on his neck.

"Well, Vinna Aylin, I'm twenty-six, same as the other guys, but you know that already. I'm a Paladin Conscript, but you know that, too." He smiles at me cheekily. "What you may not know is that I'll be the first in my family line to become a paladin."

"I did *not* know that. How do your parents feel about that?"

"They were surprised at first, but they've always been supportive. I think they were more shocked when my reading showed that I had strong Elemental magic instead of Spell magic like they assumed I would have."

"Why did they think you'd have Spell magic?"

"Because the entire coven has Spell magic, and when both biological parents have the same magic, it's incredibly rare that the child would have something different."

"I thought covens were made up of casters with different magic, for balance or something like that?"

"No, only paladin covens are built that way. Outside of the paladin, casters can build covens however they want to. Covens like my family's aren't rare at all."

Darcy snorts and flaps his tail around like he's participating in our conversation, and I chuckle.

"Are you ready to pick up some speed?" Sabin asks me, and I nod eagerly.

Darcy begins to trot when Sabin clicks at him again, and I find myself suddenly bouncing around. Sabin walks me through how to find the rhythm in Darcy's faster gait and how to use my body to work with the rhythm instead of against it. The ride smooths out, and I'm able to let go of the horn of the saddle, no longer feeling like I might fall off.

A huge smile takes over my face, and I look over to find Sabin has the same happy smile and pride shining in his eyes. He's lighter, more carefree in this moment than I've ever seen him, and I can't lie, it's hot as fuck. I shake off my hungry thoughts and focus on what we were talking about before.

"If your coven isn't paladin, what do they do?" I ask.

I've only really been exposed to ways of the paladin so far. I've visited in town. I haven't given much thought to the various types of magic that other people have and what they might do with that magic.

"They own and run a spell shop in town."

"Oh, that's cool..." I'm quiet for a minute. "I know you said shop, but I'm totally picturing a rickety cabin-like building with a small fire and a bubbling cauldron sitting over it. Are there rows of dusty shelves that are filled with bottles and jars containing weird ass shit?"

Sabin laughs. "No, nothing like that. Picture more Bath & Body Works, but everything's a spell or potion. My family members are some of the strongest Spell casters in Solace." His statement isn't boastful. It's just matter of fact like he's telling me the trees are green. "Some people come in to order bespoke spells from them, and then there are the generic spells available to purchase anytime."

"Like what?" I ask excitedly.

"There are things for healing and illness."

I turn to him confused, and Sabin answers my curious look.

"Not all casters have access to a healer, and some can't afford one even if they have access. What Ryker can do is special, and we're lucky to have him," he explains. "Healing and wellness spells are the most popular, but other spells range from dying your hair, to birth control, to spells that help you study. If you can think of *something*, there's probably a spell for it."

"Excuse my ignorance here, but I would've thought that all casters could spell. I thought it would be a staple of magic in general, or maybe that's me falling back on what I picture about witches, and let's be honest, most of that comes from the movie *Hocus Pocus*."

Sabin laughs. "I love that movie."

"Right, it's a Halloween staple."

"Damn straight it is," Sabin agrees, and I can't help but smile.

I adjust myself in the saddle and run my fingers through Darcy's mane as we continue to trot around the paddock.

"When it comes to Spell magic, I'd compare it to cooking. Some nons can cook, some can't, and then you have your master chefs. The ones who are so talented and innovative that people will pay anything to consume their creations. Spell magic is like that."

I smile at Sabin and his comparison. The image of a dusty room with a cauldron bubbling over a fire fades away, and in its place, I picture a state of the art kitchen with cauldrons bubbling over an enormous gas range.

"I'd love to see their shop sometime," I blurt out, not thinking through the fact that I'm inviting myself to meet his family.

"I'd love to take you. I'm going to up the ante again and have Darcy canter. It will be faster but feel a little smoother than his trot. Just remember to find the rhythm and use your legs to move into it. Okay?"

I give him a thumbs up and do exactly as I'm told. A thrill of giddiness flows through me as Darcy and I move faster. I have a couple *oh shit* moments in the beginning, but eventually, I figure it out. This experience is incredible, and the feeling I have right now as Darcy and I flash around the ring is joyous and liberating. I can feel some of the armor I always wear slip off and my defenses lower.

"So what about you? What was non-life like? What did you want to be when you grew up?" Sabin asks me.

Darcy slows down to a walk, and I pat the side of his neck appreciatively.

"It probably sounds weird, but I never really thought about it when I was younger. I was quiet and skittish, and honestly just trying to stay out of Beth's path as much as possible. We moved around a lot, so I never really got my feet underneath me.

"I had Laiken until she learned that things went better for her with Beth when she stayed away from me. That was pretty much how it went until Beth kicked me out. I met Talon a couple of weeks later, and then everything changed for me."

"How'd you meet?"

I snort a chuckle. "I ran up on his car when I was trying to escape this group of guys who were chasing me. I had never been in a fight before that day, but I knew it was only a matter of time being homeless and a girl. I carried a rock around with me, ready for whenever it happened, and then I ran into this group of guys. They wanted my backpack and other things.

"I knocked two guys out and broke a third's nose. I

surprised the shit out of myself, but there were still four left. I had magic, even though I had no idea that's what it was back then, but it was so inconsistent and unreliable. I knew I was in trouble with those odds, so I ran for my life. I thought I was fucked as the guys closed in on me, but next thing I know, a big SUV was rounding the corner and out tumbled four big scary dudes."

"Is that what that rock is on your shelf? I noticed it on the first day I met you. It made me curious," Sabin asks.

"The very same one. My lucky rock. Talon taught me how to fight for real, so I've never had to use the rock again, but it's a fucked up memento of when my life got better, so I've kept it."

Sabin pulls on the rope in his hands, and Darcy walks toward him. He stops, and Sabin rounds his side and looks up at me.

"I'm sorry that's what things were like for you."

I stare into his fathomless green eyes, not sure what to say.

"It wasn't all bad. Talon showed me what I was capable of. I found myself. My strength and my magic did the rest. I wouldn't change any of it, even if I could."

33

We follow a narrow path through the trees, riding side-by-side, and it feels intimate and secluded. Sabin seems so completely in his element out here. It's surprising to see how relaxed and happy he is. Most of our interactions are tense or aggressive, and I'm not really sure what to do with this chatty comfortable version of Sabin.

"You're a natural," he tells me. "You picked everything up really fast."

"Well, you're a good teacher, and there's also the fact that if I see something, I can pretty much do it. My magic's weird like that."

He chuckles and leans over to lift some low hanging branches out of the way. I duck under Sabin's outstretched arm, and my leg rubs up against his as Darcy and I pass by. It sends tingles and unwanted awareness throughout my body.

Sabin releases the branches that he's holding back, and one snaps down and clips Darcy on the butt. Darcy rockets forward, and I squeak in surprise at the sudden acceleration. He thunders down the narrow path, all muscle and power, and trees shoot past me in a blur as I try to keep from falling off. Everything I just learned in the paddock rattles around in my head as I hold on for dear life.

Fuck, this horse is fast. I squeeze my thighs against Darcy's sides and push up in the stirrups to crouch in the saddle. I have no idea if this is going to help or make it easier to fall off. But trying to keep my ass in the saddle or find any kind of sweet spot in the rhythm as Darcy runs for his life, just isn't happening.

Out of nowhere Sabin and Bennet flash past. Sabin maneuvers Bennet in front of Darcy cutting off his open track to run. Bennet starts to slow to force Darcy to slow down too, and I pull back on his reins to assist the stop running message I'm hoping will sink in. It works, and Darcy gradually slows down and comes to a stop. Sabin whips around on Bennet and comes to a stop next to Darcy and me.

He pulls me off of Darcy's back and into his lap. He starts running his eyes all over me and patting me down to make sure I'm okay. I breathe heavy as adrenaline-soaked blood flows through my veins. Now that I'm no longer at risk for falling off and getting injured—or possibly killed—I can't fight the smile that takes over my face.

I start to laugh, and Sabin freezes his panicked assessment for injuries and looks down at me wide-eyed.

"Are you okay?" he asks me, cupping my face with his hands.

"That was fucking crazy. Holy shit, he can move. Let's do it again, and you can teach me how to manage at that speed, instead of just hanging on and hoping I don't bite it."

I giggle, and it's ten percent hysterical and ninety percent amused excitement. Next thing I know, Sabin's mouth is on mine. His lips slowly and hesitantly caress my own, and he nips and nibbles, coaxing me to respond to him. I hesitate for the slightest of seconds before I answer the question in his kiss.

I claim his mouth like he's claiming mine, and heat and want shoot through me. He pulls me even closer to him, one hand around my waist and the other tangled in my hair, as he thoroughly and skillfully kisses me into oblivion.

For someone I was convinced didn't like me, Sabin's kiss is incredibly erotic and powerful. Every inch of me is on fire, and there isn't a single thought in my head other than how to get more of him. Unexpectedly, a slightly wet and warm horse nose nudges against my hip, making me squeak in surprise and snap back into reality.

I push against Sabin's hard chest, and he reluctantly lets me go. I jump out of his lap and off of Bennet's back. My feet thump against the packed dirt of the narrow trail, and I pant as I look everywhere but at Sabin and his mind-blowing lips. I touch my sensitive mouth and look over to see that Darcy is just watching us. *Perv*.

"Figures Captain Cockblock would have a cockblock for a horse," I mutter, not sure if I'm grateful or irritated with the interruption.

"I'm never going to get rid of that fucking nickname, am I?" he asks and lets out a sigh that ends with an amused chuckle.

I've never heard Sabin laugh as much as he has on this outing, and as much as I like the deep rich tone of it, his levity is also unsettling.

"Well, up until thirty seconds ago, you earned it fair and square. I didn't know you had *that* in you, Captain."

Maybe I did actually fall and hit my head, and this is all some elaborate coma-fantasy, I offhandedly wonder as I grab Darcy's reins and pat his neck. Sabin jumps down off of Bennet's back and runs his hands over Darcy, checking his legs and feet for injuries.

"I was terrified you were going to fall off and smash into a tree. You did everything absolutely right."

Sabin stares at me with obvious relief and something else I'm not sure if I'm seeing correctly. We both just stand there, staring at each other, neither one of us sure what the hell to do now.

"So what the fuck was that?" I blurt uncensored.

He rubs the back of his neck and stares at the ground for a second before answering me.

"Well, that's what we casters like to call a kiss."

I roll my eyes at Sabin's smart ass response, but I don't miss the slight blush that creeps up his neck and into his dimpled cheeks.

"Have you been body snatched?" I ask randomly and take a dramatic step back.

Sabin snorts and shakes his head.

"No, no body snatching. Although if I was, I probably wouldn't admit to it."

I huff at his solid logic. He studies me for a couple more seconds and then takes a deep breath.

"I wasn't planning on kissing you. I just wanted to talk to you, to get to know you better. That was my only goal with all of this." He gestures to the horses. "But I was just so fucking relieved you were okay. Then you were smiling and laughing and just so damn beautiful. I just didn't want to stop myself anymore. I didn't want to hold back. I'm sorry."

Sabin's candid confession astounds me, and I look back and forth between his deep forest-green eyes, not sure what to think or say.

"Valen was right when he told me I needed to stop being afraid. I thought I was being smart and protected by keeping my distance, but really I was just scared and fighting what I now realize was inevitable."

"Sabin, you don't even like me," I say, confused.

"Vinna, that's not true. I was drawn to you from the first minute I saw you, but it scared the shit out of me. You fit so seamlessly with us, and I convinced myself you were too good to be true. I know I fucked up and pushed you away. I hate that I did that. I hate that it hurt you. I realized just how wrong I was the night my runes showed up."

Sabin brushes the back of his hand lightly against my cheek.

"I could feel that *rightness* that you and the others were talking about. I could feel my magic responding and being strengthened by yours. Magic in its basest form is pure, and my magic wants to be tied to yours. That blew all of my doubts and reservations away. It forced me to wake up and see you for what you are."

"What's that?" I ask quietly.

"Ours."

Sabin's gaze is filled with such raw intensity that I look away, not able to take it and process what he's saying at the same time. Forgiveness is not a talent of mine, and I'm not sure where that leaves any of this. I knew when all of us agreed to try for a relationship that Sabin was included in that scenario. I guess, I just never gave much thought to what it would look like if he pulled his head out of his ass.

"I think Darcy may have a shoe loose. It's probably best not to keep riding him. We can double up on Bennet and head back."

Sabin ties Darcy up to Bennet's saddle and swings himself up onto her back. He puts a hand out for me, and I grab it. I expect him to position me behind him, but he swings me up in front of him instead. His saddle is different than mine. There's no horn to hold onto in the front, so it's not completely uncomfortable, just awkward. I'm half in Sabin's lap and half on Bennet's shoulder area.

He clicks Bennet into action, and we slowly start to trace

our steps back to the stables. The feel of Sabin at my back is comforting and welcome in a way that it shouldn't be. Not with everything that's gone on with us. Apparently, a mind-blowing kiss is all I need to abandon good sense. I get what he's saying about our magic making it clear what we should do. I felt drawn to these guys before I could make sense of it, and right now with him is no different.

"Sabin, how am I supposed to trust this?" I ask earnestly after we've been riding in weighted silence for a while.

"I don't expect you to let everything slide, or give me your complete trust after everything that's happened. I just need you to let me earn it. Give me a chance. Let me show you the other sides to who I am. I am more than Captain Cockblock."

I can't help the snicker that escapes my lips, and I feel Sabin's vibrating laughter in his chest.

It's tempting to draw out my hurt over what's happened between us, but I realize in this moment, that I can't. Yeah, it seriously sucks that things have gone down the way that they have. But like Bastien said, if we're going to make things work, we have to own our shit, fix the issues, and move on. Plus, I can't lie, kissing him is a level of amazing I could seriously get used to.

I huff in resignation.

"Fine, you rein in your controlling bullshit, and I'll put on my big girl panties and move past what's happened," I offer hesitantly.

"I can do that," he agrees, and I can hear the smile in his tone.

He places a soft kiss on my shoulder, and the minute his lips connect with the runes there, I shiver at the contact.

"Something about you guys touching my runes fucks with my magic. It sets off a cyclone in my chest every time. I'm not sure what it means, but unless you want to find out right now, it's probably best not to feed the tornado," I tell him.

I can feel the vibration of his laughter in my chest, and it makes me feel warm and lighter.

"Alright, until I'm battle ready, I'll steer clear of your runes."

I nod in agreement and absently trace his gorgeous tattoo with my eyes. His arms are wrapped around me as we ride back, and I'm finally close enough to take in the details. I find a silhouette of a deer tucked into the trunks of the trees, and the stars are so life like I almost make a wish on one that's falling. I feel like I'm staring at an incredible picture instead of ink in skin.

"I'll take you there sometime," Sabin tells me, catching my intense focus on his sleeve of tattoos.

"Where is this?"

"It's here in Solace. It's somewhere I love to go to just sit and sort things through. You may not know this, but I can be a bit serious and overthink things sometimes. This is my place to sit and make sense of it all."

I chuckle and lean back into Sabin's chest. We both relax into each other and fall into a companionable silence as we make our way back to the stables.

34

Sabin laughs as we walk through the garage door into the kitchen.

"I like when you pout, it does great things for this," he tells me and runs his finger down my bottom lip. "Keep it up."

"I will pout. I thought you were going to teach me what to do when they run."

"And I will, just not today."

I narrow my eyes and poke out my full bottom lip even more.

"You look more like a flirty Disney princess than the brooding badass you're going for right now," Sabin tells me on a laugh.

I swat his shoulder incredulously, and he lunges toward me playfully. I dodge his attempt to manhandle me, and sprint around the corner to escape. I come to a screeching halt when I find a group of familiar and unfamiliar faces rising to their feet in the living room.

Sabin rounds the corner, not expecting me to be standing right there and slams into me from behind. He curses and grabs my hips to keep me from tumbling forward. He starts to ask me what I'm doing, but he follows my questioning gaze and takes in the same scene I'm staring at. He straightens stiffly, as he drops his hands away from my body.

"Elders. Paladin," he nods and greets our new audience.

"Sabin, the boys are upstairs," Lachlan tells him in dismissal.

Sabin walks past me, and I catch his nervous glance. I see the same questions in his eyes that are currently in mine.

"What's going on?" I ask no one in particular.

Keegan is on the opposite end of the couch from Lachlan. Aydin and Evrin are standing in front of armchairs, and Silva is leaning casually against the fireplace. I quickly observe how tense they all are, and it puts me on edge.

Lachlan motions for me to come to him, and it's not lost on me that no one has bothered to answer my question. I walk toward him, but I find myself stopping next to Aydin instead. Lachlan gives me an unidentifiable look, but it quickly disappears from his face as Aydin gestures for me to sit in his chair.

The paladin rearrange themselves, and I observe the strangers still standing in front of the other couch. Two of them have blank looks on their face, but the one in the middle has an odd look, something akin to satisfaction. I'm not sure what to make of that, so I turn my attention to the men standing guard behind the couch.

"Vinna, I'd like to introduce you to the Elders Council." Lachlan gestures to the short, stout man on the left. "This is Elder Balfour."

The Elder dips his chin to me, and I mirror the movement in greeting. He's short and balding, and kind of reminds me of the monopoly man, minus the mustache.

"This is Elder Cleary."

Lachlan indicates the tall man in the middle. He has short white-blonde hair and an all-black suit. He looks like a solid contender for the Malfoy family, and I want to search his arm for the death eater mark. He gives me a smile and a quick once over but doesn't offer any greeting beyond that.

"And this is Elder Nypan."

Elder Nypan steps forward and offers me his hand. He looks younger than the other two, with smooth dark skin, a bald head, and a significantly less intense vibe than his companions. I shake his hand, hoping that my magic behaves itself, and I mentally pet it when I pull my hand away and nothing weird happens.

"Elder Albrecht and Elder Kowka couldn't be here this evening, but I'm sure you'll meet them at a later time," Elder Nypan tells me, and I nod in acknowledgment.

Lachlan doesn't introduce the other four men standing behind the couch, and I'm guessing it's because they're some kind of security. I fidget a little when each of them watches me with intense interest.

The elders take their seats, prompting everyone else—except the bodyguards and Silva—to do the same.

"The Elders accompanied Reader Tearson here," Aydin offers, finally answering my question.

"He's here?"

"He's preparing for the reading as we speak," Lachlan tells me, a stiff smile on his face.

My heart starts an epic assault on my chest. I work hard to keep my poker face intact and to not show any outward indication of how unsettled I suddenly feel. "Holy shit, it's actually happening?" I say astonished. *Nice, Vinna*, poker face intact, but filter clearly is broken.

Aydin and Silva both laugh and then cough to cover it up. I look over to the Elders to find Elder Balfour scowling at me and my unladylike words. When I don't apologize—

which is what it seems like he's expecting me to do—his frown deepens.

"We were just discussing the preparations for your reading. It's been many years since we've witnessed Reader Tearson in his element; it will be a delight to see him again," he tells me.

Lachlan glowers at Elder Balfour. I don't know what exactly is going on here, but it doesn't seem friendly, and I feel like I'm missing something.

"We were just discussing with the elders that their presence is unnecessary, and we'll be sure to update them as soon as the reading is concluded," Lachlan explains with a saccharine tone.

"Why wouldn't she want us there? It's an honor that we're offering our support and witness, one not bestowed often," Elder Cleary challenges Lachlan.

Lachlan visibly bites his tongue and stays quiet. His eyes quickly flick to me as the tension swells in the room. It's evident that he really doesn't want the elders in my reading. I just wish I knew why.

"Well, I don't know you, so there's that," I offer Elder Cleary.

Elder Balfour sputters, seemingly surprised that I've spoken and inserted myself in whatever the hell is going on here.

A calculating smile appears on Elder Cleary's face. "We are your Elders, child, your leaders. What more do you need to know?"

His eyes are fixed on mine, and I don't dare to look away.

"Why do you want to be there? Like you said, it's *an honor you don't bestow on many*. What makes me worthy?"

Elder Nypan interjects before Elder Cleary can speak.

"I'm sure you're aware of how unusual your circumstances are. It's safe to say we're all curious about your reading and what it will show."

"We will, of course, share any pertinent information with the Elders Council, as is expected with all readings," Keegan tells them, trying and failing to ease the strain in the room.

I quietly debate what I should do. If we're going to tell the elders what happens in the reading anyway, wouldn't it be wise to play nice and let them do what they want? I look at each of the elders trying to intuit what the best move is.

Elder Balfour seems haughty, but I suppose that's to be expected in his position. He's an elder, and apparently, they're super powerful. I'd probably have a big head, too. Elder Cleary, however, is harder to get a read on. There's hostility in his presence, but I'm not sure if it's aimed at me. It's possible it could have something to do with what happened between his son's friends and me, but I'm not sure.

What's even more confusing about Elder Cleary is that, aside from the veiled undertone of aggression, he seems incredibly eager about something too. He's trying to mask that eagerness with the apathetic look on his face, but the gleam that occasionally sneaks out of his gaze is giving him away.

Elder Nypan seems nice enough. Of the three Elders here, he's probably the most likely to respect my decision either way, but something about this whole situation is off. Why is there so much strain and rancor between the coven and the elders?

"Elder Nypan, I get the intrigue, but I respectfully decline your *request* to witness my reading."

I try to sound diplomatic, but I can't help throwing in a not so veiled dig at the Elders. None of these fuckers have even bothered to ask me if I'd want them there. They talked to me like it was a done deal, and then Lachlan kept shutting them down, but no one has spoken to me like I have any say in any of it. Elder Nypan watches me for a second and then gives me an accepting nod before he stands up.

"We look forward to hearing the results of your reading." Elder Nypan smiles at me and then promptly moves toward the front door. *Well, that was anticlimactic. I kind of expected more of a fight.* I watch the other two elders cautiously, wondering if they will follow Elder Nypan's easy and accepting lead or bitch and whine about his acceptance.

Elder Balfour is the first to concede, and he quickly exits the room while being shadowed by two of the bodyguards. Elder Cleary, however, watches me. The cunning light in his eyes is like a lighthouse that's warning me of danger, but I don't know if he's the danger or if something else is.

"My son mentioned that he had the privilege of meeting you," he tells me, his smooth cadence piercing the silence. "It seems you left quite the impression on him."

"The encounter was enlightening," I answer, my voice monotone.

He stares at me, seemingly in no hurry to leave. "Yes, I can see what all the fuss is about," Elder Cleary muses, and a cool mask of satisfaction slides over his face.

The whole exchange is odd and unnerving, but before I can analyze it more or ask him what the hell is going on, he leaves and joins the other elders in the foyer. Silva is at the front door, holding it open and thanking them for their visit, and they all shuffle out into the evening. When the door finally clicks shut, and it's just the paladin and me, a collective sigh of relief permeates the group.

"What the hell was that all about?" I ask, looking around at all of them.

"They were here assessing a threat," Silva offers me, still

staring at the door like he's anticipating someone is going to come crashing back through it.

"A threat? They're a little late if they're looking into what happened the other night."

"They were here to assess you, Vinna," Lachlan tells me, looking at me like I'm an idiot.

"Me? How am I threat?"

"You're a powerful unknown. That in itself can be threatening," Keegan explains.

That's why they wanted in on my reading. They didn't merely want answers; they wanted secrets. If they know what my magic *can* do, then they'll also get a good idea of what it *can't* do. Irritation and mistrust seep into me as things start to click together.

But why the hell would the paladin have a problem with them having that information? It's not like Lachlan would be loyal to me over them.

"So why were you all so against them witnessing my reading?"

"Because we have no idea what's going to happen. We didn't want to risk it."

It takes a second for Lachlan's words and tone to sink in.

"You didn't want to risk them, or you didn't want to risk me?" I ask.

Lachlan's silence is deafening.

"You think I'm a threat, too?" I clarify, not sure why his doubt stings so much.

Of course he thinks I'm a fucking threat. It's not like he's treated me as anything but from the beginning.

"We've never seen anything like what you can do. We have no idea what that means for any of us," Lachlan justifies coldly.

I look around at the others, but none of them look back at me.

"Wow, good to know. Not that any of you fucking care, but this is bullshit."

"Little Badass, don't be mad..."

"Aydin, look me in my eyes and tell me I'm misunderstanding what you all are saying."

Silva steps forward. "I don't think you'd do anything to hurt us on purpose, but your magic is dangerous. Look at what you've done to the boys. You're only in your quickening right now. Who knows what your magic will be like after your awakening."

"We have to be realistic about what all of this means. We don't know where you come from or how you ended up here. You seem to have been designed as a perfect weapon, and we'd be stupid not to recognize that and prepare against it."

I flinch as Silva and Lachlan's words hit me like a brutal slap across the face.

"Why am I here?" I growl.

Lachlan stares at me as confusion flashes on his face at my question.

"Did you rip me away from the life I built because I'm your blood and I deserve a life filled with family, magic, and love? Or am I fucking here to become whatever weapon you seem to think I am? To be used if possible and put down if not?"

Once again Lachlan doesn't answer, and that's answer enough for me. Any hope I ever had that we could develop any kind of familial relationship shrivels into nothing.

"You're right, Silva. We don't know what my magic will be like after I come into my full power, but you fail to realize that it will still be *my* magic. If any of you would pull your head out of your ass long enough to know anything about me, you'd know that I'm not some heartless, bloodthirsty monster."

No one says anything, and it stings like the betrayal it is. I scoff at my stupidity. I'm here because they wanted to keep their *potential* enemy close. It was never about me finding my place as a caster or being wanted. Rage sears my insides as I look at each of them. I would have been better off not being found.

"Fuck you guys."

I start up the stairs, and someone calls my name and moves to follow me. I call on a throwing knife and fling it at the feet of whichever asshole is behind me. It thunks into the wood and someone yelps in surprise.

"Just trying to live up to my hype," I seethe over my shoulder.

35

I reach my room and slam the door shut. I close my eyes and lean back against it while I take deep slow breaths and try not to scream. I'm startled when I hear someone approach me, and I find five pairs of eyes filled with concern.

"What are you guys doing in here?" I ask and then clear my throat at the emotion that just leaked through in my voice.

"Being nosy. We thought the best way to get some answers was to ambush you," Valen explains. The playful smile on his face quickly falls away when he takes a closer look at me. "What happened?"

"Well, long story short, the elders wanted in on my reading to better assess how much of a threat I might be. Don't worry though, Lachlan's coven didn't allow that to happen."

I watch as a few of their shoulders relax and then tense up again as I go on.

"Oh, they didn't keep the elders away for the reasons you're thinking. They weren't protecting me. They're fucking protecting the elders. Big, dangerous, and scary Vinna will be dealt with by the asshole paladin who are supposed to be her coven, so there's that to be grateful for."

"Wait, what makes any of them think you're dangerous or a threat?" Knox asks, just as confused as I was.

"To quote Lachlan—the newest recipient of the shittiest uncle award—they don't know where I come from, and I've been *designed* as the perfect weapon. They all think that because I'm capable, I'm automatically culpable."

"Fuck that," Bastien snaps.

"Yeah, that's more or less what I said, then I threw a knife at someone who tried to follow me upstairs. Probably not my finest moment."

I hear several snickers as I walk over to the bed where a white dress, a pouch of herbs, and a glass vial that's filled with clear liquid sit. I've been waiting for this reading and what it will tell me about my magic since I got here, but there's no excitement about it anymore. All I feel right now is a little broken and a lot pissed off.

The wood box containing Laiken's ashes catches my eye, and I stare at it and berate myself. Why am I so hurt by this? I should fucking know better by now. I followed perfect strangers to the middle of nowhere out of sheer desperation. Should I really be shocked that this is how it turned out? I take in the details of Laiken's box, and a decision cements itself in my mind. I'll get through this reading, and then I'm done with the paladin.

I can tell that the guys want to say or do something that will make all of this better for me somehow, but everyone stays silent, understanding that the damage has been done. I pick up the white dress that's laid out and throw it over my elbow. Grasping the pouch of herbs and the corked bottle, I head into the bathroom to get ready for my reading.

* * *

An hour later I step into the dress. It's white, long, and flowy. The top part is a halter that ties around my neck and fits snugly against my chest and sides. There isn't a back, and the waist drops low on my hips. The accordion-esque fabric starts just above the crack of my ass and flows nicely over my curves to the ground.

I've used my magic to style big loose curls into my hair, and I've parted it to the side. I grab what's left of the contents of the stoppered glass vial, and open the door that separates the bathroom from the bedroom.

"Knox, can you put some of this on the middle of my back? I'm not sure if I reached everything."

My voice trails off, as I stare at the five gorgeous men in front of me, decked out in white from head to toe. They're all in identical white linen tunics with fitted pants in the same material. The clothing has an old and otherworldly look about it, and a mixture of heat and awe fills me as I take the guys in.

"Where did you get these?" I ask, pointing at their clothes, confused.

"The sisters made them up for everyone in the house. They weren't sure who you'd want in your reading, so they made sure everyone was prepared," Valen explains. "If you don't want us there, we completely understand and support that, but we wanted to be ready, just in case."

"Of course I want you there."

I look at each of them and try to silently convey how much it means to me that they want to be there for me, for no other reason than to offer their support.

Knox steps forward and takes the glass bottle from my grasp. He pulls out the stopper and tilts the contents into his hand. I turn around and pull all my hair to the side. He rubs the potion into my bare back and sides with his strong hands.

I tilt my head back and do everything I can to stop myself from leaning into his touch. Knox finishes and places a kiss where my neck meets my shoulder, right over the runes there. His lips coax out the faintest moan, and when I turn around to thank him for his help, he smiles wolfishly at me. I look over at Sabin and fix him with a glare.

"You told them about the magic tornado that happens when my runes are touched, didn't you?"

"Uh, was that supposed to be a secret?" he asks innocently.

"Not cool, Captain, not cool at all," I admonish him, trying to look serious and not at all amused.

"You look incredible," he tells me, and all of the guys voice their approval and agreement.

I give them a big smile, and then I take a deep breath, steeling myself for whatever's about to go down.

"Alright, let's do this," I announce, and we all make our way downstairs.

Lachlan and his coven congregate in the living room, and my guys gather around me like they're guarding me against anything that might come our way. I've strapped back on all the armor I had been shedding since I moved here, and my demeanor is hard and unyielding.

I observe several looks of surprise from Lachlan's coven when they take in *the boys* all dressed in white as they surround me the way that they are, but no one says anything.

Lachlan moves toward me and starts to say something, but he's interrupted when a man I have never seen before walks into the living room from the kitchen.

"Reader Tearson is ready; please follow me."

He takes all of us to a closed door that doesn't lead to a linen closet like I thought it did.

"The casters who will serve as witnesses will enter first. Once they are arranged, the door will open again, and that is when you will enter." The stranger looks to me, and I nod in understanding.

The door opens on its own and reveals a dimly lit hallway. Lachlan steps toward the new opening, but my voice stops him.

"I don't want them there," I announce, and the robed assistant turns to me, a questioning look on his face. "I don't trust them, and I don't want them in the reading."

Lachlan opens his mouth to say something I'm sure is going to piss me off, but the robed caster holds up a hand and stops him.

"Vinna, as he is your blood, it is customary for him and his coven to be present for your reading. However, I will not dismiss your feelings. I will ask that Reader Tearson place a binding upon the ceremony so that nothing can be discussed without your permission or presence once the reading is complete."

He looks at me silently for a moment, and I nod my head in agreement with his compromise. Aydin's gaze is burning a hole in me, but I refuse to look at him or any of the others.

The robed caster leads the paladin into the hallway, and my guys all hug me before walking in after them. The door closes behind Ryker as he gives me a reassuring smile, and I suddenly find myself alone. I feel apprehensive and restless, as I wait—what feels like forever—for the door to open again. In reality, it's probably only five minutes before it cracks open on its own, and I step through.

The hallway and floor are comprised of gray stone, and the coldness of it seeps into me through my bare feet. Soft gas-lit lanterns guide my way, and they create an old and eerie feel to the space surrounding me. The hallway opens up into a large dimly lit stone room. Traces of residual magic surround me, and I get the feeling that the stones comprising this room are old and have witnessed more than I could ever know.

The paladin and the guys all stand around the edges of the room, still and staring straight ahead. There's a marble table with two chairs in the center, and on the far side of the table stands an elderly caster dressed in a red ceremonial robe. Reader Tearson's kind eyes are taking in every move that I make toward him, and I find it interesting and unsettling all at the same time.

He reaches out to me, and I automatically offer my hand in greeting. Instead of shaking it, like I thought he was going to do, he bends and brings his forehead down to the knuckles of my hand and then places a kiss on them.

Taken aback and not sure what the hell to do now, I just stand there.

"Sentinel, *Your Greatness*, I can't begin to describe how elated I am to meet you."

36

Ten heads snap to where we're standing, but I stay focused on this man who's still bent worshipfully over my hand. I set my other hand on his shoulder, hoping he'll stand up and explain what the hell he's talking about, and thank fuck it seems to work.

"Forgive me, Your Greatness. I'm sure I'm confusing you, please sit and allow me to explain."

We separate, and the stranger that guided everyone into this room steps away from the wall and bows to me before he pulls my chair out. He looks at me, awe and warmth radiating from him, and smiles.

"I beg your pardon for taking so long to get to you. As soon as I was made aware of your discovery, I started making all the necessary arrangements on your behalf. It took longer than I had hoped, but I think you will be pleased with everything once you understand."

I try to keep the *what the fuck are you talking about* look from my face and nod, offering him a small smile. Reader Tearson beams at me and clasps his hands together.

"Your Greatness, you are not simply a caster, but we

suspect the last of the line of *Sentinels*." He pauses dramatically, and I stare back at him blankly. Not deterred by my lack of reaction, he continues excitedly.

"It was thought that the Sentinels died out almost a thousand years ago, yet here you are, proving how wrong we were. But I'm getting ahead of myself; let me start at the beginning. Sentinels were caster royalty. They had stronger, more gifted magic, and therefore, they ruled over and protected the caster race since the first spark of magic.

"Unfortunately, over time their power and skills were coveted by many outside and inside the caster ranks, and they were brutally and systematically hunted, used, and often murdered for that power. Diminishing numbers made it difficult to maintain Sentinel rule, and ultimately the royal family stepped down and went into hiding.

"A select line of Readers were tasked with assisting and chronicling the family tree of the Sentinels, and Reader Conlin and I come from that line," Tearson explains as he gestures to the robed man who pulled out my chair.

"I have brought scans of some ancient texts from our archives in Europe that will offer greater detail and understanding about your history. I have put all of your family accounts into your name, and I will ensure you have access to all of it before I leave here at the conclusion of your reading."

I stare at him dumbfounded.

"It is beyond an honor to meet you. I never thought I would be blessed with such a gift as meeting the last Sentinel. My ancestors continued to pass down the knowledge, regardless of the loss of contact. They also maintained the inheritance in the hopes that some Sentinels survived in hiding and would someday reappear, and here you are."

Reader Tearson claps his hands excitedly, and his eyes well with tears.

"And you've already selected some Chosen I see." He runs his hand over the runes on my ring finger.

My eyes get even wider. "What does that mean?" I ask shakily, as I look down at the runes on my hands.

"It is one of the rare things that set Sentinels apart. When you find a compatible mate, your magic will mark them. This allows you to build the necessary connection that will be required to complete the transferal. Which happens when you bind yourself and your magic to them."

I stare at him for a minute before I admit, "I don't understand."

Tearson takes my hand in his and pats it affectionately.

"You see, when you bind yourself to your Chosen mate, you will bestow your runes and your magic onto them. When the binding is complete, they will have identical runes and abilities as you have. A Sentinel's ability to transfer their magic is one of their most coveted gifts."

Stunned, my eyes find the guys. I'm not sure what to think about this. I knew that marking them was a big deal and that it connected us in an unusual way, but this is on a whole other level of intensity.

"Don't fret, Your Greatness, your magic would not have marked a caster unworthy of your gift. It is a great honor to be Chosen. Multiply that infinitely, to be marked as Chosen to the last known Sentinel in history."

Reader Tearson's claims of infinite honor go in one ear and right out the other. The guys and I were just starting this whole relationship thing out. Now they're permanently bound to me whether they like it or not. *Nice, Vinna, way to skip a shit ton of steps when it comes to dating and relationships. Fuck!*

Oblivious to my distress and internal berating, Reader Tearson continues.

"I've only seen documentation of two mate runes on a

Sentinel, but from the look of things, you have five Chosen, is that right?" Tearson asks me.

"How do you know?" I query, surprised.

"This rune represents you," he points to the eight-pointed star on my finger. "Each of the other runes represents a Chosen. Each Chosen will have his rune directly underneath yours in the markings on his body. With your permission, I'd like to document your runes, as well as the runes of your Chosen before we leave. They need to be added to the archives, for posterity's sake."

Out of the corner of my eye, I see a couple of the boys looking over the runes on their hands.

"You'd have to ask them if they'd be comfortable with that," I answer absently.

"Of course. Well, I'm sure you're eager to start the reading. With Sentinels it's done a little differently than it is with casters. This will be the first time I've done this type of reading, so I beg your patience. Reader Conlin is my successor, so he will be assisting and taking note of everything as we go."

I look over to the other man, and he bows his head to me again.

"Typically, from what I understand, there are usually other Sentinels available to help the young interpret their runes and what they do. Being that this is not the case for you, it might be easiest if I go through a checklist of possibilities, and you can indicate any qualities or skills that you currently possess."

I look to Lachlan and then quickly away. "Before I tell you what I can do, can you tell me who will have access to this information?"

Tearson offers me a gentle smile. "This information stays within the people in this room and will be documented in archives only select Readers can access. Each of the Readers who have access have sworn blood oaths to protect those secrets."

I nod in understanding.

"Reader Conlin informed me that you wanted a binding placed on this ceremony. I have already started it, and when your reading is over, I will seal it. That will keep the people in this room from speaking freely to anyone but each other or you about anything they've witnessed or heard."

Reader Conlin hands Reader Tearson a list, and he proceeds to go through it, marking down the abilities that I indicate I have. About a third into the list, it becomes clear from the looks on both Readers' faces that I can do more than the average Sentinel.

"Just to confirm I have this correctly, you can: mimic most anything you see, increase your speed and strength, increase your hearing, land and avoid sustaining injury when you jump from great heights, siphon and alter another caster's magic, and you have an innate ability to fight and defend yourself. Anything else?" Reader Conlin asks.

Someone in the room scoffs, but I ignore it as I shake my head no.

"And over what time frame did your runes begin to appear?" Conlin asks me.

"I think from start to finish it was maybe forty minutes," I explain.

"Forty minutes for each one, but over what period of time?"

Taking in my confused look, Tearson further elaborates. "How many months did it take from your first rune until you got your last rune?"

"Um, they all showed up at the same time. I think it took

about forty minutes from start to finish, but I wasn't exactly keeping track of time due to all the excruciating pain I was experiencing at the moment. It started sometime around three in the morning on my sixteenth birthday. I haven't gotten any new runes since then, until the other day when I received my...Chosen marks." It feels really weird to call them that.

Both Readers stare at me, openmouthed, and I look back and forth between their displays of shock.

"Is that not normal?" I ask.

"I'd have to do some additional research, but from memory, I'd say your experience is rare," Tearson tells me, and Conlin resumes his frantic writing.

I nod my head, very used to accepting my freakish ways. I'm a freak among nons, among casters, and now among Sentinels, why not?

"Do you need to see my weapons too?" I ask, already moving to stand up.

"Please," Tearson responds, but I can tell he's a little surprised. Do other Sentinels not have weapons? I wonder and then chuckle internally. Well, he's going to be in for quite the surprise then.

I begin to call on my personal arsenal, snickering at the look on the Reader's face as I pull one weapon after another. I lay the sword and staff from my back down first. Then I call on the short swords from my ribs. I set down the bow and a handful of arrows that come from my shoulders. The mace and axe from the back of my thighs are next, and lastly, I summon a couple of throwing knives. I stare at the table now covered in weapons and feel like some medieval assassin who's just disarmed. There are a lot of options, even though I tend to use only a handful of these weapons.

"I also have shields on my arms, legs, and shoulders, but I can't take them off to show you," I tell Tearson and watch as Reader Conlin comes closer to the table, quickly documenting everything that he sees.

A slight movement to my left draws my attention, and I find Lachlan and his coven staring at me. I suddenly feel stupid. What am I thinking, putting my secrets on display like this? Maybe the paladin won't be able to *tell* my secrets to others, but they can still use all of this information against me.

This is exactly what they wanted, to deal with me themselves if need be. I might as well be giving them a roadmap to the ways they could kill me when they decide that's what's best for them. *I'm such an idiot!* With a thought, I call back all of the magic in the weapons, and they disappear in a blink from the table. Reader Conlin makes a noise of surprise and stares at the now empty marble table.

"Sorry, I just realized I've left myself exposed. In my experience, that never works out very well for me," I offer in explanation, my eyes roaming coldly over the paladin.

"Vinna—" Lachlan starts, but a quick look from Reader Tearson silences him.

"You're fine, Your Greatness. Let's move on."

I take my seat, and Reader Tearson proceeds to pull five medium-sized rocks from a velvet bag and place them on the top of his side of the table.

"Each crystal represents a branch of magic. When you're ready, bring one hand up to the table. The crystal you attract represents the kind of magic you possess."

This is it, what everyone has been waiting for. What kind of magic will I have? I thought I'd be super nervous about what will change after I find out, but after the whole *Sentinel and Chosen* bomb, I'm feeling pretty calm.

My hand is steady as I bring it to hover over my side of the table. Three crystals shoot across the surface, stinging my hand with their impact. I squeak, surprised. A fourth crystal moves more slowly across the table before it stops, centimeters shy of my hovering palm. The fifth crystal wiggles, but stays firm in its place on the Reader's side of the table.

Reader Conlin removes the crystals that are attached to my skin like magnets to metal and hands them back to Reader Tearson. His eyes are beaming excitement as he takes the crystals and tells me what this all means.

"You have very strong Offensive, Defensive, and Elemental magic, as well as a strong affinity for Healing magic. I would not be surprised if your Healing magic develops into a very strong affinity with some work. It seems Spell magic, however, will not be your forte."

"Holy shit!" someone exclaims.

Reader Tearson's brow furrows, but he ignores the outburst and begins to place the crystals back into the bag, his focus and huge grin still trained on me.

"You're nothing short of extraordinary, Your Greatness, but I would expect nothing less of the last Sentinel. I'm in awe of everything we've discovered here today."

I smile bashfully at his statement. His reverence and awe feel unearned, and I can't help feeling awkward about it. I try to ignore the praise over my existence and focus on being glad to have some answers finally. I remember him telling me that he has scans from archives that will tell me more about everything I've learned today, and I feel lighter with the realization that I'll have access to more answers as time goes on.

I take a deep breath and look around the room. I've been waiting so long to know what was revealed to me today, but this moment feels somewhat anticlimactic. Maybe I'm in shock, or maybe my anger from what happened earlier is tainting things.

Reader Tearson stands up and walks over to Silva. He

begins to chant slowly, finishing with some unusual hand movements, and then moves to Evrin, repeating the same thing. I assume this is the sealing he was telling me he would do at the end of the reading. I'm relieved that it's now over, and I realize just how drained I feel. Images of my comfy bed flood my mind, and I stifle a yawn.

I still have questions about my parents, among other things, but I'll deal with that tomorrow. I don't think I can process any more information tonight. Reader Tearson finishes the binding and approaches me. He bows again and asks Reader Conlin if there is anything more they need.

He gives a quick shake of his head and then bows to me as well. I'm instructed that we should leave the room in the opposite order that we entered it, so I thank the Readers and then follow the dim lamps back out of the door into the empty hallway.

I know that I should wait and have many of the conversations I'm sure the others are dying to have, but right now, I just want to be alone. I sprint up to my bedroom and lock the door behind me. I strip hurriedly out of the white dress and turn on the tap to fill the tub. I sprinkle bath salts and splash in some bubble bath, and I breathe in the relaxing aroma of lavender as it fills the air around me.

I'm perched naked in the dark on the edge of the huge bathtub when the first knocks sound at my door. I hear a muffled voice, but I can't make out who it is or what they're saying. I ignore them. I toss my hair up into a messy bun and sink into heat and bubbles. I adjust the tap making it even hotter and lay back while the rest of the tub fills.

I'm a Sentinel. The last in a line of hunted and murdered magic users. I have a ton of unusual abilities, and I've forced five guys into a permanent magical connection with me whether they like it or not. I possess affinities for four of the five branches of magic, and the only family I have in this world either wants to use me or kill me.

Fuck.

I never thought I'd see the day when being an unwanted, homeless teenager that fights for a living seemed like a simpler way of life.

37

I pause at the top of the stairs, hearing voices coming from Bastien's room. I knock lightly on his door and follow the shout to come in. Bastien is sitting on his bed, and his face morphs into a heart-stopping smile when he sees it's me who's knocking.

"I wondered when you'd resurface," he teases.

I give him an apologetic smile. "Yeah, I just wanted some time to...you know...deal, I guess," I offer in lame explanation as I walk further into the room.

As soon as I get within reaching distance, Bastien grabs me and pulls me into his lap. I chuckle and settle into him, his closeness soothing some of the anxiety I've been feeling since the reading yesterday.

"Just as long as you know you don't have to *deal* with everything alone," Valen tells me with a comforting smile.

I return it and start looking around Bastien's room. His bed is simple and masculine and sits up against the gray stone wall like mine does. Where I have side tables, he has thick polished wood floating shelves. There's no fireplace like there is in my room. Instead, there is a huge built-in entertainment center with a behemoth TV and different game consoles placed amongst some pictures and other knick-knacks.

A large brown sectional where Knox and Ryker are sitting stretches in front of the entertainment center. By the wall of windows to the right of the bed are two fluffy, cushioned hanging hammock chairs, one of which is occupied by Sabin reading a book.

I shake my head at myself and chuckle humorlessly. Aside from some basic facts like age and the kind of magic he has, I know next to nothing about Bastien or any of them really. I learned more about Sabin when we went riding, but all of this feels so out of order suddenly.

"What's that noise for?" Valen asks from next to me and Bastien on the bed.

"I'm just realizing that I've kissed most of you and forced all of you into a permanent bond with me, but this is the first time I've been in anyone's room. I pretty much know next to nothing about most of you. How fucked up and backward is that?"

Several of them chuckle.

"What's so backward about it? You kicked my ass, found yourself consumed by attraction for my awesome personality—and rock-hard body. You've marked me as your Chosen, and eventually, I'll be turned into a magic weapon wielding, powerful, ultra-cool badass the likes of which the world hasn't seen for almost a thousand years. I'm sure there are tons of stories out there just like ours," Bastien finishes nonchalantly, and I can't help but smile.

"Learning all about each other will come with time, and Bruiser, you're welcome in my room *anytime* you want."

Bastien leans me back in a mock dip, and his smile turns lascivious. He plants a quick kiss on my lips, and I laugh at his playfulness. I needed this. I've been so wrapped up in my head, trying to piece things together and sort through everything I learned yesterday.

I feel completely stressed and overwhelmed. But this, this easy way that I fit with these guys, it soothes me in a way I desperately need right now. He pulls away, and I grab his face for one more slow kiss before letting him sit back.

"I'm sorry about last night," I address all of them. "Valen's right, I don't always have to deal with things alone. It's been my default for my whole life, and I need to recognize that it's not my only option now."

"We get it, no worries," Ryker smiles at me. "The Readers told us to tell you goodbye and that they'll be in touch. They left a folder of documents for you and a tablet."

"Wait, what? They left?" I ask, astounded. "I thought they were here to help me with all of this?" I point to myself.

"Yeah, that's what we thought, too, but Reader Tearson insisted he had to do some research, and Reader Conlin needed to document everything from the reading. They left almost right away."

"Well, shit. I wanted to ask about my parents and about a thousand other things."

"They did leave a contact number, and I think the tablet they left behind has all the information they scanned for you from their archives. That might be a good place to start looking for answers," Sabin reassures me.

Valen pulls me from Bastien's lap and into his own, and a surprised squeak sneaks from my lips. I swat him, and he just smiles at me.

"Your squeaks are adorable, Vinna," Knox teases me.

"I'm not adorable. I'm a terrifying Sentinel, haven't you heard?"

Laughter wafts around the room, and I crawl out of

Valen's lap. As much as I like the manhandling, nosiness is building inside of me, and the pictures scattered about the wall of built-ins are calling to me. I find an adorable picture of the twins when they were younger.

Their wavy curls were much shorter then. But their hazel eyes, cute, little, upturned noses, and pouty lips are still prevalent, but on a smaller scale. I set the picture down and reach for an older looking picture of Silva with a beautiful curly haired woman.

"Is this your mom?" I ask the twins.

They both nod their heads in unison. I stare at the picture and marvel at how beautiful and happy she and Silva were when this moment was captured. I can see her in Bastien and Valen's features. They have her nose and her lips and definitely her beautiful dark curls.

I set the picture down gently and fall back into the mystery I spent a lot of the night trying to unravel. My father, the twins' parents, and their coven, all went missing together. Fifteen months later, give or take a month or two, I was born. My mother was a Sentinel, since that definitely didn't come from my father—Vaughn's side—but how the hell did they end up together?

"How did a whole coven disappear into thin air, while simultaneously discovering a Sentinel that supposedly didn't exist? That Sentinel then gets knocked up, and none of them are ever heard from again. And somehow I end up with Beth?" I ask, still staring at the picture and the happy faces it captures.

"I wish we knew," Valen answers, and I can hear the sadness that's tucked deep in his voice.

I pinch the bridge of my nose, irritated, and no closer to solving this mystery than I was last night. I went over and over everything I could remember about Beth. I searched my memories for any clues that might help me figure out how I ended up with her. She had to know more about my father than she admitted, but how did she get involved in all of this?

Strong hands grip my hips, and I lean back into Knox's chest and let out a frustrated sigh.

"Do you know anything about the nest of lamia they were supposed to be dealing with? They're obviously the missing link in this story," I ask.

"We have names for some of the lamia, but that's been a dead end. The paladin were called in to deal with them because they were abducting casters, but we haven't found any information as to why," Bastien tells me.

"They sent paladin out to look for the missing coven, but the paladin and the lamia disappeared without a single trace," Valen confirms.

Knox pulls me back to the couch, and I plop down next to him. He hooks an arm around me, and I relax into him, lost in my rumination.

"You smell good," I absently tell him as I breathe him in deeply.

I can't place what it is, but it's deep and manly, and I really like it. Knox chuckles and nuzzles the side of my face. It has to be me. Somehow I'm the key to sorting all of this out if I can just figure out how it all fits together.

"Did the abductions stop when the lamia nest and the paladin disappeared?" I ask no one in particular.

"I think so," Bastien replies. "I remember reading that the elders at the time, associated that with the nest either being eradicated or damaged enough to keep them from continuing the way they had been."

"Or the nest accomplished whatever they were aiming for, and the abductions became unnecessary," I say offhandedly.

The room grows quiet as we all seem to fall into our own

thoughts. I'm not sure how long we stay that way before Ryker breaks up the introspection.

"Do you want to go dive into all the documents the Readers left for you, Squeaks? See if we can find anything helpful in there?"

I look at Ryker and raise an eyebrow. "Squeaks?"

His smile is audacious, and his sky-blue eyes have a cheeky twinkle to them. "Yeah, I agree with Knox, all those little noises you make are fucking adorable."

The other guys chortle at his comment.

"You can't give me a nickname that makes me sound like a timid mouse."

"It's already done, Squeaks, and there's nothing you can do about it," he taunts me.

I shake my head and chuckle, looking as passive as possible before I lunge for him. Knox slows me down just enough that Ryker slips away, laughing.

"I'll show you *squeaks*," I playfully threaten, while trying halfheartedly to get out of Knox's hold.

"Just wait until we both have the same runes, and we'll see who roughs up who then," Ryker counters with a wink, and settles into the hammock chair next to Sabin.

My playful smile slips. "Shit, we need to talk about that, don't we?" I ask, looking at each of them.

Sabin surprises me by saying, "Not really."

I stare at him stupefied.

"It doesn't change anything. We all wanted things to move forward with you. We wouldn't have wanted that unless we saw a future with you."

"I thought you were the poster boy for wanting things to go slow?" I ask Sabin.

"There's nothing saying that we need to bind tomorrow, we can still go at our own pace. It's a non-issue."

Sabin's relaxed attitude astonishes me. I know we talked about things when we went riding, but I'm still a little bewildered by this accepting reaction.

"The issue is that being with me is setting you up for an uncertain future. Did you not hear the same history lesson I did about Sentinels involving death, death, and more death?" I point out.

"We're going to be paladin, Vinna; that in itself invited risk and danger into our future. Being bound to you doesn't change that," Valen reminds me.

"You already knew how I felt about things. I'm in. I want you, and I'm fucking excited for the new abilities and magic. The sooner you want to solidify things the better, in my book." Knox gives me a dirty smile and suggestively waggles his eyebrows. I don't fight the huge smile that takes over my face.

"You guys aren't freaked out about this at all?" I ask, fishing for reassurance.

They all shake their heads no and look at me like *what's the big deal?*

"Does it freak you out?" Ryker asks me.

His question makes me pause for a minute. I've been worried about them and what all of this meant for their future. I haven't even thought about my take on it all.

"I don't like the reality that I'll be making you targets by being with you. But giving you amped-up abilities that will help you deal with that is reassuring. I guess I'm just worried if all of you are really okay with this. One minute we're just deciding to give a relationship a go, and now you're stuck with me." I cringe as the words leave my mouth, terrified that one of them will agree with the *stuck* sentiment.

"Vinna, you're so cute when you're clueless," Knox teases

and starts to tickle me. I quickly scramble away from the delicious torture and shoot a playful glare his way.

"So Reader documents?" Ryker asks me, repeating his unanswered question.

I huff, not really wanting to deal with it today. "I vote for tackling those tomorrow. Let's do something normal today, something fun," I propose.

"You want to stay in the house or get out?" Bastien queries.

"As long as it's safe to go out, let's go out."

They all become thoughtful.

"Dancing?" Knox throws out there.

Five heads look to me.

"Dancing," I agree excited.

* * *

The name *The Black Hat* is lit up in deep purple lights above a small warehouse. From outside I don't hear any music or noises that would have anyone believing it was anything but empty inside. I stare at the building questioningly, but the guys insist it's a pub that turns club on select nights.

The doorman motions us through, and I feel the static of a magical barrier press against my skin. Sound slams into me like a freight train after we cross through it. We stand at the entrance for a moment, letting our eyes adjust to the dimness, and I look around.

The inside is polished concrete, metal, wood; it has a very industrial chic vibe to it. There's a long bar to the left, and straight ahead toward the back is a mass of undulating bodies that are moving to the hypnotic rhythm that's being pumped into the warehouse.

"What do you want to drink?" Sabin asks me, his palm

settled on my lower back, guiding me through the crowd of bodies to the bar.

"Water and a Coke maybe," I tell him, shouting close to his ear over the noise.

He nods and breaks away from us, and Knox moves up to take Sabin's place at my side. I tilt my head in admiration as I watch Sabin navigate away from us toward the bar. The strong muscles of his back are visible through the dark gray V-neck he's wearing. His black skinny jeans show off his powerful legs and his scrumptious ass.

I'm guided past the bar to a dark booth in the back corner. We all slide in, and Ryker places his arm behind me on the back of the booth cushion. It feels territorial, and I like it.

"Did I mention already how incredible you look tonight?" Knox tells me, his mouth close to my ear, heat in his deep gray eyes and in his tone.

I laugh quietly. "You may have mentioned it fifty or so times already." I smile teasingly at him.

He runs a finger over the high neckline of the bright red sleeveless bodycon dress I'm wearing. I'm not showing a lot of skin. The dress has a crew neck and a hem that drops a couple of inches below my knees. But it hugs every inch that it covers like a second skin, and I feel sexy and confident.

I have a bright red lip stain that draws extra attention to my wasp-stung lips, and my go-to soft curls are in full effect. From the minute I stepped off the stairs in the house until now, the guys have been very vocal about their appreciation for how I look tonight. I'm loving each of their subtle and not so subtle touches and looks that scream sex and possession.

I can't fault them when I find myself feeling the same way. Each of them looks downright delectable in their various versions of t-shirts and jeans. They all know how to dress to accentuate their gorgeous physiques and mind-numbing good looks.

Each time I interact with any of them, I have to talk myself down from attacking like a starving animal on easy prey. I wipe the corner of my mouth for the thousandth time, double checking that there's no drool. Maybe it's the club atmosphere, the dim lighting, and the vibrating bass of the music that I can feel in my bones, creating a surge in my desire.

Or maybe I'll always get like this when I'm near my Chosen. It feels weird to think of them that way, but something primal in me, in my magic, demands that I recognize that they are in fact, my Chosen.

Sabin arrives at the booth, sliding over a bottle of water and a Coke to me, and then hands out beers to the guys. We all settle in and absorb the atmosphere while we sip our drinks. Kiiara's "Gold" pumps through the speakers, calling to me, and I nudge Ryker and Valen, signaling that I want to get out of the booth.

"Who's dancing?" I shout over my shoulder, and I don't wait for an answer before I'm moving toward the packed dance floor.

I squeeze through and find a perfect spot, and my hips and body move to the sensual rhythm. I smile when all of my guys surround me. I didn't figure they'd all be into dancing, but what's even more shocking is they can all *move*.

I'm loving every minute of this as we get lost in the beat of the music. Songs flow from one into another, and we dance without a care in the world right now. I glide to and from each of the guys in seamless choreography that has us pressed against each other.

Our bodies communicate in a way that's sensual and consuming. Hands glide over hips, asses, backs, shoulders, and stomachs. Mouths caress ears as sweet seductions are whispered, and I lose myself in their touch and movements.

A new song takes over that has everyone jumping around like maniacs. We join in, and I'm laughing so hard at the antics and silly faces the guys are making that I can barely stand straight. I have no idea how long we've been dancing.

I'm clammy and thirsty, and I signal the universal sign for *drink* to the boys and make my way out of the horde of sweaty, dancing bodies. I collapse into the cushions of our booth, and Knox and Bastien sandwich me into the middle.

Ryker and Valen volunteer to hit up the bar again, and disappear back into the throng of people. Sabin flicks a switch on the outside of the booth, and a glorious breeze begins to circulate over our table. I look up to find a fan, and I close my eyes and lift my hair off the back of my neck, relishing in the cool breeze.

"That feels like heaven." I moan leaning back into the booth.

"You're an amazing dancer, Bruiser."

"Me, what about you guys? Do you moonlight as part of the Magic Mike crew or something?"

They laugh.

"You can thank Knox for that; he taught us all how to not look like complete idiots on a dance floor," Sabin admits.

I look to Knox's beaming smile. "It wasn't that hard; they all have rhythm," he dismisses as his hand skims up my thigh.

Valen and Ryker appear out of the crowd, and as soon as they hand me a bottle of water, I chug it down. I finish the last drop, still thirsty, and Ryker hands me his water with a chuckle. I stretch across the table and give him a quick peck. Valen hands me a Coke and sits down next to Sabin.

"Did you want something else to drink, Bruiser? A beer or something?" Bastien asks me.

"Um, I've never really had alcohol before, so I wouldn't even know where to start."

"What, no school parties or sneaking liquor from the liquor cabinet of your friend's parents?" Valen teases me.

I roll my eyes.

"Beth never kept us in one place for long, and by the time parties were an option, I didn't know anyone well enough to get invited. No friends equals no parties and no parents' liquor cabinets to raid." I explain.

"What about when you turned twenty-one? No all-nighter of binge drinking for you?" Ryker asks.

"I had a fight that night." I shrug again.

"Here, try this, tell us what you think."

Bastien hands me his beer. I sniff it, not overly impressed with the scent, but I tilt back the bottle and swallow a sip.

"Gahhh," I announce and make a face. "It tastes worse than it smells!"

The boys burst into laughter, and I wipe my tongue with my hand before I remember that Valen brought me a Coke. I take a huge swig of the sweet soda and try to banish the gross beer taste from my mouth.

"Why would you pay to torture your taste buds like that?" I ask, and the boys laugh even harder.

Bastien and Knox clink bottles and drink deeply from their long necks. I notice they're both drinking the same kind of beer, and I worry for their palates. Ryker hands me his bottle and encourages me to have a sip.

"I'm not falling for that again," I tell him and slide it back across the table to him.

Ryker chuckles. "It's ginger beer. The flavor is sweeter than the stuff they drink," he tells me, jerking his chin toward Bastien and Knox.

I eye him warily but accept the bottle he hands me. I smell it, and it's not bad, but that doesn't necessarily mean anything. I take a hesitant sip, surprised when the flavor is actually nice. It's a little tart, but there is a subtle sweetness, too, and that same fizzy quality that Bastien's beer had. I put the bottle back to my lips and take a bigger sip.

"It's good," I concede, handing the bottle back to Ryker.

I try Valen's and Sabin's beers, too, but in the end, the ginger beer is the only one I like.

Ryker slips out of the booth—I suspect on the hunt for a bottle of ginger beer—and I sit back and listen to the guys' banter, and let the fan cool me down.

"You guys come here a lot?" I ask as I try to picture them here on their own. They can all dance, but somehow I don't get the impression that clubbing is exactly their scene.

"Not really. We've probably been a handful of times over the years, but it's not a regular hang out for us. I just thought you might like getting dressed up and letting loose for a bit," Knox tells me.

"Good call, my Chosen," I tease him, and he gives me a wink.

"So if this isn't a regular hang out, what is?"

They seem to think about it for a minute.

"It sounds kind of lame, but honestly we hang the most at our home," Bastien tells me.

"It has everything: billiards, basketball, movies, a pool, and a gym. We go to the occasional party, and we love to do stuff outdoors, but that's about it," Valen adds.

"We sound kind of boring," Knox chuckles.

"Please, all I used to do was train, read, fight, and train some more. These past few weeks are the most fun I've ever had!"

My admission brings big smiles to each of their faces, and Knox gives me a squeeze on my thigh where his hand rests. Ryker walks back over and passes out new drinks to everyone. He hands me two bottles. One is the beer I liked, and the other he explains is a mixed berry hard cider. I try the cider first, and it's fucking delicious.

"A drink in each hand already, Bruiser; we're corrupting you faster than I thought."

I laugh and raise both bottles in salute.

"Toast!" Valen demands.

The guys heckle each other, and after a few shoulder punches, Bastien relents.

"Alright, alright, I've got one..." Bastien announces. "To corrupting lost royalty, bumping and grinding on and off the dance floor, and to having the best time of our lives!"

He raises his bottle and shouts of *fuck yeah* drown out the clinking of glass and laughter as we all cheers and drink in solidarity. We all fall into easy shouted conversations about nothing and everything while we laugh, tease, and drink.

I feel eyes on me, and my gaze wanders from the table, looking for the source. I land on a pair of fixed brown eyes that belong to a large blond man, who stares for a beat longer before he looks away. I dismiss it, but something about him reminds me of Talon's crew.

He always seemed to be surrounded by big Viking warrior types, and this man fits that description to a T. I shake myself out of my thoughts and tune back into what the guys are saying. I'm almost finished with my cider when Knox grabs my hand and starts pulling me from the booth.

He leads me back amongst the dancers. Knox expertly spins me away from him and then brings me back into his arms, my back to his chest. I laugh and press into his hands as they grip my hips. None of the other guys join us this time; it's just me and Knox wrapped up in the tempo and each other.

He twines his fingers in mine, raising our clasped hands above my head. I move with him, our bodies in sync, and I close my eyes and focus on the feel of him against me. His lips caress my neck and then settle next to my ear. He's singing the lyrics of the song to me, and I smile and lean into his mouth and his sultry voice.

His hands skim down my sides and find their way back to my hips, and I reach back and run my fingers down the back of his black buzzed hair. I twist in Knox's arms until we're dancing chest to chest. I hook my index fingers in the belt loops of his jeans and take in his gorgeous face.

Knox brushes his thumb over my lips, and I smile against the pressure of his thumb on my mouth. He bends over, and our bodies slow against each other as he presses his lips against mine. I open, wanting more from his kiss, and he sweeps in and completely enthralls me.

He tastes faintly of the beer he was drinking, and even though I didn't like it from the bottle, I like the taste of it on his tongue. His mouth moves against mine in a dance as perfect as the one our bodies are wrapped up in. His kiss is skillful, and I'm easily and happily lost in it.

Knox stops but doesn't pull his face away. His lips barely graze mine, as he sings more lyrics of the song against my kiss-swollen, smiling lips. Fuck, Bastien was right. Knox really could sing any woman out of their panties. I'm sure as hell ready to throw mine at him.

Knox tilts my head and moves his mouth to the shell of my ear.

"Enoch Cleary is watching you."

Knox pulls back, and it takes me a minute to connect what he's saying.

"What? Where?" I stammer out.

Knox spins me again, giving me the ability to look around without being obvious.

"That was an epic super sneaky spy move," I confess, and I lean in for a soft kiss.

We dance and kiss for a couple more songs, and Knox's gaze keeps flitting from me to the space behind me, where Enoch was standing with his coven. The feel of eyes on me and Knox's distraction is starting to suck the fun out of this.

"Let's go find the others," I prompt. "I don't think the Clearys are fans of me, and I don't want any problems."

Knox scoffs. "He's not looking at you like he has a problem with you. I'd say it's more the exact opposite."

Knox gives me a quick peck and starts to lead me out of the crowd. His comment baffles me, and my gaze wanders over to Enoch as I try to figure out what Knox is talking about. I stop suddenly, stupefied. Behind Enoch are a pair of familiar eyes set in a face I'd know anywhere.

What the fuck is Talon doing here? Frozen in place, my hand pulls free from Knox's grasp, and he turns to find out why. Someone steps in front of me, blocking my view, and I sidestep to get past them. When my line of sight is clear again, it's not Talon standing behind Enoch but that same blonde guy I saw earlier. I shake my head to clear it, but when I look up and around, there's no Talon to be found.

"What's wrong?" Knox asks, tilting my chin in his direction.

I look in his eyes as I try to piece together what just happened. I felt sure of my recognition, but that doesn't make sense. Talon wouldn't be here.

"Nothing. I thought I saw someone I knew, but it was just my eyes playing tricks on me," I tell him and follow the tug of his hand back to the booth.

"What's wrong, Bruiser?" Bastien asks me, observing the look of confusion I still have on my face.

"Nothing, apparently two drinks and Knox's kissing abilities have addled my brain," I say absently and then laugh, shaking off what just happened.

"Awww, Squeaks, you're a lightweight," Ryker teases me.

I cuddle into his side when he puts an arm around me.

"Maybe I need to eat or something," I add offhandedly.

"Good call, Bruiser. I'm starving. Halliwell's?" Bastien asks the others, as he slides out of the booth. "Halliwell's!" they all chorus back, and we make our way to the exit.

38

The house is unsurprisingly quiet when I make my way downstairs. The guys and I were out until early this morning, and they're probably still sleeping. I would be too if I wasn't starving. It's mid-afternoon, but past the usual lunch time, so I'm startled to find the paladin in the kitchen, eating when I walk in.

I haven't seen any of them since the reading, and I'm tempted to back up and leave, but my stomach rumbles, begging me not to. Adelaide quickly fixes me up a plate and hands it over with a small smile to counteract the somber atmosphere of the kitchen. I take it into the dining room, away from where the paladin are all eating at the kitchen island.

I get halfway through my sandwich when the chair next to me is pulled out, and Aydin sits down. Several other chairs groan their protest as they're pulled away from the table and suddenly occupied. I keep my eyes on my plate and focus on eating.

The longer the paladin stay quiet as their heavy presence surrounds me, the more I start to seethe. I push my plate away and sit back in my chair, crossing my arms over my chest. I give each of them a cold, hard stare and wait. Eventually Keegan finds his balls and speaks up.

"We fucked up, Vinna. There's no way around it, and none of us want to make excuses for what happened."

I say nothing for a while. I just continue to stare at them. At this point, I don't know what I'm hoping they will say. Honestly, I can't imagine any words that could repair the damage that's already been done.

"I fell for it all, the promises of protection and acceptance, the vows to treat me like family, like I was wanted here. But it's all bullshit. You've been watching me this whole time, and for what? Waiting to see if I'd turn on you, take you out? Or were you just hoping I was malleable and could be twisted in any way that you saw fit?"

I turn my gaze to Aydin, searing him with my betrayal and anger.

"Did you fight with me because you enjoyed it and it bonded us? Or were you sizing me up, letting me teach you my tricks so you'd be better prepared to deal with me when the time came?"

"It wasn't like that Little Badass—"

I scoff and shake my head, interrupting him. I'm not going to believe anything he has to say now. They've all broken my trust.

"I don't know how to reconcile what I thought I knew about each of you with what you showed me before the reading. I guess not you, *Uncle*..." I speak the word with cold sarcasm.

"You've been clear all along about how unwanted I was, so I shouldn't be shocked. But the rest of you"—I laugh humorlessly, shaking my head—"I thought Beth was bad, but at least she was always honest about how much of a piece of shit she thought I was. There were no shopping trips or promises that things would get better. There was no pretending like I mattered or deserved to be cared for. Beth never lied about how welcome I was. I always knew exactly where I stood with her. I'd take that over your lies any day."

Lachlan flinches at my comment, and my first instinct is to feel bad. That thought alone enrages me. I push my chair away from the table, ready to leave. Aydin's hand shoots out and grabs my wrist to stop me.

"Don't touch me," I warn venomously.

"Vinna, please hear us out," he begs and immediately pulls his hand back.

I stand silent as I stare at the wood of the table and try to calm my rage.

"I've spent all night beating myself up for letting this happen. I was desperate for acceptance, for answers. I clearly made all of this more than it was. The truth is we don't know each other, and I'm not owed anything..."

I look from the table up to Lachlan.

"We share blood, but that doesn't connect us. It doesn't make us anything more than the strangers we are." My eyes move from Lachlan and settle on each of them as I fall silent.

"Give us another chance," Keegan tells me softly, his tone hopeful.

"Why? Why should I do that?"

"Because we're family, and that's what family does."

"Family?" I snicker humorlessly. "I don't even know what that word means, Keegan. I never have. All that word has ever done for me is beat me down like I was less than nothing and then throw me away. So what the fuck am I supposed to do with that?" I ask him.

"Then let us teach you what it really means," Aydin reassures me.

"I was trying to, but all you've taught me so far is that none of you are worthy of my time, because none of you really give a fuck about me. You all think you're so much better than Beth because you don't beat me like she did, but you're not. You still treat me like I'm nothing."

I look at Aydin. "Or worse, convince me that I'm something to you when you know it's all a lie." My eyes fall on Lachlan. "And just like Beth, you're ready to throw me away when it's convenient for you. Or I should say, whenever you deem me *too much of a fucking threat*."

I feel gutted. The hurt and betrayal are fresh and festering.

"I'm done. I'm leaving. All of you just stay the fuck away from me."

"Leaving is not an option, Vinna, you are claimed and underage," Lachlan declares, and I can feel his rising anger.

"Just try to fucking stop me. You think you know what I'm capable of? You have no fucking clue."

"Vinna, you can't just walk away from being a caster," Silva tells me.

"I'm not. I'm walking away from all of you and this fucked up coven you want to pretend could ever be my family."

"You are not leaving!" Lachlan slams his hands on the table and stands up squaring off with me.

Here we go. Magic sparks awake inside of me, and I ready myself.

"Lachlan!" Birdie yells as she stomps into the dining room, Lila and Adelaide close on her heels. "What are you doing? We've given you time to work through how difficult all of this is for you, but enough is enough! What are you hoping to accomplish behaving this way with her?"

I expect Lachlan to rage at her like he does with me, but he drops his gaze guiltily.

"What if it were you? What if you disappeared and

Vaughn discovered your daughter? Would this be what you'd hope for her?" Adelaide asks lovingly.

"It should be him here, not her!" Lachlan bellows, a tear sliding down his face, and his admission breaks something in me.

"Well, it fucking isn't. You selfish piece of shit. You think I asked for this, any of this?" I scream at him.

"Neither did I!" he yells back.

"Yeah, but the difference between you and me is that I've made the best I possibly could with the shit I've been given. All you do is pout, feeling sorry for yourself, and destroy the only connection you have to your brother. You'd rather have him here than me, and now you have neither!"

"Vinna, he's just hurting—"

"Who isn't, Keegan? How much longer are you going to sit with blinders on and let me get crushed under the weight of his pain? Why am I so easy to sacrifice? You liars want to pretend I can be family. But you sit by, over and over again, and watch him try to *break me*!"

I leave, my hands shaking from the adrenaline and magic coursing through my body. No one tries to stop me. No one says a word. I pull my spare keys off the ring in the garage and jump into the Jeep. I fidget impatiently, waiting for the garage door to open when someone pulls on the handle of my door.

I look over to find Aydin's pleading face. I stare at him hollowly as he tries to say something, but I'm backing out of the garage and barreling away from the house before I can make sense of his shouts.

I don't know where I'm going. The fucked up reality is that I don't have anywhere to go. I drive with no destination as I race in a random direction, speeding to get away as fast as I can. I drive and seethe for who knows how long until everything inside of me feels empty, and everything outside of me becomes unfamiliar.

The tingling staticky feeling of a barrier washes over me, and I realize I've left the Solace boundary. I start to slow down so that I can turn around when my steering wheel suddenly jerks and the Jeep starts to shudder. I wrestle it over to the side of the road and climb out in search of the cause. My back wheel is mangled. Shredded pieces of tread trail from the Jeep back to the road.

"MOTHERFUCKER!" I shout out to the sky and stupidly kick the offending tire.

I run my hands through my hair and look around like the solution to all my problems is in the trees. I'm pretty sure they're laughing at me as they bear witness to the horrible luck I'm having.

I'm standing on the side of the road in short cotton shorts and a tank top. I don't have my phone or wallet. I don't even have shoes on. I chuckle humorlessly at my stupidity. Well, I've never changed a tire. Hopefully it's not that hard, I muse, pissed off.

I dig around in the back until I find all the tools I think are necessary. I make my way to the tire and sit down in front of it. I'm at the perfect angle to clearly see my front tire slowly but steadily deflating as I loosen the lug nuts on the back tire.

Fuck! I press my forehead against the mangled rubber. One flat I can try to tackle, but I don't have two spare tires. I get up, brush my ass off and rehome the tools. I lock up the Jeep, and I start walking.

* * *

The blacktop of the road is warm on my feet, and a soft breeze has my hair tickling my back and shoulders. I've been walking for a little while, replaying the harsh words that the paladin and I traded hours ago. I've been cementing my resolve and filling in the details of what I'm going to do now when the steady thrum of a car sounds from somewhere behind me.

I stick out my arm, thumb up, in the universal sign of *I need a ride*. A Range Rover materializes in the distance, and my nerves and adrenaline start fluttering around at the thought of one of the paladin being behind the wheel.

The vehicle gets closer and starts to slow. It comes to a stop perfectly parallel to me, and I hold my breath as the passenger window rolls down. I curse in my head when the absence of the tinted barrier doesn't reveal a paladin, but Enoch Cleary.

"Are you okay? What are you doing all the way out here?" Enoch asks, speaking across the dark-haired guy sitting in the passenger seat.

"Um, my car has two flat tires." I point behind me in the direction I've been walking from.

"Was it that Jeep just outside the boundary?" the dark-haired passenger asks. "What'd you run over?"

"Yeah, and I have no idea," I answer flatly, cursing my luck that theirs is the only vehicle that's passed me since I started the trek back to civilization.

"Nash, move to the back. We can take you home," Enoch tells me.

I scoff, and I'm not sure if it's from his use of the word *home* or that this group of casters is offering to help me. Nash opens the door and slides out. He's tall and fit and the opposite of Enoch in coloring. His hair is black and his skin fair. His eyes, I notice, are deep dark blue as they roam down my underdressed body to my bare feet.

He steps away from the now open door and offers me a hand like some gallant gentleman helping a woman into a carriage. I look around me, silently begging the universe to send another vehicle this way, so I don't have to accept Enoch's help.

No other car magically appears, so I force myself to walk past Nash's open hand and climb into the passenger seat. He chuckles at my obvious dismissal of his chivalry and waits until I buckle myself in before he closes my door and then squeezes into the back seat where two other guys are already sitting.

"Where are your shoes?" Enoch asks me, his eyes on my bare feet.

"I forgot them."

He's quiet for a minute. "Forgot them in your car or somewhere else?"

"I was in a hurry when I left."

Enoch seems bothered by my confession as he presses the gas and navigates smoothly back onto the road.

"So why the hurry, where were you going?" A Jared Leto look-alike from the back seat asks me.

"Why do you care?"

He raises his arms in surrender. "Whoa, I was only curious why you're out in the middle of nowhere with no shoes, bag, or phone?"

"Trouble at home?" the observant Nash queries.

I scoff again. Apparently, that is the noise I'm now going to make any time someone speaks the word *home* around me.

"Trouble would be an understatement," I mumble quietly to myself, as I focus on the road in front of me.

"What's going on?" Enoch questions, picking up on my quiet grumbling.

"What makes you think I would tell you?"

Enoch releases a deep sigh and drums a rhythm on the steering wheel. "I think you have the wrong impression about us, Ms. Aylin."

"I wonder how that happened, Mr. Cleary?" I mock his overly polite cadence.

"We've never laid a hand on the shifters," Jared Leto look-alike defends.

"Maybe, but I watched you sit back and allow it to happen, and it clearly wasn't the first time."

Enoch brakes at a stop sign and turns to me, about to say something, but he gets cut off.

"It's not our place to step in," Nash mumbles.

I turn around and scowl at him. I'm ready to explain all the ways that I think his comment is bullshit, but a big SUV is coming up behind us, and they don't look like they're going to stop. I barely have time to shout out a warning before they plow into us from behind.

I jerk back and then sideways, completely askew as Enoch's SUV jerks to a stop. Everyone inside is cursing and taking stock of themselves.

"Is everyone o—"

Before Enoch can finish his question, something plows into us hard and fast on the back driver's side of the car. We start spinning like we're on the teacup ride from hell, and my head smashes back against the window. I can't do anything as we're thrown around, and I'm jerked every which way amid the sounds of crunching metal and breaking glass. The side of my head takes another hit from somewhere, and the world around me blinks to black.

39

A shout jerks me from unconsciousness, and I come to, disoriented and hurting. My chin rests sticky against my chest, and pain shoots through my neck and head when I try to lift it. I squeeze my eyes closed and try to fend off a throbbing headache battering my skull.

Another shout has me trying to cover my ears from the assault of the noise, but my hands don't follow my brain's instructions for protection. I jerk my arms again and realize my hands are fastened to something behind me. I move around on what I assume is a chair, and discover my feet are also tethered in place.

Adrenaline and fear slam through me like a tidal wave as it dawns on me how bad this situation is. I don't know if the pain dulls or if I just grow accustomed to it, but I manage to lift my head off of my chest and dizzily try to take in my surroundings. Another shout has me flinching to get away, and I follow the noise to one of the guys from Enoch's back seat, tied in a chair across from me. He's yelling for help which seems counterintuitive to the situation we find ourselves in.

"Shut the fuck up," I grumble to him, and wide, terrified

eyes turn to me. "If you keep yelling, whoever did this is going to come in here. Let's try to put that off as long as possible," I tell him, trying and failing to be more reassuring and less growly.

He nods and thankfully stays quiet as his scared gaze flits all around us. Wherever we are is cool and damp. The moisture in the air adds to the sticky feeling on my skin, and I look down to find that drying blood has turned my gray tank top dark red. I don't feel any trickles anywhere on my body, so it seems wherever most of this came from has thankfully clotted or at least slowed.

The ground beneath my feet is hard packed dirt, and the walls of the room are an aged gray concrete with cracks spidering around the joints. Everyone from Enoch's car is down here tied to a chair. They're disheveled and bruised and showing signs of some injuries from the accident.

We're arranged in a haphazard semicircle, and I can't tell if that's by design or mere coincidence. There's waning natural light in the room, but I can't tell where it's coming from. I try to turn around to see if the source of the light is behind me, but an excruciating pain in my neck and head keeps me from discovering anything.

"Hey..." I whisper to the kid who was shouting.

He looks up, and I can tell how much he's trying to rein in his panic. I give him the softest most comforting smile I can.

"What's your name?"

It seems to take him a moment to register what I'm asking.

"Parker," he whispers.

"Parker, were you awake when we were brought here?" I ask, hoping that he might be able to tell me where we are and who the hell tied us up. He shakes his head, and a sob shudders out of his throat. I give him another reassuring smile.

"It's okay; this is awful, but we're alive and together. I'll get us out of here."

I don't know why I'm making promises I have no idea if I'll be able to keep, but it kills me to see him so terrified.

"I woke up a little while ago. I've been shouting, but no one has come to check on us," Parker quietly tells me, and I nod my head.

My magic bubbles up inside of me, restless and agitated, and I have to stop myself from calling on my runes and cutting myself and the others free. There may not be many opportunities to escape, and I know I need to be smart about this. Patience feels like the best step forward or at least waiting until everyone is conscious so I'm not forced to carry anyone while potentially trying to fight my way out of wherever *here* is.

A groan sounds from Enoch, and I see his head wobble. I watch the moment he realizes he's tied up to a chair and his head jerks up and swivels around taking everything in. Our eyes meet, and I watch relief peculiarly flicker in his eyes.

"What's going on?" he croaks in question.

"I don't know. I woke up not too long ago."

"You're bleeding," he informs me and then starts to struggle against his bindings.

"Quiet!" I hiss at him. "We don't want to bring anyone in here yet."

Enoch stills, but I can see the helpless rage on his face. Something moves slightly in the corner, and my head jerks in that direction. My pain renews its assault, and I instantly regret moving my head so fast. I notice for the first time that something is hanging from the ceiling in the corner.

I squint, trying to force my eyes to work like they

normally do without whatever head injury I'm currently suffering from. I gasp when I gather that it's a person slumped and hanging from a hook in the ceiling by their arms, their back to us. The person is emaciated and filthy, their clothes and skin blend right in with the grays and browns of the room.

Enoch follows my horrified gaze. "What the hell is going on here?"

As if in answer to his question, clunks and clangs sound off in an alcove to my right, and a screech of metal on metal echoes through the room as a door opens. I can see stairs through the now open entryway, and it makes me think we're in a cellar or an old basement. Seven men walk into the damp, dirty space, and a spark of recognition ignites in my head.

The bulky blond from the bar is among them. My eyes are locked on his as he files in and takes his place with the others around the edge of the room. If I had any doubt about who's responsible for our being tied up in this room, the appearance of that blonde guy solves it. It's me. *Shit!*

"Wakey, wakey, little Sentinel," a smooth voice taunts me.

I look over to the doorway and recognition punches me in the gut as I watch the beautiful Middle Eastern man step into the room. He runs the back of his hand over his tawny skin and the scruff on his face, drinking me in with his eyes. The same eyes that watched me as I fought the Colossal Douche over a month ago in Las Vegas. I knew this fucker would come for me.

His gaze falls on my blood-soaked shirt, and his whiskey-dipped irises flicker red. He inhales deeply and closes the distance between us. He places a finger under my chin and tilts my face back until my eyes find his again. I wince slightly at the pain the movement causes, and he stares at me.

"Well, aren't you a sight for sore eyes, baby Sentinel. We all thought you were lost, but here you are, right under our noses this whole time."

How the fuck does he know what I am when I just found out days ago? With those words, he leans in and smells me, which is high on the list of the creepiest things I've ever experienced. He pulls his fingers away from my chin, and they're stamped with my blood. I'm fully prepared for him to pull out a handkerchief and wipe the remnants of my injury from his hand. He seems like a handkerchief toting kind of guy. What I am not prepared for is for him to bring his hand to his mouth and lick my blood off, like he's enjoying an ice cream cone.

Nope, *that's* now definitely the creepiest thing I've ever experienced.

His eyes flash red again, and something clicks in my brain. I already deduced that he was lamia, but I'd bet anything that this group of lamia is the nest that disappeared when my father did, or they belong to it. I look over and catch Enoch looking angry and calculating. Around him, Nash and Jared Leto look-alike still seem to be unconscious, and Parker looks petrified as tears drip down his cheeks.

"Well, you look to be playing a convincing game of finders keepers. Mind telling me who you are and why they're here?" I ask, jerking my chin in the direction of Enoch and his friends. My voice is smooth and unperturbed, and I'm so grateful that I don't sound as scared as I feel.

Several chuckles echo around the room.

"Yes, finders keepers does sum it up nicely. I'm Faron, and you are?"

I'm surprised that he doesn't know my name. He watched me like a creepy hawk the night of my last fight in Vegas. They announced my name when I entered the arena that night. He knows that I'm a Sentinel, and he obviously knew where to find me—although that raises a whole other set of questions I'm forced to dismiss at the moment—but how does he not know specifics or details about me?

Reading the confusion on my face, Faron tuts.

"Yes, I know. We've used all the best motivational tactics on our...mutual friend. But he's not been very forthcoming," he tells me cryptically, the hint of a whine in his voice.

"I'm Vinna," I finally offer.

"Lovely. In both name and body," Faron declares with the slightest little bow and a lewd look in his burnt honey toned eyes. "To answer your question, they are here as motivation for your transference," Faron states simply, gesturing to Enoch and the others. "Sorik relayed that you had an attachment to a group of casters, so we thought we'd invite them along to the party."

Faron tilts his head in the direction of the familiar blond brute standing against the edge of the room. Well, Sorik clearly wasn't paying close attention, because none of these casters look anything like my Chosen. I stare at Sorik for a minute, trying to gauge if he's really that much of an idiot.

I debate pointing out the error, in the hope that Faron might let Enoch and the others go, but he'd probably just kill them after I pointed out the mistake. Sorik gives me an almost imperceptible shake of his head, and my eyes immediately jump to Faron, to see if he caught the same thing I did. Faron isn't watching us though. Instead, he's approaching the person hanging limply in the corner.

Is Sorik helping me? I look back at the blond vampire from the bar, hoping for another sign that might help me figure everything out, but his eyes are blank and focused on the empty wall across from him.

The slap of skin against skin pulls me from my jumble of thoughts, and my head jerks in the direction of Faron and the hanging body in the corner.

"Wake up, you traitorous piece of filth. I want to see your face when you see what we've found in spite of you."

Faron slaps whoever it is again, and a deep, pain-filled groan and the clinking movement of chains shatters the quiet of the room. Faron steps away, his body no longer blocking my view, and I'm utterly horrified by what I see.

"Talon!" I scream, and I try to go to him.

My chair tilts forward, but someone catches the back and rights it before I can slam face-first into the dirt. Talon's sallow eyes find mine, and they're filled with complete and utter despair. He's a shell of the man I last saw over a month ago, and it's evident they've been brutally torturing him.

His head falls, and I don't know if it's in defeat or if he's just not strong enough to hold it up anymore. Rage is slowly replacing horror, and my eyes move from my broken friend in the corner to the lamia responsible. Faron's eyes are glittery with excitement.

"I'm going to kill you," I smoothly declare.

Faron hoots with glee at my threat, and the other lamia laugh on cue. I tilt my head to the side and smile at him as I embrace my inner psycho bitch. My look seems to unsettle him, and Faron's laughter dies.

"Don't worry, delicious Vinna, we'll be with my sire soon, and there will be plenty of fun to be had by all."

Faron stalks out of the room, and the other lamia fall in line to follow.

The door clangs shut, and a sob tries to escape me when my eyes fall on Talon's battered body in the corner. I call on my runes, and a throwing knife forms in my palm. I make quick work of the ropes binding my hands, and I lean over gingerly to release my feet.

"What the hell?" someone whispers.

My head snaps up to find Jared Leto look-alike staring at me in shock. I grimace as pain punishes me for moving too fast. My index finger shoots over my lips, and I narrow my eyes at him as the throbbing in my head dulls again.

I cut Parker free next and then move to Enoch, who runs his eyes over me as I cut his ropes away. I'm not sure when Nash and the other kid woke up, but at least now they won't need to be carried anywhere. I slash everyone from their chairs and immediately move to help Talon.

Enoch and Nash both reach out to stop me.

"Vinna, don't. He's lamia. He's dangerous."

I stare at Enoch, hesitating for a second more before I decide I don't care. I pull from Enoch and Nash's grasp.

"Vinna!" Enoch warns again in a harsh whisper.

"I am only alive today because of him." I point to Talon's gaunt body. "If he wanted to hurt me, he had years to do it."

My voice breaks, and I push the unhelpful emotions down. Enoch stares at me, completely confused by my admission, but he doesn't stop me as I start to circle Talon's unconscious body, assessing the best way to get him down. I figure out a plan, but I'm not sure if it will work.

I'll need to tap into my Elemental magic, but I've only read about how to do it. I've never actually done it. I call on one of my short swords. It forms in my hand, and the other guys start whispering back and forth. I wave my hand silencing them. I'm not sure how good a lamia's hearing is, but if we're going to get out of this, we need the element of surprise, which means they need to shut the fuck up.

I stick the point of the dagger between the links of the chain that's digging into Talon's wrists. I apply some pressure and picture the blade of the dagger getting hot until it melts the metal of the chain. I hold my breath, coaxing my magic into the blade of my dagger, but nothing happens. I clench my eyes shut tightly and focus my magic on the image of what I need it to do.

Still, nothing happens. *Oh, so you want to be a fickle bitch now,* I screech at my magic. I open my eyes, abandoning that plan, and instead I pull my arm back and swipe at the chains with the short sword. The magical blade cuts through the links, and Talon abruptly crumbles to the ground with a thud before I can catch him.

I freeze and run my fingers over the runes to increase my hearing. I stand silently searching for any indication that any lamia are coming to investigate the noise.

All I hear is someone making what sounds like travel arrangements, and I tune it out to focus on Talon. I roll him onto his back and cup his face in my hands.

"Talon! Talon...wake up. It's me, Vinna... Talon," I quietly plead, as I try to wake him up, but his eyes stay shut.

I call on a throwing knife and quickly run the sharp blade across my wrist. Someone hisses behind me, but I ignore it as I bring my bleeding wrist up to Talon's mouth. I pry open his lips and let blood flood his mouth and throat, but he stays completely unresponsive. I close my eyes and let out a frustrated breath.

Nash walks over to me. "Let me heal you. You're still bleeding from a gash on your head, and you probably have a concussion. I'm sure you can't afford to be losing any more blood."

My initial reaction to Nash's request is to blow it off, but I'm most likely going to have to fight our way out of here, and it would be stupid to do that injured. I give him a nod, and he places his hands on each side of my face. I feel them warm, and my body begins to relax as his magic starts to heal me, eliminating the cacophony of pain I've been working in spite of.

When my head is pain-free, he grips my wrist. Nash's hands cool, and he pulls them away from my slash-free arm. I take a deep, relieved breath, my body feeling energized and ready.

"Thank you," I whisper to him.

Nash nods and then moves to the others, silently healing their injuries.

I run my hand lightly against Talon's cheek. "Hang in there; I've got you now," I vow, and I send out a silent plea to the universe that I can get all of us out of here alive.

Talon's face scrunches up slightly, but he still doesn't wake up. I leave him on the floor and walk to where the others are standing.

"Nash, can you heal yourself?" I ask him, noticing his hand gripping his side. He has bruises all over the side of his face, too.

"I've never been able to, no."

"Can you walk me through how to do it?" I ask him.

"You have Healing magic?" he asks me, a little shocked.

"I have all of them except Spell magic," I tell him offhandedly.

I stare off into the distance as I hear voices approaching us. I freeze, but the voices thankfully continue past us. I look back to Nash waiting for him to instruct me, but instead of telling me how to heal his ribs Nash just stares at me wide-eyed and open-mouthed.

"Seriously, Nash, I don't know how much time we have. If you want help, you need to walk me through it!"

This seems to snap him out of whatever brain stall he's experiencing.

"Just place your hand on me, skin to skin, and picture pouring your magic into me and healing any injuries. The process is more complicated than that, but that's the best way I can describe it," he admits.

I take a deep breath and run my hand up beneath his dirty and tattered shirt, placing my palm on his ribs. I close my eyes and do exactly what he just told me to do. I don't feel anything responding. I reach into myself more and think about the visuals that Ryker told me he uses. I tap into my source of magic and picture scooping some of it out in my hand and pushing it into Nash.

My hand starts to warm against Nash's skin, and in minutes his breaths go from labored to deep and smooth. I can somehow instinctually feel his bones knit back together and his lung repair the puncture. He must have been in severe pain. I stay there just a minute longer, making sure he doesn't need any more from me before I pull away.

Nash is staring at me in awe now, and a thrill of shock flits through me when I realize all the bruises on his face are gone too. I move back over to Talon and repeat what I just did for Nash. I don't know why I didn't think about trying to heal him before. But no matter how much magic I try to push into Talon, it won't sink in. I try for as long as I dare before finally accepting that it's not going to work. I growl quietly, frustrated by my magic and my inability to make it work.

I somehow healed Nash, so I'm not a complete dud, but nothing I'm trying with Talon is fucking working, and it's maddening. I shake off my anger and refocus on the next phase of the *get the fuck out of here* plan.

"Do any of you know how to fight?" I ask, mapping out the room and calculating the best plan of attack.

"We're all Paladin Conscripts," Enoch informs me.

His admission stops me in my tracks. They're training to be paladin? I look at each of them. Well, okay then, I did not see that coming. I shake myself out of my shock, and we all huddle closer together so we can whisper plans back and forth. We all realize pretty quickly that our options are mostly limited to fighting, fighting, and more fighting.

Once that settled in, we quickly worked out the details. Parker—the biggest of the group—is going to carry Talon. Enoch, Nash, Kallan—which is apparently the name of Jared Leto look-alike—and I will fight our way out to where we can hopefully find some means of escape.

We place Talon in the now-dark corner by the door, and I hope with everything that I have that he goes unnoticed the next time the lamia come in. It's getting darker and darker by the minute, and I'm hoping the lamia don't have amazing night vision and the darkness works in our favor. The rest of us make our way back to our chairs, intent on pretending that we're still tied up. The plan is to attack when we have a good shot at the lamia closest to us the next time they come in.

My runes to increase my hearing are still activated, and thankfully we only have to wait a little while before I hear several footsteps and chatter coming toward us. I hear them clunk down the stairs and disengage the lock on the door. It squeaks open, and I hope with everything that I have that they won't spot Talon's feet sticking out from the corner. Several of them stride confidently in, thankfully not noticing anything amiss.

"Alright, pets, it's time to go," one of the lamia announces, as he bends over to untie me.

His head jerks up in surprise when he discovers no rope where it should be around my ankles. I bring one short sword quickly through his neck, blood spattering my face and body as his head drops to the floor. The room explodes in chaos as each of us attack as ruthlessly and quietly as possible. I decapitate two more lamia, and Enoch and Kallan finish off the other three. I watch dazed as the bodies slowly turn to ash and disintegrate around us.

There were eight lamia down here before, including Faron, and we just eliminated six. I cross my fingers and hope only two more stand in the way of our escape. Parker picks up Talon's limp body, draping him across both shoulders, and follows us up the stairs. I go first, silently making my way up, followed by Enoch, Parker, Nash, and Kallan. I barely poke my head above the top stair, quickly taking in what's around us, before ducking back down.

We're in some kind of storm cellar set in the middle of a wide open space with a dark house to the right of us. I spot a group of lamia loading things in big SUVs and talking about fifteen feet to my left. I notice another cluster of lamia congregated closer to us on the right. As soon as we show ourselves, they'll be the first ones on us.

I lean down and turn to Enoch, trying to communicate with my hands what I see. I'd love to think I'm using some pretty sweet special forces hand signals, but in reality, it probably looks like the worst game of charades in history. I can't help but think how much easier this would be if I could speak in his mind like I can with my Chosen. I mentally facepalm when I realize I haven't even tried to use my link to them to get help. I consider quickly trying to send them a message, but the slamming of doors and impatient voices brings my attention back to trying to get us out of here, right now.

I call on several of my throwing daggers and dash quickly out of the protection of the stairwell. I pull and release daggers as quickly as possible as we run in the direction of the cars. Lamia fall and start turning to ash before the others seem to realize they're being attacked, but as soon as they do, all hell breaks loose, and they converge on us. Enoch is throwing fireballs, and Kallan is hurling glowing orbs as we run. I begin cutting the heads off of anything that gets near me or appears injured, and I curse when a bunch of lamia start pouring out of the old, dark house.

I'm cutting lamia down in a lethal and steady rhythm, as we push our way closer to the cars. I see Faron flash around the corner of the house, and I watch as his eyes turn red and his fangs drop. I separate another head from its body, and Faron bellows a feral roar. I let go of my short swords and hurl a throwing knife in his direction. In a flash, he dodges the killing blow, but it still manages to sink into his shoulder. He seems unfazed by the injury as he continues to bear down on me like the predator he is.

"Well, baby Sentinel, aren't you just full of surprises," Faron taunts, taking in my weaponless hands.

Quicker than any of the other lamia have displayed, Faron races toward me and then pounces. He gets a hand around my neck before I can do anything, and thank the stars he's trying to capture me and not kill me, or I might be dead right now. I call on my short swords and run both of them into his chest, slicing up as he tries to pull me into him. The cocksure look in his eyes fades when he realizes he doesn't exactly have the upper hand. His claws on my neck drop, and he sinks them into my wrists, trying to pull himself free of my blades.

Something hits me from behind, but my shields automatically activate, and whatever it was bounces off of me. I release the magic holding the swords in his chest, and they disappear. I feel the shredding of my wrists as I pull free from his claws, but I force myself to ignore the pain. I bring my hands up to his neck. I call the swords back into my hands, the blades forming an X at the base of Faron's throat. I scissor the swords and watch triumphantly as his head rolls off of his shoulders.

"That's for Talon," I declare and turn, looking for the next threat.

A shout calls my attention to the left, and I see the others pressing to the vehicles. I run to join them when, out of nowhere, a lamia charges Parker and slams into him. I watch as Talon and Parker hit the ground and Talon's body skids away. I'm racing to reach them, but I'm too far away, and I watch helplessly as the lamia sinks its fangs into Parker's throat and tears it out.

I scream in rage and horror, sprinting toward Parker. My magic surges, answering my call, and a pulse shoots out from me, turning every lamia it touches to ash instantly. I slide into Parker and clamp down on his tattered neck with my hands. I immediately start calling on Healing magic and shoving it into him. My hands burn white-hot, and I scream at Parker to hold on. A lamia goes up in flames dangerously close to me, and I look up to find Enoch's avenging face as he throws more fireballs at the few lamia that seem to be left.

"Come on, Parker, fight! I'm here, and I'll get you out like I promised, but you have to help me!" The wound in his neck is closing, but Parker is still limp and not moving. I jump up to defend against two more lamia coming at me from behind. *Where are they still coming from?* I look around and see Kallan make it to the driver's door of a black Suburban. The engine turns over, and I continue to cut away at attacking lamia.

Nash grabs Talon's body from the ash-covered ground and throws him over his shoulder. A lamia jumps toward them and rakes his claws over Talon's side before Enoch lights the attacker on fire. Talon yells in pain, and Nash hurriedly pushes him into the open back of the SUV. I call on the runes on my arms for extra power and pick up Parker, carrying him toward the car.

Enoch meets me halfway and steals Parker from my shoulders. I cover both of them as Enoch makes it to the car and gets Parker in. Nash dives into the passenger seat, quickly followed by Enoch jumping into the back. Enoch leans out of the still-open door and lights the remaining Suburbans on fire before slamming the car door and sealing himself inside. I kill two more lamia before jumping into the very back with Talon and pulling the door down. Kallan peels out, no instruction or encouragement needed, and we speed maniacally down the dirt road.

I watch the other cars burning bright against the night, bodies turning to ash in our wake. The few remaining lamia step out of the shadows and eerily watch us drive away. I catch sight of a large blond lamia making his way toward the transfixed survivors: Sorik. A weak grip on my arm drags my attention away from the scene, and I look down to find Talon's hazel eyes staring back into mine.

40

Panicked shouts and yelled instructions bounce around the front of the SUV, but I tune it all out and stare at Talon's conscious face.

"Little Warrior," Talon whispers to me, reaching a feeble hand toward my face.

I place my palm on the outside of his hand and hold it to my cheek.

"What did they do to you?" I ask absently, taking in how battered and broken he looks.

"Nothing I wouldn't have endured a thousand times to keep them away from you."

Talon coughs a wet cough and groans. I try to comfort him with useless words, frustrated that I can't do anything to ease his obvious pain. Talon offers me a weak smile, and I see bloody gaps where his fangs must have been pulled out. The truth of what he is squeezes my heart.

"Talon, you're lamia."

My voice is an accusation, question, and broken heart all woven together as it leaves my lips. I stroke a shaking hand over the hollows of his cheeks, and he closes his eyes at the contact.

"I am, Little Warrior."

"Why didn't you tell me?"

I'm not sure if I'm asking him why he didn't tell me about him, or why he didn't tell me about me. He obviously knew what I was, but how? None of this makes any sense. Talon's body is wracked with coughs, and I stare helplessly until they subside. Blood trickles from the corner of his mouth, and alarm bells sound in my head.

"Talon, you're a fucking vampire; aren't you supposed to heal superfast?" I ask with a panic-laced voice.

"Faron was dosing me with shifter blood. It keeps lamia from healing."

"Can I give you some of my blood? Will that help?"

"I'm sorry, Little Warrior. I'm past the point of hope. The shifter toxin makes it impossible to regenerate, and I'm too wounded. I can feel myself shutting down."

Talon's voice is a dry, brittle whisper, and the sound of it and his words cement what my mind has been screaming at me. *Talon is dying.* His head sways uncontrolled as we make our way down the bumpy dirt road. I hold his hand in mine and lean closer to him.

"Talon, what the fuck is going on?"

He tries to laugh, but it's sucked into wet coughs. I try to soothe him with promises of *hold on. We're going to get help. You're going to be okay.* But I feel the lies on my tongue as the words leave my mouth.

"Vinna, I was twenty-three when I was turned into a lamia. In the beginning, I felt like the god they told me I was, and I gloried in everything that made us what we are. I gained the trust and confidence of my sire and was entrusted with his biggest secret. A female he held captive. She had special markings that gave her immense power and abilities."

I gasp in understanding and stare at him with laser focus, not wanting to miss a single word from his mouth.

"I was assigned as her guard while my sire set about accomplishing his goal. You see, I was told that this female, with her great power and amazing abilities, could bestow those abilities and that power on another being if she willed it. My sire was intent on becoming that being, and he was trying everything he could to force or coax this female into giving him what he wanted."

My stomach roils with the thought of what this evil fucking lamia was trying to accomplish. Talon groans, and I realize that I've unknowingly tightened my grip on his hand. I loosen it immediately and try to soothe any injury with my other hand.

"After some time and repeated failures, my sire changed his plan. He decided that this Sentinel's hate for our kind was too embedded in her, and because of that, success was impossible. So he decided to breed her. He intended to take on the offspring and raise it amongst the lamia, where he was certain he would be granted the power he sought."

"We began taking male casters, but a binding and transference still never occurred. Until a coven of paladin attacked the nest. We took serious casualties, but in the end, we prevailed, and the paladin survivors were locked up with the Sentinel so Adriel could decide how he wanted to end them. Surprising to all, the Sentinel's magic called to one of the prisoners. She marked him and bonded with him, bestowing on him the gift that my sire had spent hundreds of years trying to take from her.

"Adriel was enraged, and the only thing that calmed him was that in their binding and transference, the Sentinel conceived, and my sire's new plan was finally coming to fruition."

I stare at Talon's now closed eyes, completely dumbfounded. Am I really the result of some fucked up lamia breeding program? I look away from him, my focus unseeing in the dark night shrouding the car. The atmosphere is silent and still, and I notice that we're driving on smooth pavement instead of the bumpy road we were on earlier.

Talon begins to cough again, and the episode seems to last longer and take more of a toll on his already failing body. I use my hands to wipe the blood from his mouth and side where he was clawed. I add his blood to mine and the blood of lamia I killed, as I swipe my hands down my stained and blood-soaked clothes.

"Before I was assigned the task of guarding your mother, I was a good soldier. A stalwart defender of my sire and all that he wanted. But after guarding Grier for hundreds of years, an unexpected fondness formed. She was strength incarnate, and it was impossible not to respect and admire her with time.

"When she found your father, and you were on the way, I began struggling to stomach the ramblings of Adriel and the plans he had for you. Grier and Vaughn, as well as the other prisoners, made plans to escape, and instead of reporting it like the good soldier I had always been, I found myself rooting for them.

"As you grew in her womb, their desperation to get away became palpable, and one day, an opportunity presented itself. Another nest attacked us, and in the pandemonium that ensued, I was able to assist Grier, Vaughn, and the paladin in escaping. I was leading them out when lamia from the other nest made their way to us.

"It was decided that the paladin would stay and fight, making it possible for Grier to escape with you. Grier fought to stay with them, but the centuries of torture and being a prisoner weakened her, and I was able to force her away."

Talon wipes at my wet cheeks, and I realize that I'm crying.

"She wanted to stay with you. You were everything she was living for. But the birth took its toll, and her body was so tired from the years of fighting. She held you for as long as her body would let her. She named you and placed you in my arms for safe keeping, and I swore a blood oath that I would keep you safe and protected as I watched her die."

Blood leaks from Talon's eyes, and I wipe it away hurriedly, trying to soothe him.

"I failed you, Vinna. Adriel survived the attack, and I was being called back to him. I found a blood-slave and did my best to glamor her to care for you. I checked in on you from time to time, when it was safe, but by the time I realized what Beth was doing, you were too old for me to take.

"You would have been put at more risk, and so I left you with her. I tried to force Beth to care for you better, to stop hurting you, but she had grown less susceptible to my glamor after years of exposure. When I tracked you down after she had kicked you out, it was the opportunity I needed to care for you properly. I'm so sorry it took so long, Little Warrior."

Talon's sobs morph into bone-breaking coughs. I try to soothe him, but we both know it's useless, and I can barely contain the sobs spasming from my own chest. A noise draws my attention, and I look up to find several black SUVs surround us. I shout out a warning to the others and begin to call on my magic, preparing for an attack.

"Vinna, they're with us. They're protecting us while we're outside the boundaries."

My adrenaline and energy suddenly plummet, and I collapse back down next to Talon, relieved that someone else is watching our back.

"We're almost there, Talon, just hang on a little longer."

Talon opens his eyes at my pleading tone and gives me a weak, blood-tinged smile.

"Faron must have suspected something. I was always so careful, but I must have fucked up somehow because he showed up unannounced in my territory. As soon as I was made aware that he was there, I knew it was only a matter of time before he found you." Talon's eyes close, and his face goes slack for the briefest of moments before he resumes talking. "I arranged it so that your uncle could find you. I needed him to take you before Faron could."

I reel at this admission, shock and anger boiling within me.

"Talon, if you knew where my uncle was this whole time, why didn't you give me to him in the beginning?"

Talon flinches at my anger.

"It wasn't safe. Adriel would have looked for you there first, and there was no guarantee that he wouldn't get you. I almost sent you to your uncle when I found you at fifteen. But your Sentinel runes showed up a couple of weeks later, and I knew I could train you and prepare you better than the casters or paladin could. They wouldn't have even known what you are."

Talon's breathing starts to change, a rattle sounding where there was once smooth air working in and out. I pull him against me, knowing time is running out.

"Oh, Talon. You always were a sucker for a damsel in distress," I whisper, and he gives me a bloody smile and closes his eyes. "Thank you, Talon. Thank you for protecting my mother, thank you for protecting me." My words crack and splinter as tears stream down my face and sobs break up the smooth cadence of my whispered gratitude. "You didn't fail me. I'm here because of you and your beautiful, giving heart. I'm everything because of what you did."

Talon's hand flaps up into the air, and I grab it, bringing it to my face.

"I luuhhhvvv yew, Lidl Warriorrrrrr," Talon slurs, and I feel the muscles in his arm begin to slacken.

"I love you, Talon," I sob, pulling him into my lap so I can cradle him. "Please don't go. Please, Talon, please stay with me. I'm so alone. If you go, what will I do without you?"

His breathing hitches, and I feel his body relaxing in my arms. I'm crying and begging for what I know is inevitable not to happen. Talon's lips move, but no sound comes out. I bring my ear down to his mouth.

"Ahllwayyys hrrrrr," caresses my face, in the barest whisper, as the last of Talon's breath leaves his body, and he grows still in my arms.

I drop my face into the crook of his neck and shoulder, and I cry. Loss and grief are all I am and all I know in this moment. Tears form a river from my eyes down Talon's shoulder, and I rock, holding him until his body turns to ash in my arms. I lay down on my side, knees to my chest, and become as small as possible. I stare at the remnants of what used to be Talon and find myself wishing I could crumble into nothing right alongside him.

41

I feel the tickle of magic against my skin as we cross back into the boundaries of Solace. I don't know how long we've been gone, but it's been enough time for my world to implode completely. That seems to be a running theme for me these days, world implosion. I can't seem to go more than a handful of days without something or someone ripping me or everything I know apart, and too often both happen simultaneously. I've been soldiering through, making the best of what I've been dealt, but this, all of it, it's too much. I've reached my limit of shit I can deal with.

I feel us turn off from whatever road we've been driving down for a while now. I'm not sure where we're going, and I can't be bothered to sit up and see for myself. Kallan and Nash were trying to fill the heavy silence in the car, but they've long since stopped. Now we all sit quietly, trapped in our own thoughts and memories, exhausted, drained, and processing. Another tingle of magic brushes over me, but this one speaks to me in a way the others didn't. I would know the feel of it anywhere.

"Why here?" I ask, my voice dry and raw. It's the first

time I've spoken since Talon died, and I'm not sure if anyone even heard me or will answer.

"It was the closest secured property between where we were coming from and where everyone's covens are located," Enoch answers me.

I offhandedly wonder how he knows this. Maybe it's some kind of protocol, to meet in the middle when required. We come to a stop, and I blanch; I'm not ready for what comes next. I'm not ready to soldier on and make the best of things. My armor is damaged, weak, and I can't go into battle that way. I can't win a fight when I have nothing left inside to fight with.

I hear shouts and people scrambling toward our car. None of us move, I must not be the only one trying to fortify my defenses. Doors are wrenched open, and the chaos outside comes swirling in to find us. I hear relieved shouts and questions shooting rapid-fire at no one and everyone at the same time.

"Where is she?"

The question bellows over it all, smothering the less significant noises in its demanding wake. I don't know who is asking, but I know they are coming for me. I am still nestled undisturbed in my world of loss and pain, laying in the back, but I know my solitude is coming to an end. The back door rises up, exposing me to the world and blocking the stars above me.

"By the moon!" someone gasps, and I can only assume what a shock I am to the senses. A broken girl, curled fetal in the corner, covered in blood and ash, staring dry-eyed at the pile that used to be her friend, her guardian. I feel the weight of the car shift, and I know someone is crawling in toward me.

"Don't touch him, please," I tell them flatly, no modulation to my words.

"Vinna, can you move, are you hurt?"

"I can move, I just need to take him with me," I tell whoever is listening.

I'm going to spread Talon's ashes with Laiken's. I know the perfect place. I hadn't thought about the flower-dotted clearing overlooking the lake since stumbling upon it weeks ago, but the pile of ashes in front of me called up the memory, and now I know what I want to do.

"Why is she covered in blood?" someone asks.

"She was closer to her kills than we were," a solemn voice answers.

Footsteps run toward the back of the car, and several things are handed to whoever is in here with me. I see a small handheld broom and dustpan move into my line of sight, and I reach for them.

"I'll do it."

I silently and robotically sweep up everything that I can of Talon and place it in a clear bag. I seal it off and breathe a relieved sigh now that Talon is safe and secure. I look over for the first time at whoever is next to me and find Lachlan's sad eyes taking me in.

"I know what happened to them, how I got here," I tell him hollowly.

"That doesn't matter right now. Are you hurt?"

I stare at Lachlan, confused by his dismissal. How can he say this doesn't matter? It's all that matters to him, finding answers, finding his brother.

Lachlan reaches for me, and I flinch.

"Enough! You fuckers are the reason she was out there unprotected. Back off and let us in." I watch Bastien push his way to me, my Chosen all close behind him.

He reaches for me, and I don't even hesitate as I wrap my arms around him. He cradles my body against his chest, and I feel the others' hands on me, telling me they're here, that

I'm not alone. I bury my face into Bastien's neck and simply breathe him in as he carries me from the car into the house.

"Where are you going? We have questions!" an unfamiliar voice behind us demands.

"They can wait!" I hear Sabin answer, his tone brooking no argument.

I hear their shuffled footsteps around me as we make our way upstairs. Bastien angles us into the bathroom, and I hear the water in the shower turn on. Bastien sets me on my feet but keeps a steady hold on me. Sabin gently takes Talon from my hands and places him with Laiken on her shelf.

Knox begins to peel away the blood-soaked clothes from my body. Valen's hands hold me from behind to keep me from crumbling, and Bastien quickly strips out of his clothes. When he's done, he lifts me back up, and we step under the warm spray of the shower. Valen joins us, and Bastien sets me down between them. The water runs down me, slowly fading from red to pink. When it finally runs clear, I feel Valen's hands in my hair and smell the familiar honeysuckle scent of my favorite shampoo. He washes and conditions my hair, while Bastien carefully scrubs away all the evidence of this horrible night. When I'm all rinsed off, the water stops, and I'm lifted and carried out of the shower.

Ryker dries me off and starts healing my now visible injuries. The gouges to my wrists and neck from Faron were pretty bad, and it takes some time for Ryker to fix them. When he's done, my newly unmarred outside once again becomes the perfect cover for my scarred and battered soul. Knox fills the tub with hot water and my favorite lavender bath salts and bubble bath. I step in and let the heat envelop me. The guys all take turns holding my hand or running their fingers through my hair, while I lie silently, absorbing the much-needed care and tenderness.

We stay like that for a long time before I find myself

speaking; once I start, I can't seem to stop. I relay every detail like I'm purging my soul of the weight of everything that happened. They sit, silent and attentive, as I bury them in my grief and desolation. They carry the weight of it alongside me, making it all seem a little less impossible to bear as I fill them in on everything Talon told me. When I finally grow silent, they let me. There's no assault of the hundreds of questions I'm sure they have. No false promises of how it will all be okay. They're just there with me, their presence silently and powerfully supportive.

I get out of the now tepid water and pull on underwear and a comfy t-shirt. I crawl into bed and slump against my pillow, feeling safe with warm bodies cradling mine. Tomorrow, I will deal with the questions, the paladin, my magic, the elders, my future, Adriel. Tonight, I'm going to rest, rebuild my armor, protected and surrounded by my Chosen, and feel a little less lost amidst it all.

End of Book One

THANK YOU FOR READING

You just finished the first book in The Lost Sentinel Series, and I heart you so fucking much for that! If you loved The Lost and the Chosen, please take a moment to leave a review.

You can stalk me on Instagram, my Facebook Reader Group, BookBub, my Facebook page, or my website for updates on this series and more.

ALSO BY IVY ASHER

The Sentinel World

The Lost Sentinel

The Lost and the Chosen

Awakened and Betrayed

The Marked and the Broken

Found and Forged

Shadowed Wings

The Hidden

The Avowed

The Reclamation

More in the Sentinel World coming soon.

Paranormal Romance

Rabid

Hellgate Guardian Series

Grave Mistakes

Grave Consequences

Grave Decisions

Grave Signs

The Osseous Chronicles

The Bone Witch

The Blood Witch

The Bound Witch

Fantasy Romance

Order of Scorpions

Shifter Romantic Comedy Standalone

Conveniently Convicted

Dystopian Romantic Comedy Standalone

April's Fools

IVY ASHER

Ivy Asher is addicted to chai, swearing, and laughing a lot—but not in a creepy, laughing alone kind of way. She loves the snow, books, and her family of two humans, and three fur-babies. She has worlds and characters just floating around in her head, and she's lucky enough to be surrounded by amazing people who support that kind of crazy.

Join Ivy Asher's Reader Group and follow her on Instagram, TikTok, and BookBub for updates on your favorite series and upcoming releases!!!

- facebook.com/IvyAsherBooks
- instagram.com/ivy.asher
- amazon.com/author/ivyasher
- tiktok.com/@ivy.asher
- bookbub.com/profile/ivy-asher

Made in the USA
Middletown, DE
09 June 2025